BIRDCALL
MORNING

To James —

Mark J. Asher

Mark J. Asher

ISBN: 1530578302
ISBN-13: 978-1530578306

www.markjasher.com

Also by Mark J. Asher

All That Ails You
Old Friends
Humphrey Was Here
A Day in Dogtown
Love for Freedom

For Miriam and Steve

PROLOGUE

I'll never forget how eerie it was to clean Joel Berskin's room for the first time. Before my mother left me to start cleaning the office building across the street, she always took care of his room. She never told me why, but I assume she thought seeing Joel would be too hard for me. The other residents at Tender Heart Nursing Care were old and had a lot of ailments, but Joel was different. He was in his late 40's and had been in a coma for a long time.

I tried my best not to stare at him, but I couldn't help it. How heartbreaking to see him lying there so helplessly, trapped between life and death. It was as if he was there but not there. I didn't look for long, probably less than a minute, before I turned away and went back to cleaning.

The next time I was in Joel's room, he nearly gave me a heart attack. I was dusting the blinds, with my back to him, when I heard a grunting noise. I freaked out and rushed to tell Rachelle, the overnight nurse. She explained to me that Joel was in a minimally conscious state and that this happens once in a while.

Eventually I got used to seeing Joel. Sometimes his eyes were open, sometimes he made noises, and sometimes his head would be turned in a different direction. Feeling guilty about how I stared at him initially, and out of pity I suppose, I started talking to him before I cleaned his room. I always whispered because I didn't want anyone walking by to think I was crazy. If you're wondering what I said, it wasn't anything really. Most times I just complained about how tired I was or told him what the weather was like.

One night, a few months later, I found out more about Joel in a weird way. It happened when I was moving a stack of stuff from an end table onto the chair beside it so I could clean it. As I went to put everything back, I noticed an old newspaper sticking out of the pile. It was one I had never heard of called the *Santa Monica Outlook*.

Curious and nosy, I pulled the paper out and saw that it was from the day after the O.J. Simpson car chase, June 18th, 1994. I was only ten then, but I remember my mom and I glued to the TV watching it. When I looked below the picture of AC Cowlings driving the white Bronco, I spotted a photograph of Joel when he was much younger, in front of a music store. He was a cute guy with thick black wavy hair, light eyes, and a nice smile. Next to it there was another one of him lying in a hospital bed in bad shape. The headline of the story was: *Music Man Goes Into Coma From Rare Infection*.

I read the story and discovered that Joel owned a music store called Good Sounds on Wilshire Boulevard. The paper interviewed some of his customers and they were all shocked and sad about what happened to him. From what they had to say about Joel's store, it sounded like a really cool place. One long-time customer said, "Joel loves and knows more about music than anyone I've ever met. Every time I leave his store, I can't wait to get into my car to play whatever he recommended to me." Another person said, "Every week Joel puts together a radio show and plays it in the store. They're wonderful, with tracks you haven't heard in a long time or gems you never knew about. He mixes in really interesting stuff about the artists and the songs." At the bottom of the article, the paper printed the playlist from Joel's most recent radio program.

The Music Man's Last Mix?

"Birdcall Morning" *Joe Walsh*
"Johnny's Garden" *Manassas*
"The Sand and The Foam" *Dan Fogelberg*
"We Have All the Time in the World" *Louis Armstrong*
"It's Been a Long Long Time" *Bing Crosby with Les Paul*
"Peace Piece" *Bill Evans*
"My Favorite Things" *John Coltrane*
"Be My Number Two" *Joe Jackson*
"Little One" *Chicago*
"Nights on Broadway" *Bee Gees*
"Suite: Clouds, Rain" *David Gates*
"Wanderlust" *Paul McCartney*
"Lately" *Stevie Wonder*
"Piece of Clay" *Marvin Gaye*
"The Agony and The Ecstasy" *Smokey Robinson*
"This Is My Country" *The Impressions*

"Sitting in the Park" *Billy Stewart*
"Places and Spaces" *Donald Byrd*
"Song of the Wind" *Santana*
"Washing of the Water" *Peter Gabriel*
"Lucille" *Kenny Rogers*
"December Day" *Willie Nelson*
"Bougainvillea" *Dickey Betts*
"Little Wing" *Neil Young*
"Many Rivers To Cross" *Jimmy Cliff*
"To the Last Whale" *Crosby & Nash*

I put the paper back where I found it and finished the rest of my cleaning for the night.

A few days later, I went to the beach on my one off day with my friend Isabelle. On the way there, we rolled down the windows and started singing at the top of our lungs to a band our friend is in called *The Super C's*. It reminded me of how happy music can make you feel, and it gave me a crazy idea.

The next night at Tender Heart, after I finished cleaning Joel's room, I pulled out the newspaper I had found again. I quickly typed the song titles from his last music mix into my phone. When I got home, I downloaded all of them to my iPod and made a playlist called *Songs for Joel*. I listened to a few seconds of each one and recognized a couple from hearing them in my mom's car.

I was ready to try my crazy idea now, but I chickened out the next couple of times I was at work. Finally, on a super rainy Monday night, I got up the nerve to do it. I have to admit I was a little freaked getting close to Joel, but I tucked my iPod beneath the sheets, put the earbuds on him and tapped play. I quickly turned down the volume so no one would hear it (I listen to music super loud!), and then walked away before I thought anymore about what I was doing.

The night seemed to go on forever and I was totally exhausted by the time I finished everything. I don't know why but I get tired more easily than my mom. She says it's because I'm spoiled. I always tell her, "Spoiled kids don't start working at nine years old," like I did. She never responds, she just gives me *the look*. The one that parents give their kids when they know they're wrong, but they just want you to accept what they say.

After I brought my cleaning supplies outside to wait for my mom to pick me up, I remembered that I left my iPod with Joel! I hurried back to his room, which was at the far end of the building. Before I walked inside, I stood in the doorway for a few seconds, looking to see if he was responding to the music. I don't know what I expected, but there was no change in his expression.

I walked over, quickly removed the earbuds, grabbed my iPod, and headed back outside. While I was sitting on the bench by the entrance waiting for my mom, who's always late, I felt stupid about playing music for Joel. *What if Rachelle had seen me or worse, the owner, Ms. Ridwire, had walked in*, I thought to myself.

Ms. Ridwire was a total neat freak, which is the reason I cleaned at Tender Heart five nights a week. She also wasn't the easiest person to work for. She called my mom at home a couple of times a month to tell her that if we didn't do a better job cleaning the bathrooms, she would fire us. My mom never told Ms. Ridwire that I was doing the Tender Heart job alone, but the nursing home wasn't very big—it only had ten residents—and I could handle it myself, while mom brought in more money.

A couple of months after my strange experiment with Joel, I walked into the living room while my mom was watching TV. Unfortunately, we only have one TV in our house, so I joined her on the couch. She was totally engrossed in one of these science programs on cable that she likes. It was about the power of music and how it can help people with brain injuries and strokes. They were interviewing a doctor from Harvard, who was saying that music can create new pathways in the brain around damaged areas. Next they had on a music therapist who had helped patients with brain injuries, strokes, and Alzheimer's walk and talk again by using music.

Normally these types of shows seriously bore me and I end up going to my room or texting a friend until it's over. But this one was really interesting and inspiring. When it ended, my mom and I were both in tears. I thought about telling her about the time I played music for Joel, but I knew she would get upset with me. When we started cleaning together at the nursing home, she told me never to interact with any of the residents unless they spoke to me.

Before I went to sleep that night, I googled "playing music for someone in a coma" on my phone. I clicked on a few of the links and ended up finding a story about eleven people who woke up from comas after hearing their favorite song! Most of them had been unconscious for a lot less time than Joel had been, but STILL. The article said that something familiar and emotionally important, like music, is called a "salient stimulus" and that has the power to wake someone up.

The next night I told Rachelle about the program my mom and I watched and about the website I found. I asked her if anyone had ever tried helping Joel with music and she said, "No, not while I've been here. It wouldn't matter though, he's long gone honey."

"Does anyone ever visit him?" I asked her.

"For a while they did...but as time went on people forgot about him. You can't blame them, there's nothing anybody can do," she told me before pausing to answer a resident's question. "Joel's father is the one that kept him alive for all these years. He used to come here a lot before he died and take Joel out for special occasions. But Joel's mother stopped doing that once her husband was gone."

"Does he just lie there all day?"

"Well, aides bathe and dress him in the morning, give him his nourishment, fluids, meds, and a physical therapist comes a few times a week to keep his muscles stimulated."

"I wonder what caused his coma?" I asked innocently, hoping I wasn't asking too many questions.

"From what I heard it started with a viral infection. Then it turned into this really rare brain disorder called Acute Disseminated Encephalomyelitis. It mostly happens to children, but adults can get it too. The doctors expected he'd come out of the coma quickly, but he just never did."

"This is going to sound really weird, Rachelle," I said, starting to get nervous, "but do you think it would be okay if I played music for Joel while I clean?"

"I knew you must be getting at something with all of

those questions," she replied. "I guess it's okay...go ahead if you want to...it won't do him any good though."

"I just feel sad seeing him lie there," I rambled. "But I don't want to get in trouble with Ms. Ridwire or Joel's mom."

"You almost never see Ms. Ridwire here after 3 o'clock these days," Rachelle told me. "And I haven't seen Mrs. Berskin on my shift in at least two years."

The very next night I began playing music for Joel again. At first I kept checking to see if he was responding, but eventually I stopped wondering if what I was doing was doing any good or not. I just figured that Joel loved music and if he had any way of hearing it, he would appreciate it. It might have been my imagination or wishful thinking, but I swear there were times when he moved or made more noises. Either way, I made setting up Joel with my iPod a part of my nightly routine.

At one point, I thought about changing the songs on Joel's playlist, but I had no way of knowing what other songs he liked. Also, I remembered the music therapist on the program I saw with my mom saying something about repetition, so I kept it the same.

It seems like when you're out of school and all you do is work, life goes by a lot faster. Maybe it's because there's no breaks anymore for winter, spring, and summer. Whatever the reason it sucks, and like that, two years of my life went by.

Not much changed at Tender Heart. Joel was still in the same condition, except for a little more grey hair around his temples. Sadly, one of the nicest residents, Ruth Danielson, who once knitted gloves for my mother and me for Christmas, passed away.

My life wasn't very exciting. I liked a boy who turned out to like more than one girl, so I broke it off with him. I was getting really tired of cleaning and started to fear I was going to grow old and be like my mother—with a sore back and a rag in my hand. Whenever I told her I wanted to quit, she always gave me the same lecture, "Cleaning is hard, but it pays the bills. Technology can replace everything, but there'll always be work for someone who's willing to clean."

The idea of cleaning forever didn't depress my mom like it did me. She came to this country from Mexico with nothing but me, to escape an abusive husband. So just being able to afford food and a place to live was enough for her. I know she wanted more for me, but she didn't want me to have to struggle.

As time went on, I kept thinking about my future, wondering how long I would have to keep cleaning. I dreamed of a bunch of different scenarios, but what actually happened was nothing I ever would have imagined. Why is life always that way?

On a Saturday morning, almost a year and a half after I started playing music for Joel, Ms. Ridwire called my mother at home and fired us. She said we—I wasn't doing a good enough job cleaning the bathrooms, but I found out later, when I bumped into Rachelle at the market, that Ms. Ridwire hired someone else to do the job for a lot less.

I was gone from Tender Heart for only a month when I found out that Joel had miraculously woken up. I read about it on NMN's website and I literally dropped my phone. When I picked it up, I screamed as loud as I could. My mom heard me and rushed into my room. I told her what happened and she also freaked out. Once we calmed down, we read the article together and looked at the pictures of Rachelle and some of the other employees with Joel.

All of the medical experts in the NMN story speculated how Joel could have come out of his coma after so many years, but no one could say for sure. A reverend at a local church said it was God's work, so only He could know the reason for Joel's recovery.

While my mom and I searched online for more information on Joel's awakening, I told her for the first time about how I played music for Joel. She immediately brought up the science program we watched together and we both wondered if music might have helped Joel in some way. I really hope that it did.

Every day for weeks, I googled Joel's name to see if I could find out what happened to him next. There were a lot more articles, but there was no new information. I wished I could contact Joel to tell him about all the nights I played him music, but I had no way of knowing where he was, and besides, I'm sure he was totally overwhelmed by everything. I guess it will just have to be a special memory that my mother and I share.

If you're wondering what I'm doing these days, I'm getting closer to finally giving up cleaning. I still do a few jobs with my mom but over the last year I started taking courses to become a music therapist. One day soon I hope to be doing something that uses my heart instead of my hands.

Sincerely,
Maya Diaz

ONE

When I opened my eyes on February 25, 2011, I saw a stranger with a heap of red hair, opening the curtains a few feet away. "Keep them closed," I told her, rubbing the sleep out of my eyes. When she turned around to face me, her mouth hung open in a state of shock. As the woman slowly walked toward me, her eyes locked on me as if she were seeing an alien. After a few seconds of stunned silence she said, "Did…did you just say something?"

"If you heard me, why are you asking?" I replied, noticing that my voice sounded nasally and my words were difficult to articulate.

"How do you feel?" the woman asked, reaching out for my hand with a look of awe still fixed on her face.

"I'm tired. Where am I?" I responded.

"Do you know your name?" she asked, without answering my question.

"Of course…Joel."

"Do you know where you live?"

"Why are you treating me like a child?" I asked before answering. "In a house…in Santa Monica."

"Oh–my–God," she mouthed in astonishment. "Mr. Berskin, I think you just came out of a coma."

Oh no, not another one of those crazy dreams, I thought to myself. *They always happen when I have a lot of sugar before I go to bed.*

"No more ice-cream," I blurted out.

"Mr. Berskin, listen to me," the woman said, leaning forward and stroking the side of my face. "You're in a nursing home. My name is Denise. I'm one of your nursing aides."

As she continued talking, I felt the head of the bed move slightly upward. It startled me and when my body went to react and moved limply, I realized that something was terribly wrong.

"What happened to me?" I asked nervously. "How did I get here?"

"This is unbelievable," Denise replied with tears forming in her eyes. "I'll be right back."

I watched her walk out of the room and after she cleared the doorway, I saw an old woman slowly shuffling behind a walker. With my head tilted to the side, I noticed that my right arm was shriveled and limp. I lifted the blanket that was covering me and was startled to see a tube coming out of my stomach, to the right of my belly button, and a large bag beside it that was partially filled with fluid. I tried, but couldn't peel back the blanket far enough to see my legs. Looking up, I spotted a bulletin board across the way with cards and photos pinned on it, but I couldn't make them out.

When Denise returned, she was holding a small, slender device up to her ear.

"Yes, Mrs. Berskin, he's talking! Yes, I'm sure. Here—"

She put what surprisingly turned out to be a cell phone to my ear and I heard my mother's voice.

"Joel, it's me…mom. Can you hear me?"

"Yes mom, I can hear you," I said.

"My God, I can't believe it! You're talking!" she said.

"What's happening?" I asked anxiously. "Why am I here?"

"I was on my way down to San Diego, but I'm turning around

right now. I'll be there as soon as I can."

I asked my mother another question, but she said she couldn't drive and talk at the same time. She told me to talk to the woman I was with until she got there.

Realizing that the conversation was over, Denise took the phone from my ear, tapped on the screen once, and then put it in her pocket. She said something quickly that I didn't pick up and then left the room again.

I slowly rolled my head in the opposite direction of the door and looked out the window through the partially opened curtain. All I could see was a sliver of blue sky and the trunk of a palm tree. *I must still be in L.A.*, I thought to myself. Turning back toward the room, I noticed an odd-looking TV with a flat, wide screen, hanging from the wall. CNN was on. Their logo looked the same, but the studio had completely changed.

An attractive brunette anchor, whom I didn't recognize, was talking about Charlie Sheen. I listened for a few seconds and then instinctively reached over to the table beside my bed for the remote. My arm felt as if it was moving through mud, but I was able to find the remote and press a couple of buttons. When I looked back up at the TV, I was watching another news channel, which didn't look familiar. In the lower left corner of the screen it said: Fox News. The blonde anchor was talking to a preppy-looking guy about someone named Obama. They went on for a minute and then began talking about Charlie Sheen. *He must have a new movie out*, I thought to myself.

I arduously reached over again for the remote and tried to pick it up but couldn't. I randomly pressed the buttons and this time landed on ABC. A group of people were sitting around a table talking about Charlie Sheen! One of them said something about his "twitter," which made no sense to me. *Okay, either I'm dreaming or Charlie Sheen is dead.*

Denise came back into the room with a woman several years older than her, who looked as if she were smiling or about to cry. Once they were on either side of my bed, I looked up at the TV and asked, "What's going on with Charlie Sheen?" They both let out a laugh.

"He's not dead, if that's what you're thinking," Denise said. "He's just gone crazy."

"And the media's gone with him," the new stranger added.

"Mr. Berskin, this is Sally," Denise said. "She's another one of the nurses here at Tender Heart."

"Is Seinfeld on?" I asked, staring at the happy face dangling from her shirt pocket.

"No," Sally replied. "I must be one of the only people in the world who never watched that."

"My mom used to *love* that show," Denise said. "I think I was too young to really appreciate it."

"No Seinfeld?" I asked, confused.

"There've been a lot of changes, Mr. Berskin," Sally replied.

"Mr. Berskin, we're going to transfer you into a wheelchair now," Sally told me.

"Wheelchair?" I asked. "For what?"

"Your body hasn't moved in a very long time, Mr. Berskin," Denise informed me. "Your muscles are weak."

Confused and fatigued, I watched as the two of them maneuvered me from the bed into a wheelchair. Once I was finally situated, I looked up and saw an old man standing in the doorway. He was wearing a disheveled sailor's hat that had long, wiry strands of grey hair sticking out from beneath it.

"Hello there," he said, in a deep, authoritative voice while balancing himself with a cane in each hand. "I'm Bernard Gold. In my younger days they used to call me Goldie. Let me give a word of advice, son. If the world strikes you as insane, don't doubt yourself.

The trouble is no one knows what the hell to do about it!"

He stood silent for a few moments, looking as if he wanted to say something else. Then he lifted one of his canes to wave and slowly ambled away.

Two

I must have dozed off after that because when I opened my eyes again, my mother was standing in front of me. My body flinched and I did a double take.

"Mom?" I asked, in disbelief and shock.

She leaned over to hug me and I took in her familiar scent. "My God, this is a miracle of miracles, Joel," she said in my ear.

Once she released her grip, she continued talking but I don't remember a word she said. I was struggling to process the sight of my mother as an old lady. Her face was paunchy and lined and her hair was completely gray. For the first time in my life she looked heavy.

Beauty was something I associated with my mother from my earliest memories and from photographs I had seen of her as a child. She now looked nearly as old as her mother had before she died of cancer, in her early seventies.

"Where's Dad?" I asked, as she sat beside me.

"Heart attack," she replied, in more of an informative tone than an emotional one . "It happened four years ago. You know how much he hated hospitals Joel, so I'm glad he went without a long illness."

"No..." I said meekly, turning away and staring toward the window.

It might have been the fog of coming out of a coma, or just the jolt of the news, but I didn't cry. I wish my initial, unemotional response could have lessened the grief I ultimately felt. Some people have a spirit that never leaves and makes you forever wish that you could see them one more time. For me, that was my father.

The two of us shared a similar brand of dry wit, a slightly skewed way of looking at the world, and a love of sports and music. Most importantly, my father was one of the few people in the world who understood and appreciated my personality. Together we formed a bond that helped shield us from my mother's acerbic and belittling personality.

It's a horrible thing to say, but I wished it was my father telling me about my mother's passing and not the other way around.

A strange ringing tone sounded from somewhere nearby, but I couldn't tell where. My mother fished through her purse and pulled out her phone.

"Shirley, you're not going to believe this…Joel is awake!" she told her sister. "Yes…out of nowhere he started talking to one of the nurses this morning."

While my mother paced around the room, talking with Aunt Shirley, she intermittently asked Denise questions.

"When's the doctor coming?"

"He should be here shortly," Denise answered.

"Did you tell him what happened so he'll come right away?"

"Yes, of course," Denise replied.

My mother wandered out of the room into the hallway, continuing her conversation. When she reappeared a few minutes later, after the call had ended, I asked, "Where's Lauren?" thinking about my wife for the first time since I woke up.

"What do I tell him?" she turned and asked Denise.

"That's up to you, Mrs. Berskin," Denise replied.

My mother reached into her purse again for her phone. She held it in her hand and stared at it as if she were deciding who to call. Then she looked up and said, "Joel, this is hard for me. A lot has happened since you went into a coma."

"Please, tell me what happened," I pleaded anxiously. "How did I end up in a coma?"

My mother let out a sigh and put her phone away. "You came down with a cough and a sore throat. When you went to the doctor, he said it was nothing more than a viral infection. Then, a few weeks later things got worse...you became very lethargic...you started slurring your speech, and had numbness in one of your arms. Your father got you in with his neurologist. First he thought it might be MS, but it wasn't that. It turned out to be Acute Disseminated Encephalomyelitis. Neither your father nor I had ever heard of it before...it's a rare neurological disorder. Usually it doesn't occur in adults and normally it doesn't cause someone to fall into a coma, but within days that's what happened. The doctors started giving you medication—some type of steroid. They said you would recover quickly..."

"This is unreal," I replied, trying to grasp what I had just heard.

"You can say that again," my mother responded. "It's been a heartache and a headache for the last seventeen years of my life. And your poor father...it absolutely broke his heart."

"Seventeen years?" I asked, stunned and horrified. Although I should have made the connection after seeing how much older my mother looked, I hadn't. The reality of what I was hearing was devastating. "I've been gone for that long?"

My mother dropped her head and became quiet, something that hardly ever happened. When she slowly looked up, she glanced at

Denise again, hoping for some sort of help.

"Joel, it's 2011," my mother said in the softest tone I'd ever heard her speak.

"No, it can't be," I said, becoming confused and agitated.

"Joel...you're forty-eight years old now."

"It's okay," Denise said, rubbing my shoulder, as I closed my eyes and dropped my head. "It's a lot to take."

"Can I get some water?" I asked when I was able to speak again.

"I'm sorry, I can't give you any food or water until a speech therapist evaluates you," Denise told me.

"Really?" my mother asked, annoyed.

"Yes, Mrs. Berskin," Denise replied. "We have to make sure nothing gets into his lungs."

Denise left the room and I sat quietly with my mother. She reached over to hold my hand to comfort me. I wish the moment would have lasted longer than it did. A minute later, my mother blurted out—speaking to herself and me at the same time—"Well, I might as well tell him about Lauren. She moved on, Joel."

"What?" I asked.

"She had no choice, Joel. You couldn't expect her to stick around forever while you weren't alive...for practical purposes. After all, your relationship wasn't too hot as it was."

"She divorced me?" I asked.

"Yes. She remarried...years ago," my mother replied.

If I was feeling myself, my response probably would have been something like, "Who's the unlucky guy?" I didn't have to wait long to find out.

"A Beverly Hills divorce attorney. Jewish," my mother informed me.

Some mothers have trouble getting along with their daughter-in-laws. I had a different problem—my mother was more interested in my wife than me. Whenever she called our house, she always asked for Lauren. I remember the first phone call Lauren and I got after moving in together. I picked up the phone and there was silence on the other end. I was about to hang up when I heard my mother say, "Oh, it's you."

My mother sided with Lauren in every squabble the two of us had during our three years of marriage. Her defense of my wife always began the same: *Joel, you have to understand, Lauren, blah, blah, blah.*

"Joel, there's so much to tell you," my mom said, quickly changing the subject. "Your friend Gary Wycoff has the most beautiful kids…a boy and a girl…just to die for. Apparently he's got a business that's a big deal. I don't remember what it is, but judging from the clothes and jewelry his wife wears, he must make a lot. I see her once in a while getting her nails done."

"Who did he marry?" I asked.

"I bumped into Joey Raybluff's father recently," my mother continued, skipping over my question. "He must be doing well…he lives in the Gable Estates. He married his high school sweetheart…remember Suzie? They have one daughter."

"What happened to my store?" I managed to ask before she went on.

"Your father and I sold it…a few years ago," she replied.

I closed my eyes and let another wave crash over me.

"I know you loved that place, Joel," my mother said, managing to convey her dislike for it in the same breath. "But we had no choice. I wish your father would have listened to me and sold it sooner."

Although she never came out and said it, I knew my mother didn't care for my record store. In her eyes it wasn't a prestigious enough profession (translation: lucrative enough) for her son. My father, on the other hand, loved it. He came to see me whenever he got a chance, kibitzing with the customers and giving me helpful suggestions. If his father hadn't died after he graduated from college, and he didn't feel pressure to start making a living, my father told me he would have become a classical violinist or a music teacher, instead of going to work for my mother's father in the cleaning business.

My first memory of liking music came at seven years old, when I cut out a *Jackson Five* record from the back of a box of Super Sugar Crisps cereal. I played the unique cardboard record over and over again, until it wouldn't work anymore. Two or three years later, my parents took me to the Mark Taper Forum to see an all-black cast of a musical called, *Don't Bother Me, I Can't Cope.* I had no idea what I was there to see or what to expect, but when the cast broke into song on the opening number, it was like someone had poured sunshine on my soul.

Once I got older, music became—to borrow a Bob Dylan song title—my shelter from the storm. The storm being the uneasy and often turbulent relationship between my mother and my father. In those early teenage years, when I began to be affected by the exchanges between my parents, I would get stoned, put on headphones, read the album liner notes and lyrics, and drift off into another world. Those were the days of *The Stranger* by Billy Joel and *News of the World* by Queen and *Grand Illusion* by Styx.

Once disco arrived, things began to change, and after the deaths of Keith Moon, John Bonham, and John Lennon, an era of music and my childhood had ended.

After college, I tried to make it as a singer-songwriter, but my style was stuck in a bygone era and ultimately my voice wasn't strong enough to stand out. It didn't take long for me to tire of the life of waiting tables and waiting for a break. Wanting to somehow remain involved with music, I borrowed money from my father and opened a small record store in a sliver of a retail space on Wilshire Boulevard. I called the place *Good Sounds*, but the formal name was *Good Sounds*

Goin' Round, and the logo had the words "Goin' Round" inside of the shape of a record.

"We tried hiring two different people to run it," my mother explained, "but over time we found out that both of them were stealing. Your father took it over for a while, but it was too much for him to take care of the dry cleaner and your store. We ended up selling it to a Persian family...I don't think they lasted very long before going out of business."

THREE

As my mother was talking, a tall man appeared over her shoulder, smiling down at me.

"Good morning everyone," he said, with elation in his voice.

"Dr. Kurtz," my mom reacted, turning around to greet him. "Can you believe this? He's talking!"

"To be honest, I couldn't believe it when I got the call," Dr. Kurtz replied. "But I'm always happy to be wrong—especially this morning."

In comparison to the doctors I had known in my life, who were on the short side, Dr. Kurtz was a monster. He looked to be over six feet tall, and his unusually square head and heavily gelled hair made me think of Herman Munster.

"Hello Joel, I'm Dr. Kurtz," he said, reaching down to squeeze my hand. "I've seen some miraculous things in my career, but nothing like this!"

After the buzz of excitement, the doctor began asking me questions and examining me. When he finished, he explained my situation.

"Joel, you've been in what's called a minimally conscious state. It's extremely rare to wake up the way you have, after so many years."

"What do you think happened?" my mother asked the doctor.

"It's hard to say...we've been giving him a cocktail of neurostimulants—drugs used for depression, Parkinson's and attention deficit hyperactivity disorder, which have worked in a small number of these cases," he replied. "But the truth is, Mrs. Berskin, sometimes the best medicine is a miracle, and that might be the best explanation for this. Especially seeing how lucid Joel is."

"Dr. Kurtz, more recently he's also been given stimulation therapy," Denise added.

"I didn't know about that," my mother responded. "What is it?"

"It's like a cardiac pacemaker," Dr. Kurtz answered. "We place wires in the brain and attach them to an electrical stimulator which is implanted under Joel's skin."

Wires coming from my brain? I immediately thought of the movie *Young Frankenstein* when Gene Wilder attaches wires to the monster's head, and wondered what I looked like after everything I had been through. I turned toward Denise and asked for a mirror, but in the midst of the conversation between my mother and the doctor, she didn't hear me.

"Is he going to be okay now?" my mother asked Dr. Kurtz.

"The honest answer is there's no telling. There have been cases where patients have woken up from long term comas and talked nonstop for hours, only to lapse back into unresponsiveness," he informed us.

"So there's no guarantees is what you're saying," my mother responded, questioning the doctor like he was a witness on the stand.

"I can't predict what's going to happen, Mrs. Berskin. Anything is possible."

"What are the chances of losing him again?" my mother asked.

"There are so few cases like Joel's...I just can't say with any certainty."

"But it could happen?" my mother pressed.

"Mrs. Berskin, yes, but let's try to think positively and be grateful that Joel woke up and is talking."

"Why does he sound so nasally?" my mother inquired.

"Right now he's not able to control and force enough air through his lungs and upper respiratory track to produce sound properly," the doctor explained. "He'll have to go through intense rehabilitation to improve his speech and regain his mobility. Mrs. Berskin…Joel will need every ounce of energy, support and love that you can give him."

"Can I have some water?" I asked after the doctor finished.

"Yes, Dr. Kurtz, he's thirsty," my mother interjected. "And what about food…does he still need that tube?"

"We need to make sure his swallowing is okay before the PEG tube is removed," the doctor replied. "Therapy will strengthen the muscles in his mouth and alleviate the danger of him aspirating, but it will take some time."

"What now?" my mother asked. "When can he go home?"

"Once we determine that Joel's medically stable, I'd like to transfer him to Hathers Institute of Rehabilitation. They have an excellent team of therapists there and it's not overwhelmingly large."

"To live?" my mother asked, surprised.

"Yes. He'll need to be there for at least eight weeks to receive a regular regimen of physical therapy, occupational therapy, and speech therapy."

With my mother momentarily silent, Dr. Kurtz put his hand on my shoulder and asked if I had any other questions.

"Can I see what I look like?" I asked.

The doctor turned to Denise, who then left the room I presumed to get me a mirror. After he told me again how overjoyed he was by my miracle, the doctor followed Denise, with my mother behind him.

Denise returned holding a small hand mirror and helped me guide it up to my face. It would be impossible for me to explain the shock and sadness of seeing yourself at thirty-one, and then again at forty-eight, without a single day in between.

My hairline, which when I last looked was just beginning to recede, was now mostly scalp with a few surviving strands poking up. The hair on my sides was still thick, but the color was now an equal mixture of black and gray. My face looked slender, sullen, and pale, like a mug shot of a prisoner who had been behind bars for a long time.

Perhaps sensing that this was a moment I should have to myself, and seeing that I could hold the mirror okay, Denise excused herself. Once she was out of sight, I angled the mirror downward and saw the flattest stomach I'd had since my college days. Whatever they were feeding me through that tube must not have included two of my dietary mainstays—beer and ice cream. When I tilted the mirror back up, I noticed something I had never seen before on my body— chest hair sticking out from above my t-shirt. Later I discovered I had also grown hair on my upper and lower back.

I guess I shouldn't have been surprised to see that Father Time had been a thief, but I didn't know that he had a cruel sense of humor. How else can you explain losing hair where I wanted it (on my head) and growing hair where I didn't (on my back)?

Four

The day continued like a surreal scene that I was the center of, but it felt as if I was looking down on it from a million miles away. My mother talked a blue streak, telling me as many of the things I had missed as she possibly could, and filling me in on basic stuff, like who was President of the country. Residents at the nursing home must have found out that the guy who had been in a coma was now talking, and they wanted to see for themselves. They slowly walked past my doorway, stopping briefly to gawk at me as if I were from another planet. Medical oddities, I would learn in the coming months, are like train wrecks—everyone has to look.

In what felt like a couple of hours after I woke up, but I couldn't say for sure, I heard a booming voice approaching my room that I'd recognize no matter what condition I was in. It was my friend Gary Wycoff. There wasn't anything subtle about Gary's presence—he was a six foot two tsunami of energy, who rarely stopped moving. Being wide as well as tall, he often sounded out of breath when he spoke. He had a huge ego, but a heart just as big.

Within seconds, Gary was smothering me with a bear hug that blocked all of the light in the room. When he pulled away, tears were squeezing out of the corner of his eyes.

"Buddy, you're back!" he said, trying his best to be fragile with me, which wasn't easy for him. "I can't believe it! This is UNBELIEVABLE."

"Hey, Big G," I said, with tears streaming down my face.

Gary crouched down in front of me, put his hands on my shoulders and stared intensely into my eyes; as if he was making sure what he was seeing was real.

"You went gray," I said in my nasally voice, which came out sounding like, *You went gay*. Gary and my mother started laughing.

"Not yet, buddy," Big G replied, while my mother wiped my face. "But if my wife and I don't have a date night soon, anything's possible."

"Leslie?" I said, asking about the woman he had been dating for years.

"Yeah, we finally did it," he replied. "I've got two great kids now. If I had known they would bring me this much joy, I would have done it sooner. Married life though…man, it's hard. They should change the wedding vows from *I do* to *I'll try*."

Before I went into a coma, Gary was working as an administrator for an environmental nonprofit organization and he was dating Leslie. Like all of my unmarried friends, he was beginning to realize, as cynical as it sounds, that marriage was more about timing—who you were dating when you were ready to take the leap—than love. Still, out of all of the couples at the time, Gary and Leslie were easily the least suited for one another. They fought constantly, with Leslie imposing "sex embargos" on Gary whenever she disapproved of his behavior. It was entertaining, but painful to watch.

"How old are your kids now?" my mother asked Gary.

"I can't believe it, but Hannah's ten and Todd's going to be eight in two weeks."

"Tell Joel about your business," my mother suggested proudly.

"I started a video entertainment company ten years ago," Gary replied. "But we can talk about that some other time. First things first, my man, we have to get you up and going. Then we need to have a sports night, so I can bring you up to speed on the Browns."

Gary and I met at a neighborhood sports bar in Santa Monica. He happened to be sitting on the bar stool next to mine, when Earnest Byner fumbled in the infamous '87 AFC Championship game against the Denver Broncos. It was the first and probably the last time that I saw him speechless. Then again, everybody in the bar who was rooting for the Browns was in stunned silence. The Byner fumble was like an unexpected, instant death. During the following season, Gary and I struck up a friendship and discovered we had grown up twenty miles from each other in Cleveland, and that our families had moved to California around the same time.

"What's going on with Ridenn and Kleftko?" I asked Gary.

"Man, it's been ages since I saw those guys. I know Scott got married, started a family and moved to Virginia Beach. Someone recently told me that Brian's a traveling gypsy…I have no idea where he is."

I looked up at Gary flustered, thinking back to the three of us having drinks not that long ago.

"It's okay, buddy," Gary offered, sensing my confusion and patting my shoulder. "It's been a while." Then he walked behind my wheelchair, extended his arm out in front of us with his phone in his hand, and I heard a click. "Check it out," he said, showing me the photograph he just took. "I'll post this on my Facebook page and see if I can reconnect with those guys, or some of the Browns' fans from the sports bar."

"Face book?" I asked.

"Oh man, sorry," he replied. "It's a website where people have their own page and share things that are going on in their lives. Sort of like an online watering hole. Everyone's on it."

"Except your mother," I heard a voice say over Gary's shoulder.

Gary stayed until he had to leave for a business meeting that he couldn't reschedule. After he hugged me goodbye and walked out of the room, I could still hear his voice carrying on conversations with people until he left the building.

I guess now is as good a time as any to mention that Big G is the reason you're reading this book. The next time he came to the nursing home, he gave me a voice recorder and told me to keep an audio diary of everything I went through. He thought it would make a great story, and said that his secretary, who was an aspiring author, would help me put it together.

Soon after Gary left, one of my favorite relatives, my Aunt Shirley, was standing in the doorway. She was five years older than my mother and they were nothing alike. I used to joke with her that she must have stolen all of their parents' love and affection with her effervescent personality before my mother came along. It was hard to believe that two siblings could be more different in temperament and attitude. Aunt Shirley was always diplomatic about their differences, saying my mother was a little needier, which was like saying that a mountain was slightly higher than a molehill.

"Joel," was all Aunt Shirley said, before she rushed to embrace me with tears in her eyes. She held me for a long while without saying anything.

"You came back to us," she finally whispered. "Oh, honey, we missed you."

When I opened my eyes, I saw my mother watching Shirley, trying to force a smile.

"I can't imagine what you must be thinking, seeing all of us," my aunt said. "Looking at me you can see just how much time has passed."

"Oh, Shirley, you look great," my mother chimed in. "Don't fish for flattery."

"Well, Joel, you can see things haven't changed much," Aunt Shirley said with a smile.

After asking me a few questions about how I felt, Aunt Shirley updated me on her life. Having lost her husband just before I went into a coma, she told me about a man she dated for many years who sadly passed away from cancer eight months ago. She also filled me in on my cousins. At my mother's suggestion, Shirley called both of them and at first neither of them believed it was me. Then my mother put me on the phone with cousins, Aunts, and Uncles of mine from Cleveland. I'd hardly spoken to any of them since we moved, when I was ten years old. So even under normal circumstances there wouldn't have been much to say. They all kept saying how happy they were to hear my voice again, and promised to make a long overdue visit to California.

Sometime in the afternoon, after Shirley left, a new shift of nurses arrived. The fresh faces were as stunned by my awakening as the others had been. Several of them excitedly took pictures with me using their phones. Considering I had a cell phone mounted in my Maxima, which required an antenna on the rear window, it was shocking to see that they were now mobile and small and everyone seemed to have one.

I was exhausted for the rest of the day and into the evening, and mostly slept. Once my mother finally went home and it was time to go to sleep for the night, a part of me was scared that I wouldn't wake up in the morning and a part of me—after everything I had learned—wanted to close my eyes and drift away...this time for forever.

FIVE

In what seemed like fifteen minutes, I opened my eyes and saw daylight through a tiny parting in the curtains. Moments later, Denise entered the room, smiling.

The day started not unlike the previous one, but without the strangeness, the excitement, and the reunions which had greeted my initial awakening, my new reality began to sink in.

Being bathed and dressed by others was humiliating. Doing anything, even with assistance, drained the little energy I had. Freedom was leaving my room in a wheelchair for short periods of time, as opposed to lying in my bed, tethered to a feeding tube. Meeting my physical therapist, a tall guy named Jonas with a Swedish accent, who stretched my limp and stiff muscles, made me realize just how anemic and useless my body was.

Sometime in the morning, Big G came to see me again, with my mother by his side. At first I thought he was talking to her, but then I realized he was talking into a small headset on his ear.

"Here he is…" Gary said to whoever he was on the phone with. He reached down, gave me a quick hug, and then removed his headset and attached it to my ear.

I heard an excited voice roar on the other end. "Dude, this is insane! Joel, are you there?"

It was my friend, Brian Kleftko.

"I'm here, Brian. Where are you?" I asked.

"Oh man, it's incredible to hear your voice again. I'm down in Mexico."

"You're in Mexico?" I asked, surprised.

"Yeah, I've been down here for six months now…I was in Guatemala before that. I finally decided to quit life and start living," he replied, laughing.

Talking to Brian on the phone wasn't as strange as seeing Gary in person after so long. What *was* strange was hearing that Brian Kleftko, the most steady and conservative friend I had, who worked as an accountant for a big firm in Century City, was living in a place I couldn't even imagine him wanting to visit.

While Brian told me about his new life as a surfer, a poet, and a part-time worker on a pumpkin farm, my father's brother, Uncle Solomon, appeared in the doorway. Gary took the headset off of my ear, while my uncle came over to greet me.

"My boy, I can't believe it! I just knew you'd wake up one day," he said.

"Uncle Solomon," I said, trying to raise my arms up to hug him.

"How do you feel?" he asked.

"Weak," I replied. "And overwhelmed."

"That makes two of us," he responded. "Listen, I was going to bring you a sandwich from the deli around the corner, but I thought you might want to go out and grab a bite."

"Solomon, what's wrong with you?" my mother barked in admonishment. "He just came out of a coma after *seventeen years.* Look at him…he's going out to lunch like Stevie Wonder's going to take his driver's test."

"Okay, well…" Uncle Solomon replied sheepishly. "I just

thought a little fresh air would do him some good."

"Have you seen my father?" I asked Uncle Solomon, momentarily forgetting what my mother had told me.

"No…he's gone," he replied, with tears welling up in his eyes. "Joel, your father ached for you until his last day on this earth. He always believed you'd regain consciousness. He never gave up hope. I only wish he was here to see this."

"He was a true believer…I'll say that for him," my mother offered. "Throughout this whole ordeal, he always said to me, 'Joanne, where there's hope, there's life,' and for once he turned out to be right."

Gary got off the phone with Brian and greeted Uncle Solomon.

"Gary, I haven't seen you in I don't know how long," Uncle Solomon said, bracing against his cane to stand up.

"Probably Joel's wedding," Gary replied.

"Lauren's remarried now you know, with two boys," my mother announced.

Kids? I didn't recall her saying anything about kids.

"I know," Gary replied. "I see her at the gym once in a while."

I could feel my energy beginning to fade and as I tried to follow the conversation, I fell asleep.

When I woke up, the room was empty, I was back in bed, and it was dark outside. I called for a nurse and a woman named Esmerelda came with my mother in tow.

"Joel, I took a tour of Hathers this afternoon," my mother told me, while Esmerelda tended to me. "You're not going to believe it— someone I went to high school with in Cleveland, her daughter works there. Anyway, they'll be moving you there earlier than they thought—tomorrow morning."

"Why?" I asked, sleepy and confused.

"Remember, Dr. Kurtz told us he wants you to go to rehab for the next couple of months."

"I want to stay here," I replied.

"Please, Joel, don't be difficult."

I didn't reply, instead closing my eyes and waiting for both of them to leave the room.

Once they were gone, I lay awake staring at the medical apparatus that surrounded me, wondering why I had been given another chance to live. So many years had passed and so much of what made up my life was gone. If at that moment I was able to see the way back to a normal life, which I was about to embark upon, I would have begged someone to put me out of my misery. But in time, after a hard and harrowing road, filled with unimaginable twists and turns, I would make a new life in a very different world and be grateful for the gift I had been given.

Six

I sat with my mother in the lobby, waiting to leave a place that had unknowingly been my home for many years. Soon, a black man in his thirties, with biceps big enough to carry me, came through the sliding glass entrance.

"Mr. Berskin?" he enthusiastically called out.

"Yes," my mother replied, answering for me.

"Hello, I'm J.J., I'll be taking you guys over."

On the short ride to Hathers, I curiously looked out the window, while my mother told J.J. about my coma, my miraculous awakening, my prognosis for recovery, and just about everything he wanted or didn't want to know. By the time we arrived at the rehab facility, I was no longer a stranger.

My mother's lively performance reminded me of an elevator ride I took with her years ago at a condominium she lived in with my father. We began on the fifth floor and when the elevator stopped on the floor below, an older man wearing a fedora hat joined us. Out of courtesy, he asked, "How are you?" A common response would have been, "Fine, and you?" My mother took it as an invitation to *really* tell him how she was.

By the time the elevator reached the ground level, my mother had told the man a litany of troubles she was having, including a sensitive health issue my father was facing at the time. I didn't think anyone could complain so much in four floors, but my mother outdid herself. As she rambled on, the man edged closer to the elevator door, waiting for it to open, with a look on his face that said: *Let me out of here...this woman's crazy.*

As J.J. wheeled me down a long corridor toward my room, the staff enthusiastically waved hello and smiled. J.J. told me that his cousin had spent a month at Hathers a few years ago, and that it was a great neuro rehab facility. Somewhere along the way we lost my mother—most likely to a stranger she decided to talk to or an employee she wanted to ask a question of.

Once J.J. and a nursing aide transferred me from the wheelchair to the bed, they made me as comfortable as possible in my new environment. Looking around, once the head of the bed was raised, the room was reminiscent of being in a hospital. There were a couple of chairs for visitors, a TV hanging from the wall, a bulletin board, and a view across the way of another building. Hopefully the people who design these places have other creative outlets.

J.J. had turned on the TV for me before he left, and I glanced up at it. There were a group of gaudy middle-aged women talking in a restaurant bar. At the bottom of the screen, it said I was watching *The Real Housewives of Miami.*

Although a few of the nurses at Tender Heart had told me about Reality TV, I was still surprised to see these large-breasted women showing so much cleavage. I had never seen anything like it before on a regular or cable channel. Despite the titillating view, I didn't last long, and dozed off before a commercial break.

When I opened my eyes it was dark outside and Aunt Shirley was sitting beside my bed, holding my hand.

"Hi, honey," she said softly. "I just wanted to come by and see how you made the transition. You doing okay?"

"Where am I?" I asked, completely exhausted from the move and confused.

"You're in rehab. They're going to help you get strong again."

"I want to go home," I replied. "I don't have any strength to do anything."

"Rest," Aunt Shirley whispered with a smile.

"Where's my mother?" I asked.

"She went home already…I'm about to leave myself. I just wanted you to have this."

I turned my head and watched Aunt Shirley reach into her purse, pull out a tiny rectangle-shaped object, and place it beside me. "You'll like this," she said. "You don't have to do anything…just relax."

As she put the small earphones that were dangling from the device on me, I assumed whatever it was produced sound. But I was still stunned when I heard Erik Satie's "Gymnopédie #1" coming from something half the size of a matchbook. I was asleep before the piece ended.

SEVEN

I slept for what felt like days. When I woke up, although it was daylight, for an instant I thought I was still at Tender Heart and called out Denise's name. A cheerful, petite woman in her thirties soon appeared at my bedside, wearing a black shirt that said *Hathers Institute of Rehabilitation* in white letters.

"Good morning, Mr Berskin. My name is Robyn, I'm going to be your occupational therapist," she told me.

"Occupational," I repeated, confused by the term.

"I'm going to work with you on the routine things you would do at home," she said. "But right now we're going to get you up and ready for your first day."

With the help of a nursing aide, Robyn transferred me from the bed into a wheelchair. I was still groggy, looking at myself in the bathroom mirror, while Robyn brushed my teeth and washed my face. I had seen myself in the mirror several times at Tender Heart, but the shock of what stared back at me hadn't gone away. *Could I be that old, that worn, that weak, and have that little hair?*

After enduring the humiliation of being showered and washed by a new pair of strangers, I told Robyn I had to go to the bathroom.

"Okay, just one minute, let me make sure you're dry first," she said.

Once Robyn patted the remaining wet spots around my body with the care of a car wash attendant tending to a Rolls Royce, she and the nursing aide transferred me onto the toilet.

It was the same drill I experienced at Tender Heart—one person balanced me and the other one wiped me. In my condition I was helpless without this assembly line of assistance, but I still wanted nothing more than for both of them to disappear.

"This is awful," I said, staring into space.

"This is what we're here for," the nursing aide replied.

"It's okay," Robyn added. "This isn't something you can control right now."

In order to regain control, I would need to retrain my bladder and bowels. That required the nursing aides making sure I went to the bathroom every two hours during the day. Time voids they were called. Occasionally after I urinated, they would scan my abdomen with an ultrasound device to make sure my bladder was empty.

After the bathroom drama was done and I was back in my wheelchair, I followed Robyn's instructions to squeeze her hand, shrug my shoulders, and do several other tedious things to test my strength and see how well I could move. By the time she finished I was exhausted and I asked to lie down again.

If it were my choice, I would have stayed in bed the rest of the day, but soon another nursing aide—this one named Amanda—came to get me up. She transferred me back into the chair and wheeled me down the long corridor. The goal at Hathers, I would quickly learn, was to get patients out of bed as often as possible. According to Amanda, it helped to prevent bed sores and it was good for my digestion and my muscles.

For the next two months, I'd travel the same route countless times on my way to and from therapy sessions or to the cafeteria. The employees in the hallway were always cheerful, giving encouragement to the patients, who passed by one another slowly like stray ships in a foggy night.

Over time, in spite of our physical and mental limitations, I got to know a few of them during meals in the cafeteria. Most of the patients who were older than me seemed to be recovering from strokes, while the younger ones were at Hathers for brain or spinal cord injuries. All of them were in tough shape to varying degrees, and it made for a somber and depressing environment.

Once Amanda brought me back to my room, I fiddled with the music player Aunt Shirley had left me. It didn't dawn on me at the time, but the tiny blue object I was holding, which played digital music, most likely would have been the demise of my store had I not gotten sick and fallen into a coma. To my ears, the sound quality wasn't the same as the portable CD player I used while jogging, but I couldn't believe how incredibly small and easy it was to use.

While I was skimming through the songs, the next person, in what was becoming a steady stream of smiling strangers, came to introduce himself and evaluate my condition. This one turned out to be the leader of my treatment team—Dr. Spoolner.

The doctor was in his fifties, probably closer to the end of the decade than the beginning. He had thinning sandy blonde hair, which he swooped to one side to cover a receding hairline, and sagging jowls that would have looked perfect on a puppet. His demeanor was easygoing, and he spoke with a hint of a Southern drawl.

Dr. Spoolner reached down for my hand and told me that he was my physiatrist. Sensing my look of confusion, he said, "Don't worry, it's just a fancy way to say rehab doctor."

Other than talking about my treatment plan, which would include three hours of therapy a day, five days a week, split between physical therapy, occupational therapy, and speech therapy, he kept saying how lucky I was.

"Your body is very weak, Joel. It's going to take a lot of work and time to regain your strength and relearn the things you haven't done in a while. But your cognition is remarkable for someone who was in a coma for so long. Researching cases similar to yours, and there aren't many, it's fair to say you're an extremely fortunate man."

"Can I go home then?" I asked. "I can get better there."

"The therapists here are excellent," the doctor replied, not addressing my feeble attempt at freedom. "They're going to help you take those critical first steps toward becoming physically independent again. Once you leave here, you'll still need outpatient therapy for some time to come."

Dr. Spoolner went on talking, but I can't say I retained anything that he said. Before he left, I asked when I would be able to drink water again.

Frustratingly, I was still restricted to drinking only disgusting thickened liquids. The gravy-like goop came in several different flavors, including my morning coffee. The closest I had come to having a sip of water was at Tender Heart, when Big G, unaware of my situation, agreed to hand me his water bottle. Wickedly, just before it reached my lips, Denise spotted him. The puree diet I was being fed, in combination with the nutrients I received from my feeding tube, was not as intolerable, but also awful.

"We need to strengthen the muscles in your mouth first, to make sure that bacteria doesn't go into your lungs," Dr. Spoolner explained, telling me what I already knew. "The speech therapist will help with this."

EIGHT

The next morning a pair of nursing aides put me through the same humiliating routine in preparation for another day. Afterward, a black woman with short hair, which was almost entirely grey, entered my room and introduced herself as Dorothy, my physical therapist.

No matter what condition I was in, it would have been hard not to instantly take a liking to her. She had the warmth of a home-cooked meal, cute cherub cheeks and a 1,000 watt smile.

Just like Robyn had done the previous day, Dorothy put me through an evaluation, testing my functionality. She checked to see if I had feeling in various parts of my body, how well I was able to move around in my bed, and how much range of motion I had. She also had me close my eyes and asked if I knew where my arms and legs were, as she moved them up and down.

By the time Dorothy lifted my right arm to begin stretching me out, I was lifeless. She gave me a reassuring smile and began singing softly to herself.

"Just let me know if my noise bothers you, honey," she said.

"I own a music store," I replied, speaking as if I were still in the past.

"Is that so? Well, then you and I will get along just fine. What do you like to listen to?"

"Everything, but probably classical the least."

"I've got two teenagers at home, so I'm forced to listen to rap and hip hop all the time. I don't mind some of it, but it makes me long for the days of Smokey, Stevie, Marvin, and the Temps. Now *that* was music."

While Dorothy worked my anemic muscles and tight tendons and ligaments, I fought to stay awake. I lost the battle and dozed off for what felt like a while, but it was probably just a minute. When I opened my eyes, I saw my mother entering the room.

"Hi, I'm Joel's mother, Joanne," she said, extending her hand to Dorothy.

"Pleasure to meet you, Ms. Berskin. I'm Dorothy, your son's physical therapist. Perfect timing. We're just finishing up here."

"How's he doing?" my mother asked. "Will he be able to walk soon?"

"Yes, that's the goal, we're going to—"

"The case manager, Jessica," my mother interrupted, "she told me that you need to show progress or insurance will stop paying. Is that true?"

"Yes ma'am, it is, and Jessica battles with them every day. She's the best case manager I've ever worked with."

"I sure hope so," my mother replied.

"Don't you worry, Ms. Berskin," Dorothy said with a smile. "We'll do everything we can to see that your son gets the best care possible."

Dorothy talked with my mother for a while longer, explaining the details of my therapy plan and answering other questions she had.

As soon as Dorothy cleared the doorway and went on her way, my mother turned to me and said, "I don't know, Joel…she's the only therapist I've seen here with gray hair. Most of them are young enough to be my grandchildren. I hope she's still with it."

"She's fine, mom. I like her," I replied.

"I met an adorable girl down at the gift shop," she said, quickly changing the subject. "She just got married and is going to Maui for her honeymoon. Remember when your father and I took you and your cousin Bruce to Maui after high school?"

I stared out the window and didn't say anything. Not responding to everything my mother said was a strategy I stumbled upon in these first few weeks, when I was often too weak to engage her. I soon realized that when I didn't reply, she happily kept on talking. It made me wonder how interested she really was in what I had to say.

"I bought you a copy of *Rolling Stone*," she told me, taking the magazine from her purse and lying it on the bed, making me feel guilty for thinking anything other than she's a wonderful, thoughtful mother.

Before I could look at the magazine, my case manager, Jessica, walked into the room. She didn't get very far before my mother met her and said, "Can I talk with you?" and guided her by the arm, until they were out of the room.

When my mother returned moments later, without Jessica, she told me, "They don't want to overwhelm you, so they're going to wait until tomorrow to do anymore therapy." Then she mumbled something to herself that I didn't hear, picked up her purse and wandered off. I didn't see my mother again that day, although I spent most of it resting, so she may have been in my room while I was sleeping.

After sundown, I turned on the TV and tried to watch the news for a few minutes. Like at Tender Heart, I found the stimulus of the information at the bottom of the screen, the crawling type below that, and the constantly changing graphics, to be distracting. *Who could digest all of this at the same time?* I wondered. The news wasn't like this before, and it struck me as annoying and unnecessary. I also didn't care for the flat, wide screen and missed my normal TV at home.

If life were like a movie, the patient in the room next to mine would have been a stunning single female as smart as she was pretty. But a few hours after I gave up on TV, whoever was next to me began thrashing in their bed, throwing things against the wall, and screaming.

"Mr. Rifemore, that's not appropriate," I heard a female voice say moments later. "Please stop doing that right now." More tantrums followed by reprimands from the staff went on throughout the night.

The patient turned out to be a guy my age named John Rifemore. He had been hit head-on by a drunk driver while going to the store to get medicine for one of his daughters, and ended up in a coma for three weeks. Later I learned from You Know Who that as a result of suffering a traumatic brain injury, John had outbursts, slurred speech, and paralysis on one side of his body, among many other ailments. I assume my mother must have struck up a conversation with John's wife, who was at Hathers every day.

A few days after the terrible night he had, John and I crossed paths in the hallway. He got excited when he noticed I was wearing a Led Zeppelin t-shirt.

"I saaw them liive in seeven-tee seeven…best baa-nd e-ver," he said, his speech difficult and slow.

"I wanted to see them," I replied, "but John Bonham died before I got the chance."

"I reemem-ber that day…" John said.

"KLOS and KMET played Zeppelin all day," I replied, recalling the two dominant rock stations in Los Angeles at the time.

"Who doo you think got more ass, Plant or Page?" he asked me.

In a conversation between two guys, I suppose it wasn't an entirely odd question. But in the environment we were in, it caught me off guard.

"I don't know," I responded uncomfortably in front of one of the nursing aides. "They both got a lot."

John let out a laugh, and gave me a big goofy grin.

When I introduced my mother to John in the cafeteria days later, she was taken back by his demeanor. After we sat down at a nearby table, she kept glancing over at him and then quickly looking away, as if she were worried she could catch something.

"Now you know why I screamed at you for riding that mini-bike when you were a kid," she said to me, when I met one of her stares. "You could have ended up like one of these vegetables."

"He has a brain injury, mom—he's not a vegetable," I replied.

An irritated look came over her face. "Why does he have to keep clapping all the time?" she asked. "It's very bothersome."

NINE

As a result of the noisy night when I discovered that John was my neighbor, I didn't sleep much. It wasn't entirely his fault—there was a woman further down the hall, who also woke me by screaming, "Gloria, help me! I'm on the roof!" over and over again in a blood curling cry.

The following morning, my physical therapy session with Dorothy quickly depleted what little energy I had. We ended up only working together for twenty minutes. I rested for an hour, until a nursing aide came and wheeled me to an office on the other side of the building. There I was greeted by a chipper young woman in her twenties.

"Hello, Mr. Berskin, I'm Ellen," she said in a cheery voice, extending her hand. "I'm going to be your speech therapist."

Ellen instantly struck me as a spunky, gum-chewing, cheerleader type. But judgments aside, as soon as I heard her say the words *speech therapist*, all I could think of was what Dr. Spoolner had told me. Instead of saying hello, I said, "You're the water person, right?"

Ellen flipped her brown hair, and gave me a smile a model couldn't improve on. "Mr. Berskin...we need to make your tongue, your lips, your cheeks and your throat muscles stronger," she told me. "They're very weak right now, BUT, we're going to work on that and then you'll be able to drink anything you want and eat regular food. How does that sound?"

She took in my silent disappointment, and then added, "This should happen pretty quickly, AND, the good news is the exercises we're going to do will also help your speech."

"Okay," I replied, deflated.

Ellen began the session by asking me a bunch of questions—the same ones the other therapists had asked—*Where did you grow up? How did you get here? What do you like to do?* Maybe I was tired of evaluations or maybe my fatigue was beginning to overwhelm me, but either way I became irritated.

"This is dumb," I told her. "I can talk, I just sound a little muffled."

Ellen smiled through my objection and went on to tell me that my nasally speech was a condition called dysarthria, and by us having conversations it would improve.

"By increasing your volume when you speak, Joel, you'll naturally over-articulate, and that's going to strengthen the muscles in your mouth."

"Why do I have dysar…" I tried to ask before stumbling on the word.

"Being in a coma for a long time," she answered. "It caused your muscles to atrophy and THAT reduces your respiratory support."

My half hour sessions with Ellen before lunch, divided between working on my speech and my swallowing, turned out to be easy compared to physical therapy and occupational therapy.

After two weeks I had graduated from puree food to a regular diet and at last was able to drink water and other liquids. As I progressed from one consistency of food to the next (puree to fine cut to bite cut to normal), I was given a barium swallow test to make sure I wouldn't aspirate. Being able to get more of my nutrients from meals meant that I needed less and less from the feeding tube.

When I mentioned the barium swallow test to Big G on one of his visits, he pulled a slim rectangular device from his briefcase.

"Here, let's see what it looks like," he said, as the screen on the device illuminated.

"What is that?" I asked.

"It's an iPad—it's like a handheld laptop. Pretty cool, huh?"

"Geez," I responded.

"You're used to seeing laptops that were as thick as a short stack of pancakes and super-heavy. Dude, technology has progressed like crazy—it's going to blow your mind."

Using his finger as the mouse, Big G navigated until he found what he was looking for.

"Check this out," he said, resting the iPad on my lap.

Within seconds, I was watching an x-ray of liquid and food going down someone's throat and esophagus.

"Wow, that's cool!" Big G said, looking over my shoulder. "I'm going to email this to a gal in my office…she loves this sort of shit."

For me, it must have been too close to home, because I found the video eerie and wished I hadn't seen it.

Before he left, Big G showed me how simple it was to use the iPad and gave me a quick tour of some of the stuff that was now on the Internet. I was amazed to see old sports highlights and concert footage from shows I went to as a kid. The websites were light years beyond what I had seen, and the speed was nearly instantaneous.

"Beats dialup, huh?" Gary said, noticing how surprised I was by the speed.

"How did all this get on here?" I asked.

"People over time uploading it. Crazy, huh? I'd let you hold onto it, but I need it for work. Actually, I have to jump here in a minute," he said, glancing at his watch.

TEN

My first week at Hathers was a blur, filled with new faces with various titles and responsibilities, coming and going at a dizzying pace. Overwhelmed is the best word to describe how I felt, but that only scratches the surface. If I hadn't recorded everything I went through on the voice recorder Big G had given me, I don't know how much of it I would have remembered.

The staff at Hathers gave me a bright green binder called a memory book after I arrived. It included my daily schedule and had a place for me to keep track of my therapy and activities. In doing research for this book, I've opened it several times to look back on my rehab experience.

The first couple of pages are filled with autobiographical information that, judging by the handwriting, was supplied by my Aunt Shirley. It covers basic stuff, like what brought me to Hathers, my age, occupation, family members, and a list of my hobbies.

After that, there's a couple of pages where I doodled. I can't draw on my best days, so these sketches, on my worst days, are pretty rough. One is of a desolate beach scene, with a big swatch of sand, a single towel which nobody's laying on, a huge sun, and a calm ocean. On the pages that follow, I wrote words like "HELP" and "MEAN" in really big letters. In the upper right hand corner, I crossed out the *Hathers Institute of Rehabilitation* logo and wrote *Club Hell.* This was probably right after I met my therapists and endured my initial evaluations.

A couple of weeks into my time at Hathers, I wrote in my memory book: *If this doesn't kill me, I'll wish that it had.* On the next page I scribbled lyrics to the saddest Jackson Browne songs I could remember.

When Big G came to see me next, he was with a bubbly and attractive young woman, who wore a snug short-sleeve shirt, which made her breasts an unavoidable sight, super-tight jeans, and bright orange high heels.

"Dude, I'm sorry I haven't been here, I had to go on a quick business trip," Big G told me before leaning over to give me a hug and introducing his guest. "This is Carmen…my secretary. She's the one I told you about, who's going to help you organize your thoughts, so you can write a book. Carmen's great at helping me with letters and marketing copy."

Carmen gave Gary a gushing smile, and then reached over for my hand and said hello.

"You look like you're getting along," Gary said, putting his hand on my shoulder.

"I don't know," I replied, in a defeated tone. "I feel like I'm on a long, painful road to nowhere."

"No, you just need to get strong again, buddy," he responded, walking over to the window. "There's a new world waiting out there for you."

I wasn't interested in anything new, I just wanted things to be the way they once were.

Carmen took a seat in one of the visitors' chairs and I told Gary to sit as well. Instead, he took a big gulp from his cup of coffee and began pacing the room, telling Carmen about a crazy trip him and I took to Santa Barbara, in which we ended up so drunk one night that we found ourselves playing ukuleles with a mariachi band on State Street.

Being around Gary, even at full strength, could leave you ready for a nap. But in my condition, his incessant energy was like trying to follow a leaf in a hurricane. Feeling lightheaded, I closed my eyes.

"Let's take a walk," he suggested seconds later. "Might be good to get out of this room for a while, and give Carmen a chance to see the place." Before I could reply, he was standing behind my wheelchair.

Once we reached the hallway, a nursing aide came over and asked what we were doing. When Big G told her we were going for a stroll, she said she would have to come along.

As we slowly made our way down the corridor, Big G stopped to look inside the therapy gym and the patient resource center, which I hadn't seen yet. After another stretch, we came to an alcove which had an expansive view of Wilshire Boulevard.

"It doesn't look that different, does it?" he asked me, after angling my wheelchair so I had a better view. "But man, the world has changed a whole lot since the 90's. If someone would have told me then half the things that have happened, I would have said they were insane."

"I hardly remember the 90's," Carmen interjected. "I was still a little girl."

The nursing aide, who was close in age to Carmen, started chatting with her, while Gary told me about the fate of some of our favorite haunts. It had been a long time, but still I was surprised by how few places were around anymore. My favorite coffeehouse, which also had live music, called Rhythm & News, was sadly gone.

Gary walked from behind me and sat on the edge of one of the chairs along the wall. I watched him as he interacted with his phone at a phonetic pace, reading and tapping, reading and tapping. Since I had woken up from my coma there were moments like this, when I felt as if I had come back to another world.

Soon after Gary came out of his trance, we headed back to my room. Along the way, we passed a young male patient, wearing a white tank top, who was slowly propelling himself in a wheelchair. The entire lengths of both of his arms were covered with blood and large splats of black ink.

"Is that real?" I asked after we got by him, startled by what I saw.

"That's a full sleeve," Carmen answered. "Isn't it cool?"

I had never heard of a *full sleeve*, but I assumed it was something that could be washed off.

"That's another big change, dude—tattoos," Big G said to me.

"Gary's going to get one soon," Carmen replied, giggling.

"Not happening, but I think my buddy would like to see yours," Big G responded.

When I looked over at Carmen, she had a sheepish look on her face. After an uncomfortable moment, she said, "Uh, I don't think so. At least not here."

Despite seeing my first full sleeve and hearing what Big G had said about tattoos, I never could have imagined how insanely popular human skin had become as an art canvas, until I left Hathers.

The next day, when Dorothy came into my room for our physical therapy session, I asked her if she had a tattoo.

"No," she replied emphatically. "I can't tell you how horrified I was when my oldest daughter got one."

"It's not a full sleeve, is it?" I asked, using the only tattoo lingo I knew.

"Heavens no…it's just a small anchor on her ankle. She got it and showed me before I had a chance to try to talk her out of it," she replied, distressed. "I raised my kids believing that if I kept them close to God they'd always be far from danger, but with all of the darkness in the culture now it's sure giving me and the good Lord a run for our money."

While Dorothy and I were talking, a nursing aide wheeled in something that looked like a stretcher, with straps hanging off one side. I curiously stared at the contraption with trepidation.

"Joel, this is a tilt table," Dorothy informed me. "We're going to use it to slowly bring your body to an upright position."

"Really?" I asked halfheartedly.

"Yes, it's going to get you accustomed to bearing your own weight again."

With the help of the nursing aide, I was transferred onto the table and straps were placed across my ankles, thighs, midsection, and chest.

"It's going to be all right," Dorothy said reassuringly. "You just let me know how you're doing as we go, okay? We can bring you back down, if we need to."

In small increments, with the table sounding like a hydraulic lift, I was brought to a standing position for the first time since I had come out of my coma.

"How do you feel?" Dorothy asked, standing beside me.

"Awkward..." I timidly replied.

"It's going to feel strange," Dorothy said, holding my hand. "It's been a long time since you've been in this position."

"You're standing!" the nursing aide beamed on the other side of me. "Great job!"

Before they brought me back to a horizontal position, I asked, "Can you undo these straps and shoot me out of here?"

"No, honey," Dorothy said with a smile. "You're making

progress. Remember, great strides are nothing but small steps taken over time."

I appreciated Dorothy and the nursing aide's enthusiasm, but the progress I felt I was making made a turtle look like a world-class sprinter.

When the session was over and Dorothy went to leave, she crossed paths with my mother, who was just arriving.

"Hello, Ms. Berskin. Do you mind if I speak with you outside for a moment?" Dorothy asked. My mother nodded in agreement and followed Dorothy, partially closing the door behind her. Once the two of them were out of sight, their voices were faint, but I could still hear most of the conversation clearly.

"I understand your concern about my age, Ms. Berskin," Dorothy said.

"No, I just—"

"It's okay," Dorothy replied calmly. "I have been doing this for a long time, and to work in neuro rehab you need the patience of a saint, the skin of a rhinoceros, and the spirit of a cheerleader. But ma'am, I assure you I still have all of them."

There was a pregnant pause before my mother responded. "It seems like a very hard job. I'm curious why you would still want to do it?"

"I feel most at home when I'm helping people," Dorothy answered. "There's an indescribable gratification in seeing a patient recover. I can't explain it, but I know I feel privileged to be a part of it. So, until they drag me out of here or the good Lord tells me it's time to move on, I'll keep on."

My mother mumbled something I couldn't hear and then there was silence. I thought the conversation was over, but then Dorothy said, "Oh, and about my gray hair…it came prematurely, but I'd like to think that I've worked hard enough to earn every strand."

I can't lie and say it wasn't amusing to hear Dorothy take on my mother. I wished my father were still around—he could have learned something from her.

Eleven

At the suggestion of Jessica, my mother began attending a few of my therapy sessions. Unfortunately, she was more interested in finding out about the therapists' lives than the work I was doing.

When she wasn't chatting them up, she was complaining—about the parking, the family members of other patients, or the smell in the therapy gym. One day, when she was going on about something, I said, "Mom, I hear you complain more than I do any of the patients." She didn't respond immediately, and I thought maybe I had gotten through to her. Then she replied with, "Well, I'm here every day, so I have the right."

I would have thought that my condition and the human struggles that surrounded her would have tempered my mother's pesky personality, but they didn't. When I complained of being tired during a speech therapy session, my mother turned to Ellen and said, "I'll tell you, he never complained a single time when he was at the nursing home." Ellen started to laugh, until she realized what she was laughing about.

Growing up, I always had the urge to explain my mother's nature to people, not realizing that if I just let her talk she would reveal everything I wanted them to know.

The strange thing about human nature is once people *got* my mother, I still couldn't agonize about her without hearing, "But she's your mother, you love your mother." I don't know why, but there's a taboo about being honest about your relationship with one or both of your parents when it's strained.

Normally after my occupational therapy with Robyn ended at two-thirty, I would take a nap. But outside a dark sky with ominous clouds was about to pour, so I decided to stay in my wheelchair and sit by the window.

I've always appreciated L.A.'s infrequent weather changes for the reflective mood they put me in. As the first drops of rain splattered and streaked down the window, I thought about my father. I wished he were here to go through this time with me.

He had always been my confidant, my biggest believer, my best friend, while my mother had been my thorn, my nag, and my constant critic. It seemed cruel that the one I was close to was gone, and the one I had a turbulent relationship with throughout my life was now my caretaker.

I wondered what, if anything, my father would impart to me to make my situation better. I realized how lucky I was to come out of a coma after so many years, and how miraculous it was to have my mental capacity, but was the reality I awoke to—being dependent on others to do the simplest of things and being a shell of my former self—really a life anyone would want? Even with the rosiest of outlooks, my road to independence was a long way off. Once I rehabilitated myself—whatever that eventually meant—I would have to rebuild my life from scratch.

As the sky began to thunder and the rain continued to fall, I wallowed in my pity and cried.

Other than occasional outbursts from patients, Hathers was a subdued environment at night. So when I heard a spontaneous uproar that evening it startled me.

I was listening to music at the time, which was around eight-thirty, with my earbuds on. I pressed pause on the iPod and looked outside, assuming that's where the noise was coming from. But in an instant, I realized that it was the patients who were hollering and banging whatever they could bang, as if they had just learned that World War II had ended. *What in the world could cause a neuro rehab unit to erupt like this?* I wondered.

I called for a nursing aide to find out what was going on, but no one came. As the celebration continued, I thought to turn on the TV. Every channel was showing photographs of a gentle-looking bearded man with the words OSAMA BIN LADEN IS DEAD scrolling across the screen. Not knowing who this man with the long, strange name was, I couldn't understand the excitement.

Before long, the nursing aide came and tried to briefly explain the incomprehensible event of 9-11. It wasn't until the next afternoon when, with assistance, I went to the patient resource center, that I was able to fully grasp the horrible reality of it. I was also stunned to find out that an American citizen had bombed a federal building in Oklahoma City, and killed so many people, especially children.

As the days passed, I learned that even when it doesn't seem possible, mornings come, the hours pass, and life goes on.

Despite the continuing encouragement from my therapists, the work remained repetitive and draining, and the gains seemed minuscule, if at all. I had bad days and not-as-bad days, but my only good days were in memories of the past, when I was able-bodied and whole.

Dorothy worked with me on propelling myself in the wheelchair and sitting up in bed and rolling from side to side. Whenever I got dejected and wanted to quit, she gave me a spirited dose of can-do.

"Honey, I know it's not where you want to be, but little by little you're taking your body back. Just think, one day you're going to wake up and realize you can do something you couldn't do before. It's going to happen…with faith and fortitude, it's going to happen. In time you won't need this gray-haired black woman fussing with you."

When I complained about the ridiculous amount of repetition, Dorothy would mix in some medical jargon.

"Repetition builds endurance, Joel. It reinforces the neural pathways."

It was hard to get motivated by neural pathways, but Dorothy's empathy for my effort and her enthusiasm made it seem like she was going through the grind and agony with me. Once, after she gave me a hug at the end of a session, I used her last name and called her Coach Cole.

"God's the coach, Joel, I'm just one of His cheerleaders," she replied. "You can call me by my nickname though."

"What's that?" I asked.

"Sunshine."

"Sunshine," I repeated, trying to commit it to memory. "That fits."

"When I first started working as a PT, my boss, Joe Carter, used to always say 'here come sunshine' and it just stuck. Must have been on account of my big tooth-bearing grin and my positivity," she said with a smile.

"Where are you from?" I asked, curious about her accent.

"You can't tell by the way I talk?" she asked with exaggerated sass. "I'm from Shreveport, Louisiana, honey…where right about now they're sucking heads and pinching tails, cause it's crawfish season."

"How did you end up here?"

"I followed the wrong man to the right place," she replied with a chuckle.

I didn't respond, not wanting to pry any further into her life.

"My mother begged me not to marry so young," she continued, "but I was foolish and in a hurry. I got two beautiful babies from it though, so I'm blessed."

Dorothy took her phone out of her pocket and showed me a picture of her teenage son and daughter.

"That's Keisha and this is Raymond. They hate when I call 'em babies," she said, "but I always tell 'em, no matter how old you get, you'll always be my babies.'"

Robyn was less talkative than Dorothy, but her desire to help me was the same. Her reserved nature turned out to be a good thing. If she were more chatty, I wouldn't have had much to offer, because by the time our afternoon session rolled around, I was completely drained.

In our time together, Robyn worked with me on bringing my hands up to wash my face and brushing my teeth. She also connected a mobile arm support to my wheelchair, which reduced the force of gravity and made doing certain things easier.

Physical therapy and occupational therapy didn't seem that different to me. In the beginning I referred to them as TP1 (for *Torture Phase One*) and TP2 (for *Torture Phase Two*). But Robyn informed me that physical therapy focused on the lower body, while occupational therapy concentrated on the upper body. Also, occupational therapy was more task-orientated, focusing on the activities of daily living.

My speech therapy sessions with Ellen continued to show the most improvement. She worked with me on oral motor exercises, which entailed pressing my tongue against one of those popsicle-like sticks, holding my breath, and doing several other maneuvers. Their purpose, according to Ellen, was to wake up my muscles, and help my swallowing.

To help improve my speech, Ellen had me say *ahh* for as long and as loud as I possibly could, over and over again. We also sang songs together, which we called *Beatle Breaks*. In deference to our age difference and the fact that we both needed to know the words to whatever we sang, the Fab Four proved to be the perfect choice.

"I wish we had a music therapist here," Ellen said to me one day. "I've had patients that couldn't talk, but they could sing. Music is SO powerful."

"I wonder why?" I asked.

"I'm not sure…I think it's still considered an alternative therapy. Maybe the results are harder to quantify than other types of therapy."

"That's crazy," I offered. "If it works, it works."

Another way Ellen incorporated music was to have me read lyrics aloud from some of my favorite songs, as a way to work on over-articulating.

Thank God for music. It had always been one of my greatest joys in life as well as my work, but now it became my savior. When I wasn't in therapy or resting, I delved into mixes that Aunt Shirley loaded onto my iPod, and experienced old songs in a new way. I would listen intently over and over again to incredible solos (by Eddie Van Halen, Miles Davis, and Gene Krupa, to name a few), as if they were carrying me alongside them. It was the only thing that allowed me to momentarily transcend the walls of my environment and leave my anemic body.

TWELVE

After Big G stopped by with his secretary, he visited one other time alone, and then I didn't see him again for a while. Aunt Shirley and Uncle Solomon, who both came to see me often after I arrived at Hathers, seemed to visit less and less as the weeks wore on.

I suppose the miracle of me coming out of my coma had become a reality, and the reality of rehabilitation wasn't pleasant to be around. During their visits, they had to see not only me, but other patients with spinal cord injuries, brain injuries, and strokes, who were struggling to subsist. When I look back on it, I understand why they didn't want to be in a depressing environment, but I missed their company.

My mother was a different story. She was at Hathers every day, and we ate lunch together in the cafeteria regularly. On the occasions when she was off socializing, I sat with John Rifemore.

I enjoyed our conversations, which were mostly about the music we both loved from our childhood, but sadly John had a terrible short-term memory. Days apart, he repeated the same story about seeing Pink Floyd perform *The Wall* in 1980, as if he were telling me for first time. Amazingly, his recollection of an event that happened a long time ago was precise down to how many nights the band played at the Sports Arena, to the intimate details of seeing David Gilmour stand on top of the wall, playing guitar, while Roger Waters sang "Comfortably Numb" below him.

Some days John would be cheerful. If you didn't know what had happened to him, you might assume that he was stoned, the way his eyes wandered lazily in their sockets. On other days, he would curse at the staff members walking by and throw his food against the wall like an angry child.

Whenever I saw his wife, I could see the strain and heartbreak in her eyes and hear it in her weary voice. One day, I overheard her telling someone on the phone, outside of my room, how John had been acting aggressive toward his daughters. It was devastatingly sad to hear.

Being around John, and other patients with equally difficult challenges, made me think about the lottery of life, and how everything you know and take for granted can irreversibly change in a moment. John took a short drive to the store, one he had probably made countless times before, and in a split second his life was forever and dramatically altered.

Although I was still wrestling to accept my own reality, and the daily struggle of rehabilitation continued to be overwhelming, over time my perspective began to change. I could no longer feel sorry for myself, knowing that I had been spared a worse fate. Seeing John's struggles left an indelible mark on me and long after I left Hathers he continued to inspire me to appreciate my life, but he also haunted me with a deep guilt because I was able to have one.

THIRTEEN

From those around me at Hathers and from occasionally watching TV at night, I was beginning to understand some of the ways in which the world had changed. But I was still in a confined environment, which kept me apart from the reality of living in it. That changed when Jessica came into my room one morning.

"Have you heard of NMN yet?" she asked, after pulling up one of the visitor chairs to sit beside me.

"No," I replied.

"It's a gossip website...it stands for *News Making Noise*. Most of the stuff on there is about celebrities, but it can be anything that's salacious enough to draw interest."

"Okay," I replied, wondering why Jessica was telling me about NMN.

"Joel, someone at the nursing home you were at must have told NMN about your condition."

I looked at her confused and speechless.

"The website posted photographs of you while you were in a coma and after you woke up," she explained.

"Why would someone do that?" I asked nervously.

"They pay people for this stuff, so it could be anyone who was around you."

I got quiet and felt a queasiness in my stomach. Being a private person, what Jessica had told me made me feel anxious.

Growing up, my mother was the only person I knew who religiously read all of those gossip tabloids. She wasn't ashamed about it, and once declared to my father that, "Everything anyone would want to know is in The National Enquirer, The Globe, or Star."

So, it wasn't entirely surprising that my mother knew about the NMN story, either on her own or from Jessica, when she walked into my room later that day.

"Joel, you're famous!" she said, putting down her purse.

I let out a moan, dreading the conversation to come. "What do you mean?" I asked naively.

"Didn't Jessica tell you?" she asked, giddy with excitement. "The website NMN wrote an article about you. It's the most popular gossip website and they also have a TV show. It's run by Harry Glaubson. Remember him? The Jewish reporter, who used to be on the local news."

I turned my head and looked out the window without saying anything. I knew more was coming.

"Maybe the *Jewish Journal* will do a story on you," my mother added.

"Mom, please!" I replied, with as much force as I could muster, to make sure she didn't get any ideas. "I don't have the strength for this sort of thing."

"Okay, okay," she replied, backing off. But before she dropped the subject, she insisted on showing me the NMN story on her phone. I didn't read it, but I glanced at the headline: MIRACLE MAN COMES OUT OF COMA AFTER 20 YEARS. They added more time to my time away, but I suppose it didn't really matter.

Shortly afterward, my mother was off on her social rounds. I feared this meant that everyone on the staff would bring the story up to me, but thankfully nobody said a word about it.

The following day, while I waited to begin another physical therapy session with Dorothy, I had a frightening premonition. My mother, with her love of gossip, had always been, at least in my mind, in the minority. But since coming to Hathers, I had seen way more sensational and shallow stuff on TV than before. *What if the minority was now the majority?*

I brought up NMN to Dorothy, curious as to what she would have to say.

"Have you heard of NMN?" I asked her, just after we got started.

"Of course," she replied. "I guess I shouldn't say it like that, huh? All of this stuff is new to you. What about NMN?"

"What do you think about it?"

"It's not my thing, but to each his own, right?" she replied. "I just wish I didn't have to hear about so many of these famous-for-nothing train wrecks on the nightly news."

"Is Anna Nicole Smith still around?" I asked, thinking of the only famous-for-nothing person I knew of.

"No, honey, she died years ago from a drug overdose," Dorothy informed me. "But before she met her maker, she inspired an offspring that has become more popular than you can imagine."

Fourteen

Not always, but sometimes a positive can come from a negative situation. That turned out to be the case with the NMN incident—it brought Kerrie Kucy back into my life.

Kerrie worked for me at the record store for over five years, if I remember correctly. She was easily the best employee I ever had—incredibly creative, great with the customers, and a hard worker. Many of the things that made Good Sounds unique came from Kerrie. It was her idea to put shelf talkers next to classic records to give customers the backstory on them, and she's the one who suggested that I tape a weekly radio show, with music that I liked, and play it in the store.

She also convinced me to stage a "Bob Dylan Boycott," when his *Oh Mercy* album came out. I got the idea after I read an article talking about how Dylan never gave credit to the musicians who played on the Minneapolis sessions of *Blood on the Tracks*. These sessions were after the initial ones in New York, in which he re-recorded half of the songs on the album. It struck me as being incredibly unfair that these musicians didn't get their due for playing on arguably Dylan's best work.

Once I told Kerrie about the article and my boycott idea, she thought it was great and pushed hard for me to do it. I was afraid to go through with it, I'm ashamed to admit in retrospect, because I thought it would hurt business. Kerrie argued it would have the opposite effect and she was right. A few local music publications, as well as the *L.A. Weekly*, picked up on the boycott and it ended up bringing in new customers.

Kerrie was good for me, but she wasn't always good to herself. She was notorious for falling for guys that mistreated her and sticking around way too long. I'm not sure if it was a result of her relationships, but she had a melancholy disposition. When she spoke to you, she would tilt her head slightly to one side. It came off as a sexy pout, but I assumed it came from a combination of shyness and hurt.

Eventually, Kerrie left the store to start a baby clothing company. I was sad to see her go, but she had connected with a wealthy business partner, who was going to allow her to fulfill her dream of designing clothes for kids. Over time we lost touch, but still had lunch occasionally to reminisce about old times and share new music that we liked.

I was in the therapy gym working with Dorothy, when she tapped on my shoulder and removed one of my ear buds.

"What?" I asked, annoyed at being interrupted just as Jimmy Page was launching into his guitar solo from the live version of "Stairway to Heaven" at Earl's Court.

"Honey, you have a visitor," she told me.

"Where?" I asked, looking around and not seeing anyone but other patients and therapists.

"You've reached Good Sounds, your dealer for the best drug in the world—music," I heard a familiar voice reciting the telephone greeting for my store, from somewhere close by. *"We sell classic vinyl albums and a huge selection of CD's in every genre."*

In a flash, Kerrie appeared from behind a partition. She rushed toward me with tears in her eyes and embraced me.

"I can't believe this…you're alive," she said in my ear.

"I didn't die," I replied, sounding unintentionally sarcastic.

"I know…but you know what I mean," she said, releasing my arms and looking at me in awe.

"How'd you find out about me?" I asked.

"A friend of mine sent me the NMN article," she replied. "Then I had my neighbor, who works in administration for a hospital do me a favor she probably shouldn't have done. That's how I knew you were here."

Kerrie was the first person I had seen that connected me back to my store. I looked at her for a few moments without saying anything, and then I started to cry. She leaned her head into mine, and wrapped her arms around me again.

When she backed away, I noticed for the first time how well she had aged. I couldn't remember our age difference—I think she was only a couple of years younger—but except for a few wrinkles around her eyes, she was remarkably well-preserved . Kerrie had always been kind to others, so it was nice to see that time had been kind to her.

Another patient needed the space we were in, so Kerrie suggested that we move to a spot in back of the gym. Once we got there, I told her the strangeness of coming out of my coma, and what my days had been like since. She filled me in on some of the things I had missed in her life over the years. I was stunned when Kerrie told me that she almost ended up owning my store.

"Remember Tom Tezman and his sister Arial—they owned that taco place a few doors down. A broker told them it was up for sale, and the three of us tried to buy it."

"I can't believe it," I replied.

"I really thought it was going to happen, but then this Persian family made an offer that blew ours away," she replied.

"What a bummer, I wish it would have happened."

"A month after they took over, I went and checked it out. As soon as I walked through the door, my first thought was, *Thank God Joel isn't here to see this.* I almost didn't recognize the place. Half the store was music and the other half was a Persian market. The old man behind the counter made Hitler seem warm and fuzzy. He had a serious scowl on his face and looked at me like, *What the hell do you want?*"

"I can't believe it's gone," I replied, feeling the unwelcomed wave of reality wash over me again.

"I'm sorry…maybe I shouldn't have brought it up," Kerrie said, reaching over for both of my hands and squeezing them tight, as I began to cry. "Listen, the important thing is you're with us again…that means more than anything."

"It's okay," I said, composing myself. "I'm like a sieve now. Everything makes me cry."

"I can't even imagine…you must be completely overwhelmed," she replied.

We sat for a while and watched a young girl, who had a spinal cord injury, working diligently with one of the therapist.

"It's so inspirational, this place," Kerrie said, after making eye contact with the girl and smiling.

"As an observer maybe," I replied.

"Oh, trust me, I know it's a different story to be here."

"Do you mind if we go back to my room?" I asked. "I'm exhausted."

Kerrie went to get one of the nursing aides, who took me back to my room. Once I got situated, Kerrie sat on the edge of the bed and we continued talking.

"Did you visit me in the nursing home?" I asked her. "You can lie—I wouldn't know."

"It's good to see your mind still works the same," she replied with a smile. "I did in the beginning, but not very often after that."

"Was it really weird?"

"It was surreal…just to see you in this stupor. I remember the first time—for some reason I was convinced you were going to come out of it while I was there."

"I hope I'd be there for you, Kerrie, if God forbid you were in the same situation."

"I think you would," she replied. "The truth is, it was probably one of the few times in my life when a man actually listened to me without talking about themselves."

We both laughed. "That was a good one, Kerrie," I said, as she stood up and walked over to a canvas bag she had brought with her.

"I brought you something," she said, pulling out a small boom box and putting it on the table beside my bed. "I figured everyone's going to inundate you with new technology, so I thought I'd go old school."

"That's not old school," I replied.

"I also made a few CD's for you. This one has all stuttering songs, just in case your speech was affected," she said, holding it up for me to see. "Warped personality, I know, but I didn't think you'd be offended."

"I wouldn't have…I think."

"I never realized how many stuttering songs there are…'M-m-m-my Sharona,' 'B-B-B-B-Bad to the bone,' 'B-B-B-Bennie and the Jets,' 'Talkin' 'bout my g-g-g-generation,' 'B-b-b-Baby, you just ain't seen n-n-nothin' yet.'"

"Thanks, Kerrie. Music always helps."

"Oh, and don't worry, I didn't put 'Su-Su-Sussudio' on there," she said, singing a snippet of the Phil Collins song. "I knew you'd kill me if I did."

"It would have been okay," I replied. "I still love his first solo album and almost everything he did with Genesis."

"I'll never forget the day in the store when I told you that somewhere in that song there must be something great, because so many people liked it. And you said, 'Yeah, and somewhere in McFry's Chicken Tenders there's chicken.'"

"I said that?" I asked, not remembering the comment. "I remember reading somewhere that his daughter named her horse Sussudio."

"Really? It's probably a better name for a horse than a song, but not by much."

Kerrie stayed for a few more minutes and then hugged me goodbye. She told me I'd see her again soon. Her baby clothing company had taken off over the years and a large corporation recently bought her and her partner out. She said she loved the financial freedom that selling the business gave her, but she was going stir crazy with so much time on her hands.

"I miss it," she said, as she was about to leave. "But the sad irony of designing clothes for other people's kids, when I never found a man to have my own, was hard on me."

Before Kerrie disappeared into the hallway, she turned back toward me and said, "Believe it or not, Joel, I'm finally going to record an album of some of the songs I used to play for you at the store."

FIFTEEN

My mother continued her daily visits, usually showing up sometime in the morning. She never asked how I was doing; she just talked extraneously for a few minutes, then put her things down and disappeared. I didn't know exactly where she went when she left my room, but an environment like Hathers—filled with administrators, therapists, nurses, doctors, social workers and visitors—was rich with social possibilities. In intervals, she would report back to me with personal stories about people I had never met.

"I can't believe it—Lorraine, the Inpatient Director, is a distant cousin of Taylor Swift," she told me, while a nursing aide named Irene was taking my blood pressure.

I didn't know Lorraine, and at the time, I didn't know who Taylor Swift was. But that didn't matter to my mother.

After she left the room, Irene said, "Joel, it's strange, every time I take your blood pressure with your mother here, it's higher."

"That's good to know," I replied, my nasally voice hiding my sarcastic tone.

"Really?" she asked, surprised. "Why?"

"Well, now I have scientific proof that my mother is not good for my health."

Irene let out a laugh, and it made me think of and terribly miss my father. Together, he and I always used humor to diffuse the madness of living with my mother. We were never able to change her, but it was comforting to have someone else in the world who understood what you were dealing with.

Before Irene left to take care of another patient, she must have felt bad for my mother or just wanted to cover herself. "Not everyone is a natural caregiver, Joel," she told me. "A life altering situation, like the one you're going through, can make the most wonderful person a real you know what."

True to her promise, a few days later, I opened my eyes from an afternoon nap and Kerrie was at my bedside.

"Hey, it's me again. How are you doing?"

"Okay," I replied. "Just trying to recuperate from occupational therapy."

"Can I do anything…get anything for you?" Kerrie asked.

"No," I answered. "Rest is the only thing I need and my body can't seem to get enough of it."

"I don't know if you feel up to it, but I got permission from your case manager to take you on an expedition."

"Really? Where to?" I asked.

"To one of the exotic common areas in the building," she said sarcastically.

With one of the nursing aides looking on, I showed Kerrie the progress I was making in transferring myself from the bed into my wheelchair.

"Impressive!" she responded with applause.

"I can even propel this stupid thing now," I said, gripping the wheels of the chair. "But I have to warn you, I move painfully slow."

"It's okay," Kerrie replied. "I just got off of the 405, so I'm already in barely moving mode."

"Isn't the traffic INSANE?" the nursing aide interjected. "I come in every day from Downey."

"It's unbelievable—rush hour is now any hour," Kerrie said. "I don't get how there's so many people out in the middle of the day."

The exotic common area Kerrie had arranged for us turned out to be a small nook around the corner from the staff offices. It looked like a doctor's waiting room, with chairs along the wall, a coffee table covered with magazines, and a TV on the wall.

"Nice little spot, huh?" Kerrie asked.

"Yeah," I said wearily, as I struggled to turn my wheelchair to face where she was going to sit.

"You sure you're okay?" she asked, seeing me grimace in pain from soreness in my shoulders.

"I'll be all right," I half-heartedly assured her.

"Here," Kerrie said, standing up and walking behind me. "Let me see if I can help by giving you a little massage."

Kerrie's gesture reminded me of the times at the store, when she used to rub my shoulders on long days during the holiday season, or bring me food from one of the nearby restaurants whenever I got a killer migraine.

Because we worked closely and got along so well, my friends and family always wondered why we didn't date. There were two reasons: she was a Godsend to me as an employee—I didn't want to risk losing her, and similarly to Kerrie, I never seemed to pick healthy partners.

My father was enamored with Kerrie and told me several times after visiting the store that she was the one, and I was nuts not to pursue her. "She may not be what you think you want," he said, "but I'm telling you *that's* who you marry." In baseball parlance, he called Kerrie "a double off the wall." In other words, a good, solid choice.

As it happened, I followed my father's example, not his advice, and married an unpleasable woman, who was always on me for one thing or another. My relationship with Lauren was rocky from the start, and it only got worse after we exchanged vows.

"I wish we had ended up together," I said to Kerrie, after she finished my shoulders and began massaging my arms.

"Where did that come from?" she asked, surprised.

"I don't know," I replied. "I've just been thinking a lot."

"I heard through the grapevine, years ago, that Lauren remarried."

"Yeah," I replied, feeling the sting of her leaving me, even though like so many things it felt surreal.

"I'm sure she's made her next husband very *un*happy," Kerrie said, momentarily stopping the motion of her hands. "Sorry…I never cared for her, and I'm pretty sure the feeling was mutual."

"It's okay," I said. "You were the only one who tried to warn me."

Kerrie didn't respond, as if she was letting the weight of what I said sink in.

"Do you really think you and I could have had a relationship?" she asked, sitting back down.

"I think so…we got along really well. Unfortunately, friends usually don't end up together."

"Why do you think?" she asked.

"Probably because men listen to what's between their legs more often than what's between their ears, and most times it doesn't work out that well."

"I remember in the beginning, you guys were crazy about one another."

"Yeah, that lasted for about six months, and then the real me met the real her."

"And then you wanted to kill each other," Kerrie added.

"You must have some experience with this," I kidded.

"Just a little," she said, smiling.

Kerrie and I talked for a while longer, but I was fading fast.

"I need to go back and lie down." I told her.

We were on our way back to the room, when I heard an omnipresent voice behind me.

"That's my son—I have to go," my mother said to whoever she was talking to.

"Guess who?" I asked, looking over at Kerrie.

"Your mother," she replied instantaneously, with a hint of dread in her voice.

Kerrie and I stopped and slowly turned around. As my mother approached us, she said, "I thought that might be you, Kerrie. Oh my gosh, it's been ages!"

"It's definitely been a while," Kerrie replied, giving my mom a hug. "How are you Mrs. Berskin?"

"Well, other than having to be here, I'm okay," my mother responded. "Kerrie, you look great—tell me what's going on."

"Thanks…everything's good. I just can't believe I'm actually here with your son," Kerrie answered, putting her arm around my shoulder.

"Are you married? Kids?" my mother questioned, quickly getting to the heart of all that mattered to her.

"No," Kerrie replied, tilting her head to the side.

"Really? I find that so hard to believe," my mother responded, oblivious as to how it might make Kerrie feel.

"Me too," Kerrie replied. "I guess I marched too long to my own drummer, and ended up being the only member in the band."

I glanced up at Kerrie and gave her a look of encouragement.

"Well, maybe you and Joel—" my mother replied.

"Okay, Mom—" I interrupted, knowing where she was headed. "Kerrie and I were just finishing our visit…she has to leave in a minute."

"All right," my mom replied reluctantly. "Kerrie, it was nice seeing you again. Maybe we can have lunch sometime. I have to go talk to Joel's case manager now."

"For sure," Kerrie replied. "Nice seeing you, Mrs. Berskin."

Kerrie and I watched as my mother walked down the hallway, stopping to talk to the first staff member she saw.

"She hasn't changed," Kerrie said. "She looks incredible for her age though."

"You think so?" I replied. "When I saw her for the first time at the nursing home, I couldn't believe my eyes. I never thought I'd see my mother old."

"It must be hard not having your father here."

"Yeah, it is. He evened things out."

When Kerrie and I got back to my room, she reached into her canvas goodie bag and pulled out an iPad.

"Big G showed me one of those," I said. "I couldn't believe all the stuff that's on the Internet now."

"Technology has come a long way, that's for sure. It's a good thing I guess, but we're all addicted to it now," she replied as the device came on. "Anyway, I got you a subscription to this website where you can watch all the movies you want."

"Don't you need this?" I asked, as she positioned the iPad so I could easily use it.

"I just bought a new one, so you can keep this one. Oh, and before I forget, this folder has a list of movies you missed that you might like."

"What's this?" I asked, pointing to a folder beside the one she mentioned that was labeled COOL PEOPLE WHO DIED.

"It's morbid, but I thought you might be curious about people who died while you were in your coma."

"Can I look?"

"Go ahead, just tap on the folder."

Glancing at the list, my eyes landed on a name that stunned me.

"Tim Russert?" I said, surprised. "I used to watch *Meet the Press* every Sunday morning."

"Yeah, he had a heart attack. It was really sad."

I commented on Princess Diana and a few of the other names on the list, and then I must have fallen asleep.

When I woke up, the iPad was on the table beside my bed, and Kerrie was gone. For whatever reason, I started thinking about my life after Hathers, and the reality of having to live with my mother. I immediately got anxious and closed my eyes again.

My restful state didn't last for long. Before I knew it, my mother was in mid-sentence, going on about something, sitting in the chair beside my bed.

"I *was* trying to sleep," I moaned.

"Sorry, I wanted to tell you about the conversation I had with Jessica."

"Don't be sorry, just be more aware."

"She was asking me about my condo—if there's stairs, the bathroom situation, etcetera."

"Oh," I replied, uninterested and wanting the topic to go away.

My mother continued telling me about the logistics of my eventual move, and I continued responding with one word answers. Thankfully, after a few minutes, she told me that she had to leave to meet a new friend for lunch.

As difficult of a place as Hathers was to be, the thought of living with my mother made me cherish my remaining time there like water in a desert.

That night I watched the first of Kerrie's movie recommendations, which was "Good Will Hunting," and by the end of the week I had seen "Almost Famous," "The Truman Show," "The Shawshank Redemption," and "Once." Like music, the movies took my mind off of my struggle and transported me to another place.

Sixteen

Kerrie had become an unexpected savior in an unforeseen situation, and her frequent visits gave me something to look forward to. Whether it was her intention or not, her presence put a little distance between my mother and I, which was a good thing.

The next time Kerrie came to see me, she was carrying a guitar case.

"I thought I'd play you some of my new songs, if you promise not to be too judgmental," she said, putting down her things.

"I won't be…promise."

"How was today?" she asked.

"I worked on my standing balance with Dorothy. You take all of these things for granted, but it's hell if you have to relearn them."

"Well, now you get to just relax and listen. I'll play you the mellower ones."

"Do you have a title for your album yet?" I asked.

"I have a few possibilities. My current favorites are *Moods Through Sound* and *Music For Your Every Mood*."

"I like both of them, but the second one gets my vote," I said, as she took her guitar from the case and began tuning it. "I can't wait to hear the songs."

"I hope you're not the only one who hears them," she replied, reaching into her bag for a bottle of water.

"Is it going to be just you or are you going to have a band?" I asked, ignoring her comment.

"Remember the Robert Palmer video for 'Addicted to Love' with those seductive background singers wearing tight black dresses?"

"Yeah. MTV played that thing to death."

"I thought about putting together a band with the biggest hunks I could find, who can play half-way decently, and calling us *Kerrie Kucy and the Delectable Dudes*. But I'll probably chicken out and just have it be me."

"It's a great idea…you should do it."

"I'll see," she replied. "At my age, in this business, you have to do something to get attention. I just don't want it to take away from the music."

Kerrie began playing her guitar in one of the chairs, but when the arm of the chair got in the way of her strumming, she stood up and leaned against the riser below the window.

Listening to a friend play songs for you can be an uncomfortable experience, but I always liked everything I heard of Kerrie's at the store. Her music had elements of several singer-songwriters from our generation, but her style was unique and entirely her own. Shortly after she started singing, one of the nursing aides, who was walking by, poked her head in and gave a thumb's up and a smile.

After Kerrie finished three songs, she leaned her guitar against the wall in the corner of the room.

"Well…" she said, inviting feedback.

"They're great, Kerrie—and yes, that's my honest opinion. The melodies are catchy and I love that the lyrics are not obvious."

"Coming from the Music Man, I'm flattered," she replied. "I've been reworking them for months and they're finally where I don't hate them anymore," she said, reaching for her guitar again. "I'd like to do a couple of standards, but I want to find ones that haven't been covered a zillion times. Any suggestions?"

"My Aunt put some really nice songs on the music player she left me. Have you heard of a jazz singer named Blossom Dearie from the 50's?"

"What a name. I've never heard of her."

I pointed to the iPod, which was on my pillow. "Go ahead and listen…it's called 'Try Your Wings.'"

"I like it," she told me after removing the earbuds, "but she has such a girly voice. I wonder if it would resonate as well in my style."

"It's worth a try. I don't think it's been covered many times."

"I'm surprised you like it," she said. "You don't normally go for those sacchariny type of songs."

"I don't know…it might be the place I'm in, but the sweetness of her voice and the message really got to me."

"It would be the first and probably the last time that I sing the word 'hitherto.' I don't think I've ever heard that in a song before. Any other ideas?"

"How about 'I'll Be Lucky Someday?' It's an obscure track on one of those great Glen Campbell records from the 60's. It's not a standard, but it could have that feel."

"Is it on here?" she asked, pointing to the iPod.

"No, that's mostly jazz, classic rock, and some classical."

Kerrie tapped her phone a few times, and within seconds Glen Campbell was singing the song. It was amazing to see how the cell phone could do so many things so quickly.

"You've taken me from sweet and uplifting to sitting alone on a bar stool in the middle of the day," she said after the song ended.

"That's a good way to put it," I replied. "Both could work, though…especially if you decide to go with the second album title you mentioned."

Kerrie looked down and tapped on her phone again. "I'll add it to my maybe list."

"Anything you want to hear?" she asked, picking up her guitar again.

"I've got the Beatles on my brain from singing their songs during speech therapy."

Kerrie went straight into one of my favorites from the *White Album*—which she probably remembered from our days together in the store—and began plucking out "Dear Prudence." When she got to the bridge, I heard a voice singing along behind me. I turned my wheelchair to face the door and saw John Rifemore joining in.

"More, more!" he cried, clapping his hands excitedly once Kerrie finished.

"Hey, John, come in," I said. "Is there anything you want to hear?"

"Bee-toles? How about Mar-tha my Dear, for my mom," he replied.

John listened quietly and by the time Kerrie strummed the last chord, he had tears streaming down his face.

"I really miss her," he said, when Kerrie walked over to console him.

"It's okay," she said, rubbing his back. "It's good to let it out."

"I'm glad she's not here to see me this way though," John responded.

"John, this is my friend, Kerrie Kucy, or KK for short," I said.

"She's a sexy bitch," he blurted out, changing his mood in an instant and starting to grope himself.

Kerrie took a step back and her face tightened. I was caught off guard and stunned into silence, until I was finally able to say, "Oh man, c'mon…don't do that."

Thankfully, the awful and incredibly awkward moment was interrupted when a nursing aide came to tell John that one of his daughters was waiting in his room to see him.

"A little concert, huh?" the nursing aide offered, as Kerrie walked back to pick up her guitar.

"Yeah!" John replied like a giddy child. "That's KK and we're the Head Cases. New grouup."

When John left the room, I tried to explain the nature of his brain injury to Kerrie, from what I had picked up while being at Hathers.

"The signals in his brain are scrambled from the accident he had. It messed up his memory and emotions and behavior," I told her. "It's like dropping a computer from a two-story building and damaging the hard drive."

I wanted Kerrie to understand that John couldn't control his actions, and I wanted, if possible, for her to be comfortable around him. It was a difficult position to put her in, but I knew how much John loved music, and how much he would enjoy singing with us, if Kerrie brought her guitar again.

"I'm here for you, Joel, in any way I can be," she said, while walking over to close the door. "But that was so scary…the way he turned like that."

"I've heard him screaming and cussing at his own daughters for no reason at all…just talking out of his mind. It's beyond…anything," I managed to say before beginning to cry.

By now, Kerrie must have felt like she was becoming a caregiver, not by choice. She leaned over and held me.

"Do you think he'd do that again?" she asked, still shaken by the incident.

"I don't know, that's the awfulness of his condition," I replied. "He probably won't remember what happened. Most of the time he forgets what we talk about or he gets confused. In the cafeteria yesterday, he said to me, 'I gotta get back to my office, we're super busy today.'"

"Maybe if his daughter is with him, he'd be okay," Kerrie offered.

"Maybe," I replied.

SEVENTEEN

The next time I saw John, a few days after the incident with Kerrie, he was smiling and happy. We sat together in the cafeteria and talked about music. Once we finished eating, he engaged me in a game of sorts, where we went back and forth naming artists from the 70's and our favorite song by each of them. Some people like to poke fun at the 70's, but when you remember all of the great music and movies from that era, it's unbelievable.

Before John and I ran dry, we came up with groups I hadn't thought about in a long time, like Poco and Manassas and Firefall and UFO.

I was progressing with my therapy and was now able to stand at the sink, wash my face, and brush my teeth. The staff was effusive about my accomplishments, but they were judging how far I had come, as opposed to where I once was. In my mind, I was still a far cry from being whole again. I wanted to be able to walk without assistance, I wanted to be able to drive, I wanted to be INDEPENDENT.

During the next week, I got some good news—my feeding tube was going to be removed. From my work in speech therapy, I had improved my swallowing to the point where I was able to get all of my nutrients from meals. The annoying apparatus, which I was initially tethered to for eight hours a day, was right where I pulled up my pants and I couldn't be rid of it fast enough.

So when one of the nurses came to inform me that the tube would have to remain for another three days, until they were certain I didn't need it any longer, I became agitated.

"How about if I take it out myself," I told the nurse, chasing away the cheery grin from her face. "It'll save the doctor some time."

"No, Mr. Berskin, I'm afraid you can't do that," she replied.

"I can do anything I want, it's my body," I responded, with probably the most overused and unoriginal patient threat in the book. I felt childish saying it, but threats are all you have when you're powerless.

I continued to carry on with my tantrum, making it seem as if I was not bluffing. The nurse attempted to reason with me, but eventually gave up and left the room. She returned moments later with Jessica, who talked to me until I accepted the procedural delay with a little less angst.

Once the doctor finally pulled the feeding tube out, I was required to stay in bed for four hours to heal. I filled the time by watching two more movies on Kerrie's list, "Forrest Gump" and "A Moment to Remember."

With my eating habits back to normal, I spent my speech therapy sessions working on improving my articulation, which would get rid of my nasally voice. Most of them went smoothly and I was amenable to the tedious vocal calisthenics, but there were days when my mood and desire soured.

"My voice is fine," I told Ellen on a particularly trying day. "I'd rather use this time to rest or do more physical therapy, so I can walk again."

"Joel, listen to yourself, you're making improvement," she said enthusiastically.

"I don't care how I sound…people can understand me. Besides, my speech will get better on its own, even if I don't do anything."

"Okay," she said, trying to appease me with a smile. "Let's do a little more, and then we'll be done for today."

At various points during my rehab—and this was one of them—my experience at Hathers reminded me of the sentiment expressed in The Eagles classic song, "Hotel California." *I could check out, but I couldn't leave.*

However small the increments of my improvement were, I noticed that little by little I began to retreat back to my solitary nature. Patients were encouraged to eat in the cafeteria and socialize with others, but more often I preferred sitting in my room, listening to music or watching a movie. I was also beginning to use the iPad Kerrie had given me more and more, discovering sporting events, presidential debates, and cultural phenomena that I had missed.

No matter how much I dreaded my therapy sessions, I always looked forward to seeing Dorothy. She had a unique way of making the struggle seem more palpable, and she was helping me reach my biggest goal: being able to walk.

Eighteen

As the end of my time at Hathers grew near, Jessica and Robyn worked with my mother and me on the logistics of my upcoming transition. Like anything you dread, I tried to push it out of my mind. Whenever my mother brought up the move, I continued to brush it aside.

"Joel, I need to know these things so I'm prepared for when you come home," my mother pleaded with me one afternoon after occupational therapy.

"Whatever you do is fine," I replied dismissively.

"I know you, Joel—you'll start in on me as soon as things aren't exactly the way you want them."

"No I won't," I assured her. "I'm easygoing."

"Sure…and elephants leave small footprints."

My mother almost never made me laugh, but her comment caught me off guard and I chuckled. "Where'd you get that from?" I asked her.

"I overheard it downstairs in the gift shop," she replied.

"That's funny."

"Can we discuss this now, please…I have a lot I'm dealing with here."

"In comparison to whom?" I asked, provoking her.

She didn't take my bait and instead began wandering around the room, organizing things and talking to herself.

The next time I saw Jessica, I expressed my trepidation of living with my mother. She asked if I had anywhere else I could go. I thought about my Aunt Shirley, but it would cause a stir and create tension between her and my mother. Kerrie crossed my mind, but it was a tremendous thing to ask someone, and I didn't want to put her in a position of having to say no. Besides, even though she hadn't told me, I sensed that she had a guy in her life, which would have made it even more difficult. During her visits, she was always corresponding with someone on her phone, typing away and smiling and then laughing at the responses she got. I might have been wrong, but I was pretty sure it was a love interest.

Big G was another possibility, but I needed someone to care for me and he couldn't take on that role, and I wouldn't think of asking his wife, who was raising two kids.

"Maybe it'll bring you and your mother closer," Jessica said optimistically, responding to my quandary.

"I highly doubt it," I told her. "We've been orbiting around one another like two different planets for as long as I can remember."

"Don't planets align sometimes?" she asked playfully with a smile.

"No, I think you're thinking of stars, and that happens mostly in books and movies."

Jessica proceeded to give me the perfunctory speech about how hard these situations can be on family members, and that my mother loved me.

I've never been big on birthdays, so it meant even less to me to turn forty-nine in the condition and place I was in. If it were my choice, no one at Hathers would have known about it. But my mother, walking down the hallway with a big bouquet of balloons that said *Happy Birthday* and placing them beside my bed, effectively announced it.

"You didn't have to do this," I said, with a look of displeasure.

"Joel, it's your birthday," she replied emphatically, while arranging the balloons so that the message on each of them faced in the right direction.

"If it's my birthday, shouldn't it be about what I want or don't want?" I asked, expressing an old sentiment of mine.

"Of course," she replied. "These just make the occasion a little more festive and special."

"For you," I responded before letting it go.

Every staff member who came into my room felt it necessary to serenade me upon seeing the balloons. The ones who didn't have the occasion to be in my room, wished me happy birthday in the hallway, in the therapy gym, and in the cafeteria, where an announcement was made. The only upside to all of it was that my dietician said it was okay for me to have a small piece of chocolate cake.

Late that afternoon, Kerrie came by and surprised me by remembering the date.

"I can't believe you remembered," I said, as she walked into my room, holding a long, skinny wrapped gift.

"How could I forget?" she replied. "You complained about it every year I worked for you."

"Yeah," I conceded, giving her a hug. "What in the world did you bring me…it looks like a rifle."

"First, tell me again why you don't like birthdays. I forgot that."

"No reason really…I've just never liked them," I told her. "There's a Super 8 film my dad shot of my sixth birthday. There's no sound, but you can see how shy I get when the clown my parents hired, and all of my friends, start singing happy birthday to me. I don't like being the center of attention."

"I can sort of relate," she said, handing me the intriguing gift. "Do you need help opening it?"

"Let me see," I replied, managing to tear off one end of the wrapping. Once I was able to peek inside and see the gift, I started to laugh.

"Hold that end," she said, "and I'll pull off the wrapping."

Kerrie had bought me an incredibly unique walking cane. The handle was an old Shure microphone, which was inserted into a beautiful piece of wood. Along the wood body, there were lyrics engraved from several classic songs.

"I couldn't resist...a friend of mine made it," she said, grinning. "I know you can't use it yet, but you can work on your Freddie Mercury imitation for now. Remember that sawed-off mic stand he used in concert?"

"Oh yeah...I saw Queen in my freshman year of high school at the Fabulous Forum. I think it was the *Jazz* tour."

"Don't Stop Me Now," Kerrie replied, singing the title from one of the songs on the album.

"This was very thoughtful, Kerrie. Thank you," I said, looking more closely at the engravings on the cane.

"I decided to go for songs with an inspirational message."

"It's perfect," I replied, reciting a few of the lyrics aloud.

"I just hope you can use it real soon," she said, rubbing my shoulder.

"I should be ready for a walker soon. I'm working on strengthening my legs, quads and gluts now to improve my balance," I replied, handing the cane to Kerrie, so she could lean it against the wall.

"You'll get there."

"I don't know," I replied cynically. "Some days when I wake up, for a moment I think I'm me again. My mind flashes on the things I have to do before opening the store. Then I realize where I'm at and what happened, and I wish I never woke up."

"It's a heavy thing, what you're going through, Joel," Kerrie replied. "I think it's probably normal to feel those things."

"I want to get out of here and get on with my life, but I'm scared to start over again…especially in this condition," I said. "I keep hearing from everybody how much the world has changed, which makes me think it's going to be that much harder."

"I'll be honest with you," Kerrie replied. "Technology has changed everything—the pace of life now will make the 90's look like they're barely moving. The other biggie, in my opinion, is the culture has become shallower than a bird bath."

"Don't you think it was pretty shallow before?" I asked.

"Yes, but trust me, not like now."

"What do you think happened?"

"It's just a theory, but in a sound bite society, which is what we've become, substance has less value," Kerrie said before she paused and looked out the window. "God this all sounds awful. It's not that bad, I promise."

"Sure," I replied, giving her a doubting look.

Nineteen

My remaining days at Hathers passed without any noteworthy changes in my condition. Unfortunately, I wasn't able to graduate from a wheelchair to a walker, and I still needed some help being bathed and getting dressed. But even a contrarian like me couldn't deny the strides I had made since arriving.

My next step would be outpatient therapy at a place not far away called Sarswick Therapy Center. I knew approximately when it would begin, but I had no idea when it would end. That date was further off than I could allow myself to think about.

On most days toward the end of my stay, I was positive and focused on the goal of regaining a productive life, but there were times when dark clouds would drift into my head and make the light impossible to see. I would ruminate endlessly on the difficulty of my situation. The reality that even in the best case scenario, according to my doctors, I would never get back to where I was before my coma, severely depressed me. To add to that, being unconscious for nearly seventeen years made it so I was no longer a young man.

During one of our last sessions, Dorothy asked me what I was looking forward to most about leaving.

"I don't know," I told her. "I'm just overwhelmed by the thought of it."

"That's entirely understandable," she replied. "But if you make a list of at least three things, it'll give you something to look forward to. Put some desired destinations on that road map, honey."

"Maybe I can hire you to motivate me after I leave here, Dorothy. I'll need as much pep as I can get."

"Well...*you got to accentuate the positive, eliminate the negative*, she said, singing the 40's standard, in a spirited voice. "The light warms the heart, shows the way, and blinds the devil."

"Okay...let me see if I can think of three," I said, forcing myself to think beyond the dread of moving in with my mother. "I can't wait to see the ocean again...I can't wait to listen to live music again, and I can't wait to have at least three slices of pizza at Frankie's on Fifth."

"There you go," Dorothy replied, beaming like a proud parent. "Do me a favor...when you're cruising down Pacific Coast Highway, roll down those windows, turn up that music, and let out a yell for me. Okay?"

"You got it," I said. "I want you to know how much I appreciate you as a therapist, and even more as a person, Dorothy. Thank you."

"You don't have to thank me, Joel, it's my job and my pleasure."

My last few sessions with Robyn were spent getting me reoriented to cooking, cleaning, and doing laundry in a simulated apartment Hathers had. I also attended three meetings on how to manage my medication, which Robyn led with a nurse and another staff member.

The biggest surprise of our time together came when we went shopping at a Ride Aid around the corner from Hathers. The store was uncrowded and we didn't stay for long, but it was the first time I had been in a public place since Bill Clinton was president.

When the morning of my last full day arrived, a new nursing aide named Isabelle came into my room and put a lanyard around my neck. The placard attached to it said, KEEP MOVING FORWARD in big letters.

"Good luck with everything," she said with a smile before quickly leaving.

Seconds later, each of my therapists, as well as Dr. Spoolner, Jessica, and a group of nursing aides, walked single file into the room. They formed a semi-circle around my bed and stood smiling. Then, one by one they took turns giving me a hug and wishing me well.

Human kind is an oxymoron, I heard my father say more times than he'd probably admit. But at Hathers I was surrounded by selfless people, who dedicated their careers to those who were a shell of their former selves and needed to start over. Whatever they were paid, it wasn't enough. There was no amount of money that could adequately compensate them for the dedication, encouragement, love, and respect they gave to patients like me.

"I know I was a pain at times," I told the group, tearing up.

"At times?" Dr. Spoolner joked. "Not at all, Joel. We loved having you here."

"Joel's like a jelly donut," Dorothy chimed in. "A bit crusty on the outside, but soft and sweet once you reach the center."

Everyone laughed and Dorothy leaned over to give me another hug.

"Promise you'll keep in touch and let us know how you're doing," Robyn said.

"This is goodbye, not good riddance. I promise," I replied.

"I have your mother's phone number," Jessica teased.

"Don't feel special...everyone she's talked to here has it," I cracked.

For my last lunch, I sat with John and his wife in the cafeteria. When I told him I was leaving, he surprised me and said, "Mee too."

"Well, not exactly," his wife clarified. "By the end of the week though."

"I'm going home!" John protested.

"Yes—yes, honey, you are," his wife replied, trying to appease him.

"I'll miss our music chats," I told John before I reached over to pat him on the shoulder.

"Mee too," he replied.

After John's wife and I exchanged contact information, I turned my wheelchair to leave. Just before I reached the hallway, I heard John yell, "Ramble on, buddy."

"Ramble on," I called back to him, and raised my arm.

As I settled in to go to sleep that night, I tried not to think about the morning ahead. I knew if I did, I wouldn't sleep a wink. Exhausted, I conked out within minutes. Unfortunately, a patient near my room had a panic attack in the middle of the night that would have woken an old man, who could sleep through a passing train on a subway platform.

After tossing and turning for an hour, I gave up and raised my bed. I thought about how Lauren used to think I was crazy for taking walks at odd hours of the night to quell my restless mind, and wished that were an option. I reached over to the table beside my bed and looked through the CDs Kerrie had made for me. I found one labeled *progressive jazz* that I hadn't listened to yet and put it in the player. The first song was Pat Metheny's beautiful, "First Circle." I closed my eyes and envisioned myself driving through a lush countryside, somewhere beautiful, in spring. It did the trick, and when I opened my eyes next, it was morning.

When my mother came to pick me up, she brought a big bouquet of flowers for the staff. After a prolonged round of goodbyes to everyone, including some of the patients and their family members, we left Hathers eight weeks after we came.

TWENTY

On the ride to my mother's condominium, which turned out to be a few blocks from where I last lived with Lauren, my mother droned on about an argument she had gotten in with Aunt Shirley. I listened for a few moments, and then tuned out and focused on the sights around me. In spite of many new storefronts, the stretch of Santa Monica Boulevard we were on didn't look all that different.

"This place is to die for," my mother said, pointing to a restaurant as we turned onto the street where she lived. "It's the best sushi— remember my friend Ilene Stevens? We went there for her birthday last month."

"Sushi?" I replied. "Lauren's the only person I knew who ate sushi."

"It's *very* popular now," my mother informed me. "Everyone eats it."

When it came to cultural trends, I trusted my mother. She was always a reliable bellwether for whatever the *in* thing was.

Growing up in the 70s, it was trendy for women to wear tennis outfits off the court, as well as on it. Although my mother, to my knowledge, never played a single game, she was always decked out in her best tennis attire. It exemplified her social philosophy: *You don't need to read the most popular book—you just need to be seen carrying it.*

As we pulled into her condominium complex, I commented on how modern the building looked and asked, "When did you move here?"

"A year before your father died," she answered. "It's lucky for you that I'm here. Somebody at Hathers—I can't remember who—told me that newer buildings have wider doorways, which accommodate wheelchairs. If I were still in our old house, I don't know what we would have done."

As I was asking her another question, my mother spotted an older man walking a tiny dog along the pathway that circled the complex. She rolled down her window a few inches and waved hello.

"That's Harvey Weinglatt," she said, once we passed him. "He owns—I don't know how many dry cleaners. Very successful. Harvey's the one who told your father and I about this place. He calls it *Hebrew Heights*, because there's hardly any goyim."

After we parked in the underground garage, I waited for my mother to come around to the passenger side with my wheelchair. We took the elevator to the third floor and went half way down the long, wide hallway. Once we got to her unit—which faced the exterior of the building—my mother partially opened the door. She then reached inside, flipped on the lights, and cried out, "Surprise!"

I wheeled myself inside and immediately spotted a banner strung across the living room, which read: WELCOME HOME JOEL! The tables and countertops had large balloon arrangements on them, each with a different festive slogan. I looked over at my mother and she was beaming at her work.

I put down the backpack I had taken home from Hathers on the coffee table and took the place in. Instantly I was overcome with emotion. So much of my past surrounded me—from the furniture to the photographs that covered the walls to the aroma in the air.

After my mother walked into the kitchen, I wheeled myself toward a large photograph of my father and I above the couch. It was taken during the time he coached my little league team. I must have been around twelve at the time. I'm in a batting stance and my father is proudly looking on.

I slowly moved from one spot to another, looking at the collection of images from my childhood. When I got to a series of photographs from my wedding day, I glanced at them quickly and turned away.

Most of the ones taken of Lauren and I were after we had a huge fight over a seating issue regarding her family. They illustrate how photography can capture—in a split second—a spirit or mood that didn't exist. We both look so happy, when inside we were both seething.

"Are you hungry?" my mother asked, coming up behind me.

"No. I'm really tired."

"Okay. Well, everything's set up for you. I hope you don't have too many complaints about it."

She led me down a short hallway to my new room. When she opened the door, I was taken back. Unlike the banner and the balloons, this was completely unexpected. There was memorabilia from my childhood everywhere. It was as if I had stepped back in time. Most of the stuff had been in a family storage unit and I hadn't seen it for years. When I looked at a Cleveland Indians' pennant my father had bought me at my first baseball game, pinned on the wall, I turned to mush.

"I thought it would make you feel more at home," my mother said, leaning over to give me a hug.

"Yes…it does," I mumbled through my sobs. "I wish Dad were here."

"You keep talking about your father," she said, drawing back from me. "What am I? Chopped liver."

"I miss him…that's all," I said.

"Well, he's gone and I'm here. And I'm the one who redid the bathroom so you would be able to use it, and I'm the one who had my kitchen reorganized so you could reach things. I was talking to someone at the market the other day and they asked me, 'Doesn't your son realize all that you've done for him?' 'Apparently not,' I told her."

"I appreciate everything," I said, too tired to tussle with her. "I really need to rest though."

"Okay," she said, softening her tone. "I'm going to call and find out what time your therapy starts tomorrow."

I wanted to lie down and get some sleep, but I couldn't stop looking around the room. I've always been a nostalgic person, but now—in this strange time and place in my life—remnants from my past had even greater meaning to me.

Before I finally dozed off, I looked through a photo album from my last year at summer camp and wondered where life had scattered all of those fresh, innocent faces.

TWENTY-ONE

The following morning, after an early breakfast, we were off to begin the next phase in my rehabilitation. On the drive to Sarswick Therapy Center, which was less than ten minutes from my mother's condominium, I again curiously stared out the window, trying to see how the world had changed. When we came to a stop light, my mother eyed a group of people crossing in front of us.

"You're going to have to get some new clothes," she said, as the light turned green. "Denim is outdated."

"I see people wearing jeans," I replied.

"Trust me, Joel—all that denim you used to wear isn't in fashion anymore. Maybe Kerrie can take you shopping."

It didn't take long for me to notice other things that were outdated. I hardly saw any guys with goatees, which were hugely popular in the 90's. I never jumped on the bandwagon, but several of my friends did, with varying degrees of visual appeal. Pagers were also a thing of the past, in a world where everyone carried a phone. Seeing people tethered to these devices made me miss the old, semi-connected days when you could only receive a one-way message and had to wait to get to a phone to respond.

It was strange to see a herd of people, heads down, oblivious to the world around them. I couldn't understand what could be so important that couldn't wait until they were back at a computer or the next time they talked to the person.

Kerrie had warned me about the pace of life, and I sensed it in the first week after I left Hathers. At times, it looked to me as if an announcement had been made that the world would cease to exist in twenty-four hours, and everyone was scrambling around in a daze.

Although I dreaded arriving at Sarswick for more consensual torture, the staff was all smiles, welcoming me as if I were boarding a cruise ship. My mother met a few of the employees, as well as my therapists, and then left to run a few errands.

The facility was a large, open space, which was akin to being at a regular gym. Oddly, it made me miss the isolated environment that I had initially loathed at Hathers. Unlike there, Sarswick had an ever-changing patient population that I found to be overwhelming at first.

I picked up my regimen where I had left off, but I missed the familiar, friendly faces I was accustomed to working with, especially Dorothy. I knew that therapy was still critically important to my recovery, but I was determined to make it a part of my life, as opposed to my entire existence.

After finishing my first session, I was surprised to see Kerrie waiting for me in the reception area.

"Look who's out in the real world?" she said with a big smile.

"Don't tell me my mother sent you here to take me shopping," I said.

"What do you mean?" she asked.

"Oh, my mother informed me this morning that denim was dead and I needed new clothes."

"Denim's not dead," she replied, giving me a hug. "Nothing can ever replace a good pair of blue jeans."

"Does my mother know you're picking me up?" I asked, as we left the building.

"Yes, I got permission," she replied, chuckling.

As Kerrie helped me into the front seat of her black Audi, I noticed a large bouquet of flowers in the backseat.

"Who are those for?" I asked.

"An old friend," she replied. "Do you mind taking a drive with me to drop them off?"

"As long as it's not too far."

"In the time it takes you to tell me how your first day went, we'll be there," she said.

While I was telling Kerrie my initial observations about Sarswick and my so-so feeling about my new therapists, I realized we were driving alongside the Kurtz Brothers Cemetery.

"Are you taking me to see my father by chance?" I asked.

Kerrie didn't respond, which in combination with the look on her face told me that's where we were headed. After driving another hundred yards, she turned into the cemetery parking lot. When she turned the engine off, I asked, "Do you know where he's at? I remember coming here once with Brian Kleftko to see his grandfather and we got totally lost."

"Why didn't you just go to the administration office and ask?"

"They were closed, so we hopped the fence and wandered around drunk for a long time before finding his plot."

Kerrie had called earlier and parked so we could easily access my father's gravesite. He wasn't buried on the hillside with a great view and a grand tombstone. He was in a newly expanded area close to the parking lot, but knowing my father he wouldn't have cared.

Kerrie made it to his gravesite before me, and as I slowly approached it, my heart began to pound and I could feel my stomach begin to twitch. The reality that my father was beneath the ground was hitting me.

Out of breath and sweating, I took a deep breath before looking down at his marker.

"I can't believe that's all my mother said about him," I told Kerrie.

"*Loving father and husband*," she replied, reading the marker aloud. "What's wrong with it?"

"I don't know…it could have been a little more special…less generic than that."

I took a sip from a water bottle I got from Sarswick, then closed my eyes and silently paid my respects.

"I wish I would have come out of my coma while he was still alive," I said, looking over at Kerrie. "I think he'd still be here."

"It's hard to say," she replied, massaging my shoulder.

"I feel guilty that I left him alone to deal with my mother."

"How do you think he was able to stay with her for so long?" Kerrie asked.

"I asked his brother—my uncle Solomon—once, and I'll never forget his answer. He said, 'Your father survives his marriage like an elephant survives the circus—trained, bound by duty, with regret and loathing.'"

Kerrie placed the flowers beside my father's marker. I took off the Cleveland Indians cap I was wearing and leaned over to place it next to the flowers. As I did, the right wheel of my wheelchair dug into the soggy grass and I tipped over.

"Oh shit!" Kerrie cried, reaching down to grab me.

"It's okay…I'm all right," I said, lying practically face first against the metal marker, "I've wanted to give my father a hug ever since I found out he was gone. I guess this is as close as I'm going to get."

When Kerrie got down on her knees to help me back up, I looked at her for a moment without taking her hand. Then I smiled and reached up to kiss her. Her lips met mine, but before our tongues could intertwine, she quickly drew back.

"Wait—what am I doing?" she asked. "What are *you* doing?"

"It's something I started to feel at Hathers, and I—"

"Joel, I have a boyfriend. Actually we live together."

Good old intuition, I thought to myself. *Sometimes neglected, but always reliable.*

"Why didn't you tell me you had a boyfriend when you came to see me at Hathers?" I asked her.

"I should have when I sensed you had feelings for me," she replied. "But you were in such a fragile place, and I didn't want to hurt you."

"Don't worry. I can handle it," I said defensively.

"Joel, listen…I want to be your friend and I want to help you through this time."

"And then what? You're out of my life?"

"No…I didn't mean it like that."

"Then how did you mean it?" I pressed.

"I care for you a lot, Joel, and I know what you're going through is tremendously difficult. I want to be here for you."

"Should I refer to him as your boyfriend or does he have a name?"

"Jay," she replied.

"Well, I wish you and Jay nothing but good things…and I mean that. Not an ounce of jealousy. Okay…maybe just a smidge."

Kerrie gave me a relieved grin and then helped me off of the ground. Once I was back in my wheelchair I said, "Can we forget what just happened? I'm a little embarrassed."

"Absolutely," she said, as if she already had. "Hey, would you mind if I went over to my high school boyfriend's mother's grave? She passed away recently and it's not too far from here."

"Of course not," I replied.

Kerrie pushed me away from the grass that was overwatered, and we headed toward the section of the cemetery where the tombstones were larger. Along the way, we both looked at the names and sentiments of a few of the markers we passed.

"Not to defend your mother," Kerrie said, "but none of these are any more original."

"You might be right," I replied, staring at the final resting place of Edward Searsman, who was only on this earth for eighteen years.

After Kerrie wandered off a little ways ahead of me, I heard her bust out laughing. I looked up and saw her holding her hand over her mouth.

"What could be that funny in this place?" I called out to her.

"Come here…you have to see this one."

I made my way to where she was standing and looked down at the unique epitaph of Harry Hertzenbaum. It read, *Life is hell, but it's worse if you complain about it.*

"You'll have to use that one on your mother sometime," Kerrie said.

"*A mensch of a man, gone too soon. 1903 to 1957,*" I said, reading the rest of the tombstone.

"Have you ever thought about what you want yours to be?" Kerrie asked me.

"Not before my coma, but now it might have to be, *Down For The Last Time.* What about you?"

"I have no idea, but in the spirit of old Harry here, I'll go with, *I Can't Believe How I Look!*"

"I told you there's room for originality," I said with a smile.

After Kerrie found the grave she was looking for and paid her respects, I was beat tired. She suggested that she go back to the car and pick me up closer to where we were, and I accepted her offer.

TWENTY-TWO

Once I got adjusted to living at my mother's, Gary invited me over to meet his kids, and see Leslie again for the first time in years. I forewarned him that although I was excited to visit, I probably wouldn't stay for long. I knew that Gary, mixed in with two young kids, was going to sap my energy quickly.

When he picked me up on a Sunday afternoon, he was as amped up as ever.

"Well, buddy, this is it! Life 2.0!" he exclaimed, hoisting his large cup of coffee in the air, as if to toast me.

"Ready or not, I guess," I replied, staring at the young male driver beside us, who had a large, black plug where his ear lobe used to be.

"Look on the bright side, dude—you have another chance at life."

"True, but just because I'm out of that place, doesn't mean I'm out of the woods. I'm still bound to a wheelchair, I'm still dependent on others, and I'm living with my mother."

"I understand… Hey, do you remember this song?" he asked, turning the volume up on The Who's "515."

"Of course," I replied. "Quadrophenia was one of the soundtracks of my high school party days."

"They released a director's cut of the album with a few unreleased songs. Here—I made you a copy," he said, reaching inside of his door side pocket and handing it to me.

"Wow," I said, holding the disc. "I can't believe it's so easy to do that now."

"In minutes," he replied. "And the discs cost next to nothing."

From listening to Big G and my mother talk at Hathers, I knew he had a very successful business. But when we pulled up to his house, I was completely blown away by how enormous it was. He lived in a new, gated area in Pacific Palisades called *Fox Tail Meadows*, and every house on the street was a mansion with expansive land around it.

"Man, this is insane," I commented, as we parked in the circular driveway.

"I got real lucky, dude. I saw an opportunity and I jumped on at the right time."

"I know, but how did you make enough money to afford THIS?"

"We'll talk more later—there's Leslie coming to see you," he said, rolling down my window. "Man, I wish she were that excited to see me when I came home. That's all for you, buddy."

While Gary retrieved my wheelchair from the backseat, Leslie reached into the car and engulfed me with a hug.

"Oh my god, Joel, it's incredible to see you!" she said, wiping her lipstick off of my cheek. "I can't believe how well you're doing."

I told her how great she looked, which wasn't an obligatory compliment—it was the truth. When we were younger, Leslie wouldn't have been considered to be pretty by most men, but in the intervening years she had come into her own.

Once I got out of the car, I stared at the two-story Tudor Style home, which had an enchanting hand-carved wooden front door, and God knows how many rooms.

Looking around once we were in the entryway, I felt as if I were entering the lobby of a five-star hotel. What it lacked in intimacy—for my taste—it made up for in grandeur.

"Geez, this is...wow," I said.

"Here," Gary motioned. "Come into the game room and meet Todd. Hannah is down the street at a friend's house, but hopefully she'll be back before you leave."

I didn't know what to expect when I met Big G's son, but his reserved nature—considering who his father was—surprised me.

"C'mon," Big G said to Todd, pulling him away from a video game he was thoroughly engaged in. "This is my old friend—the one I've been telling you about. Get up and give him a hug."

"Are you the one that came back from the dead?" Todd asked me after we embraced.

"Yeah, I guess you can say that," I said with a laugh.

"Wanna play Blood Bath?" he asked me, walking back to his spot on the floor, in front of a huge flat screen.

"No...you go ahead," I replied. "It looks pretty daunting."

"It's super easy, dude," Gary interjected. "Come over next to the couch and I'll set you up."

I wheeled myself to where Gary wanted me and took the red control stick he handed me. Then he squatted beside me to help guide me.

"My killers are black and yours are red. Okay?" Todd said, becoming more animated as we prepared for battle.

"Can you turn down the sound?" I asked immediately after the game started, distracted by the constant sound of gunfire.

"No," Todd replied emphatically. "I like it super loud so I can hear it when I kill your guys."

Thankfully Gary ignored Todd, and lowered the volume. But that wasn't my only problem—the dizzying speed in which everything moved was overwhelming. Everywhere I looked there were things lighting up, popping up, and exploding. My hand-eye coordination was much slower than it once was, but even so, I never would have stood a chance because Todd was a killing machine.

"He's unbelievable," I commented to Gary about his son's skill.

"He should be—he was one of our testers when we developed the game," Gary replied.

"Oh wow, so *this* is your business?" I asked.

"Yep, Sharp End Interactive."

"How'd you go from trying to save the environment to this?" I asked after finally managing to make my first kill.

"It took me a long time, but I finally realized that there wasn't enough money in being noble. I worked years for next to nothing, and when the kids came along I decided to do something different."

"Do you miss it?" I asked.

"No time to," he said, taking another gulp of coffee. "The business never stops...we're expanding to other countries now."

Leslie returned from the kitchen and set a large cheese tray and a bowl of chips down on the coffee table. I let Gary take over for me and snacked on some chips. As I watched him and his son square off in an evenly matched battle, I thought back to the table-tennis game, *Pong*. It was the first video game I played as a kid, and it had just two vertical lines for paddles and a white dot for a ball. Obviously video games had come a long way—even by 1990s standards—and the subject matter had changed with it.

After Todd beat his father two games in a row, Gary and I left him and toured the rest of the house. It continued to amaze me: there was an enormous pool with a waterfall and a slide, a racquetball court, a batting cage, and a full gym equipped with separate locker rooms for men and women.

As I took everything in, I couldn't help but wonder how video games—no matter how popular they were—could make so much money. And, although I didn't ask Gary, I wondered if he felt conflicted, as a parent, producing a product that was violent.

"It's nice, but I don't think it's enough house for four people," I joked with him, as we headed back to the living room.

"Actually, we only have three bedrooms—the master and one for each of the kids."

"That's not counting the housekeeper's room and the guesthouse," I replied.

"The guesthouse doesn't count—that's where I retreat when matrimony turns to Armageddon."

"She looks great," I offered.

"Leslie? Meh…" he replied.

"Really? You don't think so?"

"We don't notice one another anymore," he told me. "Remember when you moved into your first apartment and you made a big deal about what to put on the walls? Then after a month went by, you never looked at the stuff again. That's how she and I are now—we just blend into the background."

"That sucks," I said.

"Yeah…" he replied, indifferently. "It is what it is."

When we returned to the living room, Todd was still in the same position, with the same intense gaze on his face. We watched him for a few minutes and then I told Gary I needed to get back to my mother's to rest.

Gary and I were about to drive away when a voice cried out, "Daddy, daddy, wait!" Big G rolled down his window and his ten year old daughter, Hannah, appeared.

"Sweetie, I want you to meet my old friend, Joel," he said to her.

"Hi," she said, quickly glancing over at me before turning back to her father and saying, "I need some money."

"I just gave you fifty dollars two days ago," Gary told her.

"So, I need some more."

"Get it from your mother," he instructed her.

The two of them went back and forth, until Hannah started to beg and whine, which made Gary angry. After another minute, he closed the window and Hannah turned away.

While Gary complained to me about how spoiled his daughter was, I watched her ride past the front of the car on her scooter, into the garage. She was wearing tight shorts, hiked high up her legs, and had on at least three-inch platforms with metallic silver straps that a hooker wouldn't pass up.

Gary must have noticed the look of surprise on my face.

"What?" he asked me.

"Is that how girls her age dress now?"

"Yeah…" he said, pulling out of the driveway. "I don't remember when, but at some point little girls started looking like little women. It drives me crazy."

"Does Leslie say anything to her?" I asked.

"We both do—all the time. But that's the way all of her friends dress. It's part of the culture now, so there's not much you can do about it."

During the conversation, I must have fallen asleep. When Big G shook my shoulder, I was surprised to see that we were in front of my mother's place.

"Hey, I'm going on a business trip for a week," he said, waving to my mother, who was standing out on her balcony. "But when I get back, you'll have to come out and watch one of Todd's little league games. I'm coaching this year."

"Man, you are busy."

"Dude, when you have kids it never stops," he said before driving off.

TWENTY-THREE

Over time, I got used to my new environment and routine. I bickered with my mother about everything, except for what flavor of ice-cream we would buy: most times something chocolate with the crunch factor accounted for. I visited with Aunt Shirley, going to her place for lunches and making occasional trips to public places, when my energy was good. Brian Kleftko and I traded phone calls and talked about old times. Whenever I would complain about my struggle to readjust to my new life, he would tell me to shuck it all and come stay with him in Mexico. I explained that it wasn't that easy—that I sounded far better than I functioned.

Unfortunately, as the days wore on, I didn't hear from Kerrie as often. I confronted her and asked if it had something to do with my clumsy attempt at romance, but she insisted that she was busy working on her album. Once it was finished, she was planning on touring the western states with her boyfriend, who was the drummer in her band, to play small clubs. I had a feeling once I left Hathers that the dynamic of our relationship might change, but it still made me sad.

I tried to focus on rebuilding my life, but most days were a struggle just to get through. Besides contending with my physical condition, I was beginning to feel empty without having something to fill my time. The store had been a huge part of my life and had given me purpose—I greatly missed it.

On a rainy Monday, a few weeks later, when my mother was out with a friend, I called a cab. When the driver arrived, sporting pink and purple streaks in his hair and a thick steel bolt through his lip and smaller ones in both of his nostrils, I had him take me to the corner where Good Sounds once stood.

I knew from my mother that the people who had bought my record store were out of business, and as we drove along I wondered what would be there in its place.

When the cab turned onto Wilshire Boulevard and pulled over, it took me a few seconds to realize where we were.

"Is this it?" the cabbie asked.

"Yeah…I think so," I answered, staring up at the street sign and then down at a mini-market that now occupied my old spot.

A mini-market? I thought to myself, as the cab driver came around to the passenger side with my wheelchair. *Aren't there enough of these places littered throughout Los Angeles? Nothing against convenience and necessities, but music feeds your soul.*

I asked the driver if he wouldn't mind sticking around while I checked the place out for a few minutes. I'd happily pay for his time, I told him. I just didn't think I was going to be long, and didn't want to have to call for another cab.

"Don't worry about paying me for that—you look like life owes you one," he said, turning off the meter. "Just pay me for this ride, and I'll circle back in twenty."

After he drove away, I rolled up and parked my wheelchair beside the tinted window of the store. I raised my hand to block my eyes from the sun and peered inside. Instead of seeing aisles of food, I saw bins filled with albums and CD's. Where the cold drinks were, I pictured myself sitting behind the cash register in my trusty director's chair that I occupied seven days a week. I closed my eyes and heard the erratic rattle of the air-conditioner, and remembered summer nights when we had listening parties with beer and free pizza.

I thought back to the joy I got in turning customers on to new music, hoping it would move them, or make them reminisce, or help soothe a hard time. I knew sometime in the future they'd listen to it again and it would take them back in time or to an entirely different place. Music is magical and a timeless art form. I loved spending my days being surrounded by people who appreciated it in the same way I did.

Still, with everything that I just told you, I complained often to my father about how hard it was to run a small business. How I was working long hours and not making as much as some of my friends who were accountants and lawyers. How I was tired of haggling with the landlord about one thing or another. How I hated dealing with flaky kids who wanted summer jobs, but didn't want to work hard.

As I glanced down at my watch to see how much longer I had before the cab driver returned, I wished I could go back to my old life for just a day and realize what I had. It made me wonder: *Do we sugarcoat the past or just fail to appreciate the present?*

When the driver honked and pulled over to the curb, I didn't feel like going straight home.

"Can you take a long route back?" I asked him.

"How long?"

"About forty minutes," I replied.

There was only one thing to do for the somber mood I was in: listen to Frank Sinatra's *Watertown*. And it was one of those records you couldn't start without finishing.

James Rizmini, an old customer of mine who was a Sinatra fanatic, is the one who turned me onto the album. It sold terribly for a Sinatra record, when it came out in 1970, and caused him to briefly retire the following year. But in retrospect, many—me included—considered it to be a lost masterpiece.

The last song of the album faded just as we pulled into my mother's complex. When I came through the door, she was waiting for me with a look on her face I hadn't seen since high school.

"Where were you?" she asked.

"I took a cab ride," I replied nonchalantly.

"Without telling me or leaving me a note?" she asked, incensed by my action.

"Yeah… I'm almost fifty years old, so I thought it was time to start shifting for myself," I responded sarcastically.

"Joel, it's not a joke."

"I know, but we can make it one."

"I tried calling you several times," she said.

"I forget to turn my phone on sometimes."

"You really worried me," she said, turning away in disgust and heading into the kitchen. "You shouldn't be doing something like that in your condition."

TWENTY-FOUR

Once the weather got warmer, I began sitting on my mother's balcony. The view was limited to a small portion of the pool and the backside of other units, but I enjoyed the fresh air and gazing out.

One day, while I had my earbuds on listening to music, I noticed someone gesturing toward me from the next balcony over. It was a man of about sixty, with a week's beard, wearing a fisherman's hat.

"I feel your pain," I heard him say, as I turned off my music. He was pointing at my Cleveland Browns cap. "I'm originally from Cleveland."

We chatted about our hard-luck team, and then he began telling me a bunch of long-winded gambling stories.

He struck me as a lonely but nice enough guy. I thought I had met my first potential friend in the building, but my mother wasn't happy about it.

"Joel, please, do me a favor, don't talk to that man," she said when I came back inside.

"Why?" I asked.

"I'm just asking you not to."

"Tell me why and maybe I won't."

"He gives me the creeps...and if you start talking to him, he'll start looking over here," she replied. "And who knows, if you become too friendly with him he might knock on our door one day."

"Don't worry about it," I told her.

"Joel, I'm telling you he's dangerous," she persisted.

"Mom, anyone who's not Jewish or perfectly presentable is dangerous to you."

"He's a dirty old man," she insisted. "He has a sign on his door that says, unless you're a beautiful woman who wants to get naked or have a winning lottery ticket you're willing to share, stay away."

"I bet that cuts down on solicitors," I said, laughing. "Give the guy a break, his wife just died."

"He probably killed her," my mother replied without missing a beat.

The neighbor had told me his name, but I had forgotten it.

"What's his name?" I asked my mother.

"Don Grainy," she replied. "Even his name is creepy."

I didn't see Don out on the balcony for a while after our initial encounter, so I decided I'd be a sociable neighbor and a defiant son and knocked on his door one afternoon. Before he answered, I noticed that he edited his do not disturb sign to allow food delivery drivers.

He was happy to see me and immediately welcomed me inside.

"You sure I'm not interrupting you," I asked, noticing he was larger than he appeared while sitting on the balcony.

"Nah, I got nothing to do and a long time to do it," he replied.

As soon as I cleared the doorway of his place, I was amidst a hurricane of clutter. The carpet was covered with mail, newspapers, and clothes. Don kicked aside a few things to clear a path for my wheelchair and I navigated to a spot beside his couch.

"Sorry for the mess," he said, "but after the wife died I let go a little."

Don untucked his shirt and plopped himself down on the couch.

Once he got comfortable, he offered me a beer. I hadn't had a drink since I came out of my coma, and I hadn't had one at this time of the day probably since college.

"Sure," I said, surprising myself with my answer.

"Why the hell not, right?" he replied, reaching into an ice box he had beside the couch and leaning over to hand me a beer.

After we talked for a minute, he asked me, "Does your mother know you're here?"

"No, she's gone for a few hours."

"Don't say anything to her, will you?"

"Really?" I asked. "Why?"

"Well, I can't figure it out, but for one reason or another she doesn't like me very much," he said, taking a long pull from his can of beer. "One time she was sweeping her balcony and she looked over, raised the broom up, and made like she was sweeping me away."

"She lacks tact sometimes," I told him.

"Yeah, you ain't kidding."

While we watched ESPN with the sound low, Don told me about his wife's long battle with Leukemia. They had been together since their senior year of high school, and he was visibly emotional about her passing. Afterward, I shared a little bit of my story with him. He was fascinated to know how the world struck me after being away from it for so long.

After Don got up to use the bathroom, he returned with a big bowl of barbeque potato chips from the kitchen. The heavily salted chips, which I heartily consumed, and the warm temperature in his condo had me drinking like a fish. Whenever I finished a beer, Don promptly swapped my empty can for another cold one.

After what felt like at least an hour, I was stone drunk. The warm glow felt good.

"Don, I just thought of one cool thing about being in a

wheelchair," I slurred, while making my way to the bathroom.

"What's that partner?" he asked.

"It's easier to wheel around drunk than it is to walk."

"Oh shit, I didn't know you were a lightweight. Jeez, I hope your mother doesn't find out I did you like this."

"Don't you worry about that partner," I said, unintentionally imitating his vernacular. "There's no crime in having a good time."

"You better go back now—before she gets home," he said, getting nervous. "Here—I'll wheel you out."

"No, I'm fine right where I am."

For however long Don had been my mother's neighbor, she must have put the fear of God into him. He quickly rocked himself forward, stood up and pushed me out into the hallway.

"Thanks for the visit...have a good rest of your day," he said, before quickly closing his door.

After wandering for no reason to the end of the hallway, I went back to my mother's. Luckily, she still wasn't home. I grabbed a piece of bread from the kitchen and then transferred myself onto the couch in the living room. Seeing my iPod on the coffee table, I reached over and grabbed it. The last thing I remember was singing my heart out to "Free Bird" like a drunken fool.

I have no idea how long I slept, but I woke up to the sound of my mother's voice.

"Joel...Joel," I heard her calling before I opened my eyes and saw her standing over me with my iPod earbuds in her hand.

I mumbled something as I tried to clear my head.

"What's going on here?" she asked.

"What do you mean?" I replied.

"You're holding an open bottle of mouthwash."

"Oh...I must have been in the bathroom...before I came out here. I'm exhausted."

"Joel, have you been drinking during the day?" she asked me.

"Of course not," I replied.

She mentioned something about where she had been, and then grabbed the mouthwash and walked out of the room.

I didn't have any recollection of going into the bathroom, let alone taking mouthwash into the living room. Did I take a swig and spit the mouthwash out somewhere along the way or swallow it? I had no idea, but I did know by the time I went to sleep that night my head was throbbing.

TWENTY-FIVE

The following morning, I was still feeling the effects of my afternoon soiree with Don. I was about to crawl back into bed, after having a bagel and a glass of orange juice, when Big G texted me to say he was on his way to pick me up for his son's little league game.

I had completely forgotten we had made plans, but quickly threw on sweats, said goodbye to my mother and went downstairs.

Gary pulled up as I came out of the building, and once I got situated in the passenger seat, I turned and said hello to Todd. He barely let out a grunt, preoccupied with the device in his hands.

"Hey!" Big G yelled back to him, banging his hand on the roof. "Someone's saying hello to you. Look up and respond."

"It's okay," I said, trying to taper Gary's anger. "He's probably just saving his energy for the big game."

"Damn kids these days," he said. "They have zero manners and they're unbelievably selfish. ME is all that matters. Right son?"

Todd mumbled something under his breath that sounded like a continuation of a prior argument with his father. I rolled down my window, looked at the passing scenery, and tuned both of them out.

Once we arrived at the little league field, I sat while Gary and Todd made several trips from the car to the field, carrying their team's equipment. On their last leg, I transported a heavy canvas bag filled with bats by laying it across my wheelchair.

After I found a good vantage point to park my wheelchair, I watched Gary hit infield practice. Although he had never been a great athlete, I figured his knowledge of the game and his enthusiasm would make him a great coach for kids. So I was taken back to see him berate several of his players for not paying attention and for making errors. He was the hardest on his second baseman—Todd—who he told to, "start listening right now or you'll be sitting your ass on the bench today."

In Gary's defense, the intensity of little league baseball had changed since I was the shortstop for the Cubs in 1976. Once the game began I quickly discovered that it was high stakes now, with parents screaming like maniacs. There was a large white sign hanging from the fence in front of them that read—PLEASE REMEMBER: THESE ARE KIDS AND THIS IS A GAME—but it didn't have much effect.

For six innings, Big G paced in front of his team's dugout like a hockey coach nervously watching the final minutes of the Stanley Cup. Despite his cajoling and hollering, his son's team lost a three-run lead in the last inning. Todd didn't seem phased by the loss when he came through the gate leading to the stands.

"Good game," I said to him as he walked by me.

"Thanks," he replied meekly, already looking down at the phone in his hand.

After the parents shuffled out of the stands to greet their kids, I waited for Gary to finish talking with one of them. From what I could pick up of the conversation, she was upset by her son's lack of playing time.

Once Gary freed himself from her, he tossed me a baseball as he came my way. "Well, what do you think?" he asked. "We're the

Angels, but we lost that one like the worst of any Indians team."

"Yeah," I agreed. "It wasn't for the coach's lack of intensity…that's for sure."

He chuckled and then said, "You gotta stay on these kids—they have no attention span."

"At this age shouldn't it just be about having fun and learning the game?"

"You sound like one of the parents who complained about me to the league president."

"What'd he say?" I asked, curious.

"*She*," he corrected. "She wanted her son traded to another team because she considered me to be the Bobby Knight of little league baseball."

I was going to ask Gary what became of the kid, when he pulled out his phone to read a text message.

"What'd you think of the eye candy in the stands?" he asked looking up, once he finished typing a response.

"Eye candy?" I asked, unfamiliar with the term.

"You know—the hot women."

"Yeah, there were definitely a few lookers."

"Did you check out the blonde with the big blinkers, sitting in the top row?"

"When she got up to go to the snack stand, I stared at her all the way there and all the way back," I replied. "How'd she get those pants on? Man, they were tight…they looked like they were hermitically sealed on her."

"Who cares how she got them on—I just want to be there when she takes them off."

"Does Leslie come to the games?" I asked, realizing that Todd was in earshot of us.

"Sometimes," he responded, deflated by the change of subject.

"She tries her best not to be where I am."

Being around Gary, I was struck by how different life turned out in comparison to what we dreamed it would be like back in our late twenties. The youthful idealism we once shared was now like a faded, torn t-shirt, whose message was unrecognizable. Perhaps our dreams were too simple and too perfect for the complications that eventually came, but still the reality of it was sobering and sad to see.

TWENTY-SIX

My Aunt Shirley kept telling me that I should get on social media. So one day after lunch, while at my mother's, I let her convince me to sign up for Facebook.

In setting up my page, I wasn't surprised that there were other Joel Berskin's in the world, but both Aunt Shirley and I were startled to find out there were several who claimed to have been in a coma for seventeen years. A few of them even had a link to the NMN story on me on their pages.

"Who would want to be the guy that went through that?" I asked her, dismayed by the discovery.

"Who knows," she said. "These days people want notoriety any way they can get it. Don't let it bother you, Joel."

After I friended Aunt Shirley, Kerrie, Big G, and a few other people from my past, I poked around the site for a while. It was hard for me to understand what the fuss was about, and after logging on for a few days, I felt the same way. Perhaps it was because I didn't have much to share, or maybe I was just disconnected with the way the world was now.

My rehabilitation was going along, but I was discouraged by how slowly I was progressing. I thought at this point—almost four months since leaving Hathers—that I would be using a walker or at least have the milestone in sight. But all I had were platitudes and encouragement from my therapists, and the reality of more struggle to reach my goal.

Frustrated, I began lying to my mother in order to miss sessions. She never questioned my excuses, because unlike at Hathers, Sarswick was an environment that, for whatever reason, she never tapped into. Most times she would drop me off and then return a couple of hours later with stories about her social encounters.

One morning, while playing hooky from going to therapy, I got a text message from Kerrie inviting me to see her band rehearse. In less than a week they would be leaving for their first gig in Davis, California. Instead of responding to the text, I picked up the phone and called her.

"Did you get my text?" she asked.

"Yeah, but I prefer the phone."

"Why—it's so much easier to text—especially to make plans."

"I don't know, Kerrie…part of me hasn't adapted to the digital world yet, and part of me just doesn't want to."

"Well, can you come tonight?" she asked. "I want you to meet Jay."

"Is that your guy?" I asked, even though I knew.

"Yes," she replied quickly. "We'll pick you up at seven, okay?"

An hour after having dinner with my mother, I went downstairs to wait for Kerrie and Jay. Once they arrived, he got out of the passenger's seat, introduced himself and let me take his spot, while putting my wheelchair in the trunk.

The conversation was forced, but it was more on account of me than anybody else. Jay was a super-friendly guy and you could tell that he was crazy for Kerrie.

"Joel, Jay used to shop at *Good Sounds*," Kerrie said, trying to engage me.

"Cool," I replied.

"Best record store this city ever had," Jay said. "This town really misses it."

"Thanks," I responded.

After I gave one word answers to a few questions that Jay asked me, Kerrie shot me a look–*C'mon, it wouldn't kill you to extend yourself a little.*

Kerrie knew my moods, and understood that I had a habit of crawling inside of myself when I didn't feel entirely comfortable.

I leaned back against the headrest and stared out the window, listening to the two of them talk about their set list and ideas they had for rearranging various songs. Before long, we pulled up to a funky building in Venice that looked like it was the victim of a drunken painting party.

Inside, Kerrie introduced me to the other members of the band, and then found a good spot for me to watch and hear the music.

"Are you okay?" she asked, rubbing my shoulders.

"Yeah, just feeling a little low."

"I'm sorry. If you need me, don't hesitate to get my attention," she said, before walking away.

Despite how I felt, I was looking forward to hearing Kerrie play through her entire album. After the first song, you could tell that she had assembled a group of musicians that perfectly complimented her style, and she was on cloud nine performing with them.

"Bravo," I called out, after she finished the set with a song called "Dumb Enough To Be Happy," a stinging condemnation of people who bury their heads in the sand, ignoring the world's problems. Before the band broke down their equipment, Kerrie and Jay sang "Two of Us" from The Beatles *Let It Be* album.

Afterward she came over to me buzzing with energy, and said she was taking the band out for drinks—did I want to join them. I told her I was tired and I didn't want to be a bump on a log. It was best to take me home.

On the ride back, I forced myself to be a bit more animated and friendly toward Jay, which Kerrie looked pleased about. After she hugged me goodbye, she handed me a CD and said, "Ten of my happy songs—I guarantee it'll help."

Once I got upstairs, I texted Kerrie: *Thanks for letting me enjoy your radiance and immense talent. Your songs will be a treat to all who hear them. Knock 'em dead in Davis and enjoy your musical sojourn.*

She quickly wrote back: *Thanks for the support and for the TEXT! Love always, KK.*

Kerrie and I stayed in touch via texting and Facebook during her tour, but we hardly spoke on the phone. I missed not hearing her voice and having her spirit around. I wish I could have been more effusive about her relationship. After all, Kerrie, like me, hadn't had the best of luck with significant others, and Jay seemed like a healthy choice. Unfortunately, my heart was aching for something I wanted and couldn't have.

That weekend, my mother and I met Uncle Solomon for lunch for his eighty-second birthday. Leaving early was a Berskin family trait, which left time for my mother to go to Jiffy Lube to get an oil change. Driving around with her again, doing errands, reminded me of being in her red Cutlass Supreme, listening to Neil Diamond, when I was ten years old.

Both bays were empty when we pulled in, and the attendant that greeted us said that we would be in and out in twenty minutes. I thought about asking the guy if I could stay in the car while they worked on it, but instead decided to sit with my mother in the waiting room.

The two of us were in our separate worlds—my mother fiddling with her phone and me reading a magazine—when we heard a car outside blasting rap music. Moments after the music stopped—presumably when the attendant took over the car—a clean cut white kid swaggered into the waiting room with baggy pants and a black tank top.

I watched, amused and surprised, while he set up a pair of small speakers on the glass table beside him and began playing his music loud enough to make the table vibrate.

My mother immediately looked up and said, "Please turn that down."

The kid was already in a deep trance, with his eyes closed and his head grooving to the beat.

When he didn't respond after she asked him a second time, I reached over and tapped his shoulder to get his attention.

"What up?" he asked, annoyed by the disturbance.

"Would you mind turning down the music?" I asked him.

"You serious? I just laid down this track. It's a wicked groove, bro. You ain't feeling it?"

"Would you mind?" I appealed to him again, motioning with my hand to lower the volume.

"What are you into boss? REO Speedwagon?" he asked mockingly.

When I didn't reply, he shrugged and took out a pair of earbuds and plugged them into the speakers. A few moments later, I glanced back over at him and he was softly rapping to himself.

If you ignored his appearance, he was a suburban kid no different than I once was. What changed in the world while I wasn't around that made his generation listen to rap and hip-hop, as opposed to rock 'n roll, which was the soundtrack of my youth? Whatever the answer was, I was surprised that a genre of music that was becoming mainstream before my coma was today's pop music.

The oil change seemed to be taking a long time, and I was getting fidgety. I went outside to get some fresh air and when the door closed behind me, the attendant looked up from beneath the hood of my mother's car.

"How's it going?" I asked him.

"Five minutes, tops. Sorry for the wait," he said. I was about to roll my wheelchair away, when he walked over to show me the air filter. "It's getting there, but I think she can go one more oil change."

While the attendant continued checking under the hood, I noticed the young kid in the pit below. He glanced up and gave me a nod. It took a second for it to register, but I realized he was holding his phone, texting someone.

I suppose it shouldn't have surprised me, but it did. I knew technology was *everywhere* now, but I didn't expect to see a guy underground texting while changing oil. What could there possibly be to say: *Draining oil on a 2007 Lexus...thinking about a salami sandwich for lunch.*

Our lunch with Uncle Solomon was nice. When I was younger and my aunt Betty was still alive, her and my mother would always get into it over something and make the occasion unpleasant. My father and Uncle Solomon used to act as the referees, while I watched the fireworks and wondered if all families were as crazy as mine.

We went to Uncle Solomon's favorite Italian restaurant on Ventura Boulevard in Studio City, not far from where he was living in a home for seniors. We started out sitting inside, but ended up on the patio, after switching tables three times.

"How many tables must a group of Jews try before settling on one?" Uncle Solomon joked with the hostess.

Not long after we sat down, my mother started talking to a couple at the table behind us. It gave me an opportunity to talk one on one with my uncle. When he asked me how I was doing, I told him the truth—that I was having a hard time adjusting to my new life.

Although Uncle Solomon could be in another world sometimes—like when he visited me after I woke up from my coma and he wanted to take me to lunch—he could also be wise. He listened thoughtfully as I droned on about my struggles and then said, "Joel, sometimes acceptance is greater than change. You've been dealt a tough hand—do the best you can and let the rest go."

When my mother turned around and rejoined us, Uncle Solomon made the mistake of asking her what she had been talking about for so long with her newfound friends. For the next five minutes I learned more about the finalists of *American Idol* than I ever wanted to know.

Being a huge music lover, you would think that it would be a show I would appreciate. But the competition shows—I never thought I'd see chefs competing against one another—just weren't my thing. Besides, I preferred the old fashioned way, when artists built a following by putting out great records and touring.

TWENTY-SEVEN

To break the boredom and loneliness of my days—against my mother's wishes—I began taking cabs to various places. My first outing was to a new park I had seen on my commutes to Sarswick.

After the driver dropped me off, I wheeled myself over to read the stone placard at the entrance. It said that in 2003 a wealthy businessman named John Duggleson had bought and demolished a series of old buildings to give the city's residents more open space. Below the dedication date, the lyrics to Cat Stevens' song "Where Do The Children Play?" were inscribed.

The park had more than its fair share of ponds, as well as an elaborate outdoor gym and a bandshell for concerts and plays. Its most unique feature was a cluster of manmade mounds, which had hammocks atop of them.

I decided to wheel myself over to the base of one. Looking up, I imagined myself climbing the gradual slope, collapsing in a hammock, and watching the clouds drift across the hazy sky.

Lost in thought, I hadn't noticed that there was a father with two young kids standing behind me. The little girl, who was probably five, must have picked up on my longing.

"Daddy, can I push that man up the hill?" she asked with an

innocence and sweetness only a child could muster.

"No, I don't think so, honey," the father replied.

"Thank you, though," I said to the little girl, with a smile. "How about if you guys climb up and wave to me once you reach the top?"

As I was offering my suggestion, the father was shaking his head no. "We have to go find your mother," he told his daughter. "She's jogging around here somewhere."

After the family wandered off, I headed toward the basketball courts, where a group of young kids were playing 3-on-3.

Before I got there, I heard a chime go off. It took me a moment to realize it was coming from my phone. I looked down at the screen and there was a reminder that it was Aunt Shirley's birthday. I smiled thinking that although I couldn't remember for sure, I think it was Aunt Shirley who originally entered the information into my phone. She loved birthdays just about as much as I loathed them.

I watched the kids play a couple of games and heard more f-bombs than I probably heard throughout my entire childhood. When they quit to take a break, I called for a cab.

My thought was I'd stop at the Wilshire Center, which was between the park and my mother's place, to get a gift for my aunt. I had never been to the mall, but remembered them breaking ground on it just before I went into my coma.

From the second I entered the three story structure, I regretted it. The place was packed with people and I was instantly on stimulus overload. I was about to leave, thinking Aunt Shirley would forgive me if I got her a belated gift, when I passed a sleep store.

For my entire life I had been a stomach sleeper, but at Hathers, without the pillow I had used for years, I became a side sleeper, a back sleeper, and anything but a sound sleeper.

I wheeled myself inside, spotted the pillow section and began feeling a few. An enthusiastic saleswoman soon approached me to ask if I had any questions.

"Yes…I'm wondering why there's a prejudice against stomach sleepers." I said. "Everything here is for back and side sleepers and the ones that say stomach sleeper are way too thick."

She directed me to a different section of the store and showed me some other, better options. I found one that I liked and made my way to the cash register.

Once I left the store and was back on the main traffic artery of the mall's ground floor, I thought I heard shouting coming from the direction I was heading. After pausing for a second and not hearing anything, I continued toward the exit.

I traveled about ten feet before I heard what sounded like fireworks exploding. I looked at the woman beside me—who was selling watches at one of the kiosks—and her eyes were filled with fear.

"Oh shit!" she yelled, when another series of loud bangs rippled through the air. In an instant, she took off running.

I turned my wheelchair and followed after her as quickly as I could. In what felt like minutes, but was probably seconds, people began rushing past me, screaming. I could hear the sound of what I now thought were gunshots getting closer, but I couldn't move any faster.

As the crowd began to swell, a heavy set man slammed into me and knocked me to the ground. I grabbed for my wheelchair to shield myself from the oncoming stampede, but I couldn't reach it. Instead, I curled my body into a ball and covered my head with my hands. Looking behind me, I could see people falling to the ground, either from being trampled or shot.

"Someone, please…help me!" I cried out, my heart racing and panicked with fear.

Seconds later, I felt someone trip over me and saw them land face-first a few feet away. The crush of people began to trample over the woman. There was a large spot of blood on her lower back, seeping through the white shirt she was wearing. I managed to crawl to her and ask if she was all right.

"My daughter!" she cried. "I lost my daughter!"

I positioned my body to protect her from the rush of people. Then I lifted her shirt to look at her wound. Blood was pouring from where she had been shot, and I thought to use the pillow I had bought to stop the bleeding. Looking behind me to find it, I saw someone wearing a black mask—no more than twenty yards away—spraying gunfire from side to side.

I shimmied my body toward the pillow, which was five feet away, but as I was about to grab it I felt a piercing pain in my right hand. Seconds after I clutched my hand in agony, I felt myself being lifted off of the ground.

A young guy with a thick beard was running with me in his arms, and I felt my body shaking up and down.

"No!" I yelled at him. "Go back—that woman needs help!"

He continued to stare intensely ahead, swerving right and left to navigate through the crowd.

"Please—go back!" I cried again. "That woman was shot."

Suddenly I felt my body abruptly turn and realized we were in a hallway. The man ran a few more feet, and then turned his body sideways and pushed open the bathroom door.

"Mother fucker!" he yelled, lowering me to the ground in front of the sink. I watched dazed, as he stood up and grabbed a handful of towels from the dispenser. "Here—" he said, putting the towels in my left hand and covering my wound. Then he quickly splashed a handful of water on his face and ran out of the bathroom.

I thought I was alone—nobody was at the urinals and I couldn't see any feet beneath the stalls. But as I lifted the blood-soaked towels from my hand and saw where a bullet had passed through the flesh between my thumb and my forefinger, I heard a man's voice coming from one of the stalls. He must have been standing on the toilet, fearing that the gunman would come inside and start shooting.

Soon more and more people flooded into the bathroom. Families were huddled together, shaken, and children were crying. A muscular man next to me with a Navy Seal tattoo on his arm started yelling, calling the gunman a terrorist and cursing the country for not securing the border. It was a surreal scene.

I don't know how much time passed, but amid the chaos someone ran into the bathroom and shouted, "It's over! It's over! A security guard shot the guy!"

Slowly people began filing out of the bathroom. The guy with the Navy Seal tattoo picked me up and threw me over his shoulder. My body dangled on each side of him like a sack of potatoes.

When we emerged from the hallway and were back on the floor of the mall, it looked like a war zone. Medics were treating the injured and personal belongings were littered everywhere. Sirens were wailing like crazy.

The man handed me off to the first paramedic he saw. I told the woman that I just needed to get my wheelchair and I would be okay. She quickly transported me to an ambulance that was parked just outside of the mall entrance. Not long afterward, I was in the emergency room at Cedars-Sinai Medical Center.

While the medical staff was treating my hand, Aunt Shirley came through the partition and rushed to my side.

"Joel, my God, are you okay?" she asked, smothering me with a hug. "I cannot believe this."

Luckily, I soon found out that I had the best type of gunshot wound you could have—a through and through—and my hand would heal quickly. Before long, I was given a new wheelchair and released.

When Shirley drove me home, my mother was waiting outside, looking petrified. Strangely, she had more compassion for me after I was shot than after I woke up from my coma. "Thank God you're all right," she said, helping me out of the car.

Once we got upstairs, I recounted the story of what happened inside the mall for Aunt Shirley and my mother.

"I wish you would listen to me and stop going places alone," my mother said before I finished.

"Joanne, it's not the time—" my aunt started to say.

"Shirley, please—" my mother responded, giving her a perturbed look. "He can't be taking cabs, roaming around the city. He's not physically strong enough."

The room got quiet and a short while later Shirley got up to leave. My mother and I continued talking for a few minutes, and then I went into my room to lay down.

Moments after I closed my eyes, I saw the face of the woman who had been shot and heard her screaming for her daughter. I couldn't get the image out of my mind and I couldn't fall asleep.

I got up and went back into the living room, where my mother was glued to the TV.

"He was an American," she said, in reference to the shooter. "Thirty-two years old."

I looked at the TV and they were showing a close-up photograph of the gunman. He had an eerie grin on his face and two different colored eyes, which my mother explained was from colored contact lenses.

"Why?" I asked my mother and the universe.

"He's a nut, that's why. Look at him," she replied.

I felt a chill in my soul that night that I had never felt before. Other than talking to Big G and Kerrie, who both called to see if I was all right, I was quiet and somber. For the next several days, I felt listless and depressed.

The media coverage of the shooting was continuous, and the tragedy was the topic of just about every conversation. You couldn't escape the horrible details about it, although I desperately wanted to.

It turned out that the gunman randomly and senselessly killed seventeen people. Three of which were children. The word DEATH was imprinted in white letters on the black mask I had seen coming toward me.

When the names and faces of the victims began surfacing in the media, I couldn't help but look. I was devastated to find out that the woman I had tried to help was among them. She was a thirty-five year old hairdresser named Sylvia Cutler. I looked at the names of the children who had died and thankfully didn't see any with the same last name, so I assumed that her daughter had survived. Tragically, the man who had carried me to the safety of the bathroom was also among the dead. His name was Curtis Shoner and he was just twenty-eight.

I went online to try to find out more about both of them. There wasn't very much on Sylvia, and I couldn't find a Facebook page under her name. Curtis, however, was on Facebook, and many of his friends left touching tributes to him. His most recent post was a photograph of him proudly displaying a new tattoo, which covered most of his arms. In his eyes you could see a kind soul. I stared into them, sobbing uncontrollably.

Questions about the shooting continued to haunt me: *Had Curtis gone back to try to save Sylvia? Why did he pick me up off of the ground instead of her?*

At Hathers I learned that even in your darkest hour life slowly moves on, no matter what the circumstances. And although this wasn't as difficult as waking up from a seventeen year coma, it was devastating.

TWENTY-EIGHT

I hoped that the ensuing days would wash away the horrifying images I had in my head, but they didn't. Haunted by the incident, and still struggling with my recovery, I began to withdraw further into myself.

I spent long stretches in my room with no desire to leave. Music had always helped me through difficult times, but it didn't do much to lift my spirits. Whenever Big G called with a plan to get together, I made an excuse. My replies to Kerrie's emails, when she checked in on me from the road, were brief. My mother occasionally asked if I was all right, but it was easy for me to deflect her concern by bringing up something trivial.

Under a dark cloud that wouldn't lift, I wondered often if I was meant to have woken up from my coma. What was the purpose of another chance at life if it was going to be so painful? The guilt of surviving the shooting weighed on me, but I was also pestered by nagging, self-pitying questions like, *Why did I have to be in the mall when this happened? Hadn't I been through enough?*

I tried pouring myself into my rehabilitation, as a way to focus on something other than the shooting. But even the news from my therapists that I would soon be getting a walker didn't bring me joy.

Where do you go when life feels like a small, suffocating room with no windows or doors?

I decided to call a cab and take a ride to the ocean. Once we turned onto Neilson Way in Santa Monica, I rolled down the window and took in the view. After so many years, it was refreshing to see the sun glistening on the water and smell the salt air.

The driver pulled into one of the parking lots that lined the beach, and let me out beside the snack stand.

"You gonna be all right?" he asked, either sensing my mood or on account of me being in a wheelchair.

"Yeah," I said, handing him the fare. "I just need to turn the world off for a while."

After he drove away, I wheeled myself onto the concrete boardwalk that ran parallel to the sand. For a long while I just stared out, trying to lose myself in the vastness of the ocean. Occasionally someone rollerbladed or bicycled by me, but for the most part it was quiet.

A promise I had made to Dorothy at Hathers crept into my mind. Although I wasn't driving on Pacific Coast Highway with the windows rolled down, listening to music, I had accomplished one of my three goals.

"I'm here, Dorothy," I whispered to myself. "I'm here."

Trying to channel Dorothy's positivity, I closed my eyes and listened to the sound of the crashing waves in the distance. With each one, I imagined my sorrow being swept away.

I opened my eyes again when a large flock of seagulls flew over me, screeching loudly. Glancing down the beach a ways, I spotted a guy with headphones on, scanning the sand with a metal detector. I couldn't imagine how his findings could be worth his time, but it was nice to see a relic from the past in this ever-changing world.

Although it wasn't summer yet, the sun was starting to get to me and I hadn't brought a hat. I moved to a sliver of shade beneath the overhang of the snack stand, and stared up at the palm trees that lined the bluff. After listening to a few songs on my iPod, I started to think about lunch.

Frankie's on Fifth, another thing I wanted to do once I left Hathers, was only a few blocks away.

I called for a cab and then put back on my earbuds and drifted away to music. When the driver arrived unbeknownst to me, and began aggressively honking his horn, it startled me.

"You call for a cab?" a man with a thick New York accent asked through the rolled down passenger window.

"Yeah, I did."

"Well, let's go buddy, I don't have all day."

When the cab driver dropped me off at Frankie's it was 11:40, and the lunch crowd hadn't arrived yet. After I looked at a few of the photographs from Santa Monica's past that lined the walls, I positioned myself in front of the daily pizzas, which were behind a glass partition. As I looked up to place my order for two slices of mushroom, goat cheese and garlic, the owner and I instantly recognized one another.

"Frank…" I said amazed by how little his appearance had changed.

"Joel—man, it's been ages. How you been? *Where* you been?"

"Oh, it's a long, crazy story, but I'm doing fine."

"Some other time then, huh?" Frank replied, while dishing out my slices and giving me an extra one on the house.

The pizza was as delicious as ever, leaving me full and satisfied. I pushed my plate aside and watched as the place filled up. It was more of a business crowd than I remembered it being. Clusters of people who walked in together, probably from the same office, stood in line with their heads down, interacting with their phones.

I thought about dessert—they had incredible chocolate chip cookies—but felt I was ready to go home. I gave Frank my compliments on the pizza, and waited outside for a cab.

When I arrived back at my mother's, she was talking on the phone in the kitchen, pacing, with a nervous look on her face.

"The doctor said it's the worst case he's ever seen," I heard her say just before she hung up.

"The worst case of what?" I asked quickly, hoping to avoid being questioned about where I'd been.

"I don't want to talk about it, but it's not good," she said grimly.

"You were just talking about it, and I'm your son," I reasoned, before remembering my mother's history of having mysterious ailments that were certain to kill her.

"I can't get into it right now," she responded.

"I hope it's not that awful virus everybody's talking about?" I said.

"What virus?" she asked nervously.

"It's starts with a series of nebulous symptoms, and then quickly becomes deadly."

I couldn't keep the serious expression on my face for long and burst out laughing.

"It's not funny, Joel. The doctor said it's very serious."

"I'm sorry," I said as earnestly as I could before walking away.

I did feel bad for my mother. She had a debilitating need to fear something in order to believe that it wouldn't come true.

TWENTY-NINE

The following morning, my mother and I got an awful surprise when we left to go to Sarswick. As soon as the elevator leading to the underground garage opened, we were ambushed by a group of reporters and cameramen. They swarmed me, shouting questions and shoving microphones and tape recorders in my face. The fact that I was in a wheelchair and startled by their onslaught didn't deter them.

My mother pleaded with them to let us through to her car, but they wouldn't disperse. Figuring the best way out of the situation was to give them what they wanted, I began answering their questions, which came in rapid fire.

Why were you in the mall?

Did you see the gunman up close?

Were you near anybody else that was shot?

Why are you in a wheelchair?

Is it true you were in a coma for twenty years?

I gave short answers, hoping to satisfy them and be done with it. But the questions kept coming. Finally, my mother forcefully demanded that the reporters back away so that we could leave for Sarswick.

They trailed us to her car and continued taking pictures and yelling questions even after we got inside. Once we made it out of the garage and had cleared the complex, I kept looking in the rear view mirror, thinking we were being followed.

"How the hell did they know about my coma?" I asked my mother.

"Did they ask you about it?" she replied.

"Yeah," I answered.

"Don't think about it…it'll be okay," my mother offered, seeing the look of despair on my face.

Throughout my therapy session, I was preoccupied by what had happened and worried that I hadn't seen the end of it.

My fears were realized when we returned home and found another group of reporters camped out at the entrance to the underground garage. I rolled down my window and yelled at them to leave the property, but was met with cameras and microphones. I closed the window—nearly catching a reporter's finger inside—and then reached over and honked the horn. I kept my hand on it and didn't let up.

"Joel—don't—you're going to incite them!" my mother shouted. "I don't want to get hurt."

I ignored her and kept honking. When I finally lifted my hand up, I heard a loud bang and everyone around the car ducked or ran for cover. Seconds later, a series of what I now recognized as gunshots rang out.

"Oh my God!" my mother cried. "Someone's shooting a gun!"

I rolled down my window a crack to try to figure out what was going on and heard a voice above us yell, "Stay away from that car or I'll shoot all of you sons of bitches."

It was Don Grainy, out on his balcony.

I quickly motioned for my mother to take advantage of the clearing and pull into the garage.

Once we got inside her unit, I peeked outside to see if the media had left. There was no one in sight.

"I can't believe he did that," my mother said, making reference to her renegade neighbor. "He's crazy."

"In a good way," I replied.

Later in the day, with everything still quiet, I went out onto the balcony to see if Don was there. He was sitting in his trusty rocking chair, staring out, as if nothing had happened earlier.

He didn't hear me the first time I called over to him, and I thought that maybe he had already consumed a few beers. When I got his attention and thanked him for coming to our rescue, he said, "Oh, that's nothing... I've got plenty more for 'em if they decide to come back."

I felt good knowing that Don's actions had scared off the media, but that night after dinner Aunt Shirley called with distressing news.

The media had discovered that one of the people shot in *The Mall Massacre*, as they now dubbed it, had recently come out of a very long coma. The NMN story about me had resurfaced, and my photograph was all over the local news. I guess that explained why my mother and I were ambushed earlier in the day.

After Aunt Shirley did her best to console me, I retreated to my room and listened to music until I fell asleep. When I woke up, the reality of what had happened began to unnerve me.

The article I found out about while I was at Hathers thankfully never impacted me beyond the initial aggravation. This time, I feared, I wouldn't be as lucky. The mall shooting was a huge story. The thought of being hounded by the media again severely upset me. It tipped me into a depression that I couldn't recover from.

THIRTY

Since opening my eyes at Tender Heart, my life had been a string of painful losses: my father, my store, my marriage, and my independence. I didn't feel like I could take any more.

There is an innate desire inside most of us to carry on living no matter how much pain and suffering we face. That desire had died in me.

I knew there were people and things I would miss if I was gone, but the thought of ending my struggle and pain was greater.

I began writing goodbye letters, but threw them away, feeling my actions would speak better for me than any words could.

My mind began to think of ways I could end my life.

I didn't want to use a gun because it would be violent and bloody, and whoever found me (God forbid, my mother) would have to live with that horror. I researched information online about taking pills, but feared with my luck I'd wake up worse off than I was. I thought about carbon monoxide, but read a haunting story about a woman who tried it and ended up with brain damage. My mind flashed back to John Rifemore at Hathers. Jumping off of a bridge seemed like the best way to go—at last my anemic body would be free. If I could find one with a body of water below it, hopefully my remains would just wash away.

Los Angeles isn't known for having tall bridges, but I looked online to see if one had been built during the time I was in my coma. I came across the Brackingham Bridge in Echo Park, which was constructed in 2011, and surpassed the Colorado Street Bridge in Pasadena to become the highest one in the city. It arched across a manmade river called Feather Canyon. I found several websites with stories about successful and unsuccessful suicide attempts that had been made from the bridge, but it was difficult to decipher what was real and what had been fabricated.

The next morning, a Monday, after my mother left for a doctor's appointment, I took a cab to the Brackingham Bridge. On the thirty minute ride over, I stared out the window deep in thought.

"Why the bridge?" the cabbie asked, taking me out of my head.

"Oh, just going for a ride…trying to sort some things out."

"Be careful around there—it's not the best area."

"Really?"

"Yeah… A few people have killed themselves by jumping off, so it attracts a lot of lookie loos and kooks."

"They've jumped from there?" I asked innocently as the bridge came into view. "How—there's a guard rail all the way across it."

"I don't know…but one guy I drove here told me there's a small opening somewhere in the railing," he replied. "I guess the city's too lazy or stupid to find it and fix it."

Once the driver dropped me off and drove away, I looked around the park area that connected to the bridge. Being early in the morning on a weekday, it was quiet except for a sanitary truck, emptying the trash bins.

I slowly propelled myself toward the bridge, which was thirty or so yards away. Once I was on it and had traveled a few feet, I pulled over to the side and stared down at the rushing water. A sudden gust of wind blew and nearly took my baseball hat with it.

Moving along, I scanned both sides of the overpass for the opening that the cab driver had mentioned, but didn't see any spaces in the tall metal guard rail. As I neared the half way point of the bridge, a cyclist approached from the opposite end. Once he got closer, I waved my hand to get his attention. He stopped and pulled off one of his earbuds.

"What's up? You okay?" he asked.

"I'm fine...sorry to stop you. I'm part of a film crew that's doing a documentary on this bridge. Do you know anything about a spot where people have jumped off of here?"

"I think it's down there," he replied, pointing in the direction he had come from. "At least that's what I heard."

After I thanked him and he peddled off, I took a brief rest before continuing on my way. By the time I reached the end of the bridge, I still hadn't seen anything unusual.

Drained from the distance I had traveled, I struggled to wheel myself off of the concrete platform onto some grass. I drank the remaining water from the bottle I had brought with me and closed my eyes to gather my strength. Then I lowered myself out of my wheelchair to lie on the cool, moist ground.

Exhausted, I stared up through the trees to the sky. Remembering what the cab driver had said about the area, I made sure I didn't fall asleep. After I sat back up for a few minutes, I pulled out my cell phone and called a cab.

Staring back toward the bridge, while I waited for someone on the other end to pick up, my eyes locked on a sliver of space where there was an opening in the railing. I ended the call, put my phone away, and crawled over to it.

Holding onto one of the metal slats, I was able to hoist myself up. Looking at the slender gap in the railing, I couldn't figure out how someone could fit through it. But when I turned my body sideways and shimmied back and forth, I realized that it was possible. I leaned forward and felt the heels of my shoes lift off of the ground. My heart began to beat faster. A slight maneuver and a moment of desperation were all that separated me from my demise.

THIRTY-ONE

In a split second, out of the corner of my eye, I saw something move. I flinched, turning towards it, thinking it would be another cyclist. But when I swung my head around, I realized it was a dog.

"Oh shit," I said, under my breath.

Locking eyes with me, the dog stopped and it looked as if it might turn around.

"Go on," I said softly. "I don't have anything for you."

The dog tilted its head back, sniffed the air, and then continued towards me. As it got closer, I noticed that it was dragging its rear right leg on the ground, and there were leaves knotted in its white, wiry coat. It looked like an older dog, about forty pounds, and it didn't appear to have a collar on.

When it was five yards from me, the dog began to whimper. I assumed it was crying from the pain of its hind leg, but the dog's tail was wagging briskly. I backed away from the railing and collapsed onto my rear end. The dog closed the distance between us, and buried its head in the crook of my arm. Looking between its legs, I saw that it was a female.

The stench from her coat made me cough, and she responded by reaching over to lick my face.

"Oh man, you need a bath," I said. I slowly ran my hand along the side of her body and I could feel large clumps of matted fur. Not knowing what to call her, the name Mattie popped into my head.

She sat down with her injured leg splayed behind her, and gave me a yearnful look that seemed to say, *Let me be your friend.*

I patted the top of her head, and she shook it back and forth several times before profusely scratching her left ear. Looking down, I noticed that one of the toes on her front right paw was severed.

I crawled back to my wheelchair and Mattie followed me. Once I got situated, I looked around to see if there was anybody searching for her. As on the other side of the bridge, the area was deserted.

I reached down and gave Mattie another rub on the head. She wagged her tail and then lifted her paw and rested it on my leg. I couldn't help but smile. "Sorry, I don't have any treats, if that's what you want," I told her.

I fished for my phone in the pocket of my wheelchair and called the cab company again. While I waited for someone to arrive, I moved myself beneath a large tree that was near the parking lot.

Spotting a sizeable stick on the ground, I picked it up and handed it to Mattie. She chewed on it a couple of times and then dropped it on my lap. I tossed it a few feet away, not knowing if she could retrieve it with her injured leg. I was surprised when she took off after it with zeal and a decent degree of agility. She came back, tail wagging, and dropped the stick again on my lap. We continued our game of fetch, until the cab driver pulled up.

"Where are you and your friend heading?" the man with a Greek fisherman's hat on asked, as he got out of the car.

After I gave him my mother's address, he opened the passenger side rear door and encouraged Mattie to hop in. I wasn't sure if she would be able to make the leap, but with a little help from the driver, she made it.

"Let me get the windows rolled down to give the pooch some air," the driver said, as he got behind the wheel.

Once we pulled out of the parking lot, I turned around to check on Mattie. She was joyfully taking in the breeze, with her head tilted back.

I was experiencing one of those moments in life that you can't fully comprehend or appreciate, until you look back on them. After going to a place to contemplate doing away with myself, I was returning to my mother's with a stray dog.

On the way home, I thought about taking Mattie to the nearest animal shelter, but I decided against it. I suppose I could have been more diligent in seeing if she belonged to someone, but I figured whoever owned her—considering her condition—didn't deserve to have her any longer. My intention was to get her cleaned up, bring her to a vet, and find her a home.

But first, I needed a few basic things. I had the driver stop at a pet store near my mother's place to buy a collar and a leash, some food, treats, a pooper scooper, and a bed.

I left Mattie in the cab so I could get what I needed quickly. When I returned she was practically on the cab driver's lap, looking out his window for me.

"Loyal dog," the driver said, taking the supplies from me and putting them in the trunk.

I got mentally prepared to introduce my mother to my new friend, but she wasn't home when Mattie and I arrived. Before I could decide where to put the stuff I had bought at the pet store, Mattie excitedly poked her nose at the bag of dog food. I opened it and poured a healthy portion into a bowl and put it down beside some water. She inhaled it without hardly chewing, so I hand fed her some more kibble. Afterward, she sniffed her way from the kitchen into the living room.

Quickly, I wheeled myself to the hallway closet to grab a couple of towels. After I ran one under the kitchen sink faucet, I made a feeble attempt to clean my house guest before she met my roommate.

Once I finished, Mattie walked over and stood by the sliding glass door that led to the balcony and stared out. I went over and pushed the door open, and she happily went outside.

"Joel?" I heard Don Grainy call a few seconds later. "Is that you?"

"Hey, Don," I replied, joining Mattie on the balcony. "I'm here with a dog that's visiting."

As he said something else to me, I heard my mother calling my name.

"I'm out on the balcony," I called back.

"What's that smell?" she asked, as she walked through the living room towards me.

"What smell? I don't smell—"

"Oh my God!" she cried, spotting Mattie through the screen door. "What's that dog doing here?"

"I just found her."

"Where on earth did you find a dog like that?"

"In the park."

"Did you call animal control?"

"No, I'm going to put some signs around to see if she belongs to anyone."

"Joel, that dog doesn't belong to anyone."

"How do you know?" I asked.

"Look at it."

"She'll look better tomorrow—I'm going to have her groomed."

I hadn't made any calls yet, but figured it was probably too late in the day to get her in anywhere.

"Where is she going to stay until then?" my mother asked.

"Here," I replied as if it were obvious.

"Joel, don't be ridiculous…that's an old, emaciated dog. You have no idea what diseases it could be carrying."

"It's one night, mom. She can stay outside."

"I don't know about that."

"She doesn't bark…she'll be fine out here."

"Okay," my mother replied reluctantly, "but if you don't figure out what to do with that dog by tomorrow, we're taking it to the shelter."

I didn't reply. Instead I reached over and gave Mattie a reassuring pat on the head, and looked up at my mother and smiled.

THIRTY-TWO

I suppose it was probably better than where she had been staying, but I hated that poor Mattie would have to spend the night on the balcony.

After my mother retreated to her room for the night, I watched TV for a half hour. Then I attempted to go to sleep. But all I could do was lay awake and stare at the ceiling. I couldn't stop thinking about Mattie. I wasn't worried about her trying to escape the balcony, but I felt bad that she was outside alone.

At 3:45 in the morning, I got out of bed and went to check on her. She was contently curled up in one of the corners of the balcony, against the metal railing. I stood silent for a while, watching her through the glass. Even at rest, this creature I had just found was wiggling her way into my heart.

Kerrie used to bring Elvis, her fawn-colored pug, to the store on occasion and that was probably the last dog I had been around.

As a kid, our family had an orange tabby named Jake. But as much as we liked him was as much as he disliked us. Jake was mostly an outdoor cat, who went on long expeditions. He would return without any sentiment for being gone, and look at us as if to say: *Who are you and what are you doing here?*

I opened the sliding glass door and roused Mattie from her slumber. It took her a few seconds, but she happily accepted my offer to come inside.

Back in my room, I took one of my blankets and lay it on the floor beside my bed. I set my alarm clock so that I would have time to feed Mattie before my mother woke up.

When morning came, Mattie gladly followed me into the kitchen and had breakfast. Once she finished, she wandered over to the coat rack in the entryway and sniffed around. Just then, I heard my mother stirring earlier than I expected.

I wheeled myself over to where Mattie was, so I could quickly grab her and take her outside. She alluded my grasp and in a second, over my shoulder, I heard my mother say, "Joel, please…put the dog back outside."

"I'm trying, but she doesn't seem to want to go."

Foolishly, during the night I had taken off the collar I bought Mattie because she kept scratching at it. Casually, I wheeled myself towards her and tried to grab her again, but she easily darted around me.

"Can you help me?" I asked my mother.

"Joel, I'm not touching that dog," she replied.

"Well, then I guess she stays inside."

With that, my mother cornered Mattie between the end table and the wall, grabbed the fur behind her neck, and led her outside as if she were disposing of something poisonous.

While my mother washed her hands at the kitchen sink, I told her I was going to skip my therapy session in order to get Mattie situated. She liked the idea and soon left to meet a friend for coffee.

As soon as she was gone, of course, I let Mattie back inside. She wagged her tail and danced around my wheelchair as if she had just scored a touchdown.

"Okay, Mattie girl," I said to her. "We need to get you clean and come up with a plan." I called a few nearby groomers, until I found one with an immediate opening and then called a cab.

The female cab driver, who arrived shortly after we got downstairs, didn't see Mattie as a dilapidated dog but as royalty. She asked if Mattie could ride in the front with her, so she could pet the dog and feed her treats from a stash she kept in the door pocket.

"You must have a dog," I said from the backseat.

"Dogs," she replied, emphasizing the "s" as she looked at me in the rear view mirror smiling. "Always plural."

I told her the story of how I found Mattie, minus the reason I was on the bridge.

"Poor sweetheart was probably surviving on her own," she said. "Fucking people…they take everything the dog has to give, and then dump it somewhere when it gets old or sick."

She seemed to know a lot about dogs and said that if I brought Mattie to an animal shelter, the dog would most likely be euthanized because of her age and condition. She suggested that I post something online to try to find someone to take her or keep her myself. She preferred the latter option.

"It's perfect," she offered. "She needs you, and it looks like you could use her."

Once we arrived at the groomers, she led Mattie out of the cab and got down on her knees and gave the dog a hug. When I paid for the ride, she handed me back my change along with a couple of dog treats.

"Good luck," she said, smiling and waving at Mattie. "She's a great dog…you won't be sorry if you keep her."

The Canine Clippery was buzzing with the sound of barking dogs coming from the room behind the front counter. Judging by the size of the place, the lady who greeted me did everything herself.

Once Mattie disappeared into the back with her, I pulled my wheelchair into the corner of the tiny reception area. I picked up a magazine from the coffee table, with a regal-looking German shepherd on the cover, and started to read an article on dog training.

Almost an hour later, when the woman returned with Mattie, I was stunned by the transformation.

"WOW," I said.

"Yeah," she said, wiping the sweat from her forehead with her forearm. "She was one dirty dog. I don't know if I've ever seen fur matted like that."

Mattie's white coat was now soft and shiny, and she smelled nice. Being clean seemed to make her perkier.

"Except for her back leg, she's as good as new," I said, as I paid the lady.

"I hate to tell you," she replied, "but I think that leg is probably paralyzed. Another client of mine had a dog with the same thing."

The groomer leaned over and grabbed a business card from a stand on the counter. "Here," she said, handing it to me. "Most of my clients go to this vet. She's great."

As I left the building, I called the vet's office and the woman who answered said she had an available appointment at three in the afternoon. I took the appointment and then took a cab back to my mothers. I hoped she would be home, so she could see the new Mattie.

Unfortunately, she was still out. So, after I pacified Mattie for a while with a toy I had bought at the groomers, I went into my room to lie down.

I awoke to the sight of my mother standing over me.

"Hey, mom," I mumbled, coming to.

"Have you noticed who's in the house and on your bed?" she asked, annoyed.

I looked and saw Mattie curled up at my feet.

"Did you see how clean she is?" I asked.

"Wonderful," she said, drenched in sarcasm. "Too bad it happened after she got hair all over my kitchen and on the living room couch."

"I need to work on keeping her off of the furniture," I said.

"What you need to work on is finding her a home."

"It's not that simple, mom. I found out a few things. If I bring her to an animal shelter, they'll put her down because of her age and her injured leg."

"Then take her to the dog park and give her away to somebody there," she replied. "Joel, you have to do something—she can't stay here."

I looked over at Mattie, who was adorably unaware of us discussing her fate. At that moment, I knew I wasn't going to give her to anybody. She had made herself mine.

"You have to admit she's cute," I said, trying to soften my mother on the idea of keeping her.

"Joel, you don't know this dog's history—it could have other medical issues besides the leg."

"I have an appointment with a vet this afternoon."

"Okay, but do you really want an old dog that'll be dead in a year or two?" she asked.

"We all could be dead in a year or two," I replied defiantly. "This dog found me and needs me, and I need her."

"Joel, you're in no condition to take care of a dog. You can't even take care of yourself without help," she said, before walking out of the room.

I knew it was a valid point, but sometimes the heart renders the mind useless.

As my appointment with the vet approached, I thought about

asking my mother to give Mattie and me a ride, but I thought better of it.

When the cab pulled up to the vet's address, we were in front of a small, yellow house in a residential area. It seemed like an odd location for an office, but there was a wooden sign hanging from the porch, so I figured it must be the right place.

The winding brick pathway that led to the front door was a bit tricky to navigate, with Mattie crisscrossing in front of my wheelchair to sniff the bushes on each side of us.

Opening the front door, we were staring into the living room of the house, which was the reception area. After we checked in with the woman behind a small wooden desk, Mattie pulled me toward a dog who was sitting nearby with her owner. While our dogs greeted one another, the man told me all about his Jack Russell Terrier, Penelope. The cute, high strung dog had suffered a lot of health issues, and the owner had taken her to several vets before finding the one we were at.

"It may not look like it, but you're sitting in the best vet's office in L.A.," he said confidently.

When it was Mattie's turn to be seen, a young vet tech came out and ushered us into a nice-sized bedroom, which served as an examining room.

The vet, Sima Michel, had an easygoing manner and an obvious love for animals. I was a little surprised when after shaking my hand, she plopped down on the floor and sat cross-legged, feeding Mattie treats and petting her.

Upon hearing the circumstances in which I found Mattie, she suggested that we do a complete examination, including a blood test, to which I agreed.

Mattie, as it turned out, was a perfectly healthy dog, with the exception of having permanent nerve damage in her hind right leg.

Dr. Michel, however, said that Mattie's liability wouldn't hamper her life in any way.

I briefly discussed my physical condition with the vet and asked her opinion on whether it was practical for me to keep Mattie.

"That's for you to decide," she told me. "But I will say this is a very smart and sweet dog."

Leaving the vet's office—other than the confirmed diagnosis of Mattie's leg—nothing had changed about my situation. I knew the news I would tell my mother wouldn't change her mind about Mattie.

THIRTY-THREE

On the ride back to the condo, I decided to call Big G and explain my situation to him. I didn't want to include the reason I had gone to the Brackingham Bridge, but I knew it would help with the huge favor I was about to ask.

"I'm having a real tough time living with my mother," I told him, after filling him in on my fated encounter with a stray dog.

"Right," he said, anticipating there was more to come.

"Is there any way I could live in your guesthouse for a while?"

"With the dog?" he asked.

"Well, yeah…I've decided I'm going to keep her."

"Are you sure you're up for having a dog, dude? There's a lot of crap—no pun intended—that you have to deal with. Maybe you should wait to get stronger before taking something like that on."

"Maybe. But I've made up my mind," I told him. "Just let me know if you can help or not."

"Okay, let me talk to Leslie and I'll get back to you on it."

With the size of Gary's house, I hoped there might be a chance that he could accommodate me for a short time, but I wasn't counting on it. If it didn't work out, I wasn't going to let it deter me from keeping Mattie. For the first time since I awoke from my coma,

I felt connected to something. It wasn't in my wildest dreams what I imagined it would be, but it felt good.

Surprisingly, within five minutes, Gary called back and said it would be okay for me to live in his guesthouse temporarily. He seemed convinced that as soon as I moved out, my mother would acquiesce and allow me to live there with Mattie. Before we hung up, he mentioned that he had two cats who had never been around a dog before.

When I told my mother about Mattie's checkup with the Vet, she was predictably unmoved. She was, however, startled when I said I was leaving to go live at Gary's.

"Okay," she responded, trying to hide her hurt. "If that's what you want."

It would have been nice for her to put up some resistance—even though it wouldn't have changed anything—or say I was welcome back anytime. Wishes aside, I was ready to be anywhere but where I was.

I sent Gary a text and asked when I could move my stuff. He replied with, "Whenever. The place is clean. By the way, the kids are excited to meet your dog."

"Would you mind bringing me over to Gary's later?" I asked my mother, looking up from my phone.

"It would have to be tomorrow or the morning after—I have a lot going on."

"Okay," I replied. "I'll see if Gary can pick me up."

"Don't do that to me, Joel."

"Do what?" I asked, although I had a good idea as to what her objection would be.

"If Gary comes to get you, I'll feel guilty and look bad for not letting you stay here with the dog."

We traded a few verbal jabs, and then I made an arrangement

with Gary to have him come later that evening, when my mother planned on being out.

Big G showed up with a hotel luggage cart that he borrowed from a friend who owned a boutique hotel a few blocks away.

"Just a forewarning," I said after we shook hands. "I haven't packed, but I don't have much."

"No sweat," he replied. "We'll do it like we did in the old days."

"Just throw the crap in a pile and take off?"

"Exactly."

"I'll never forget the time Brian and I helped you move from that apartment on Bentley Avenue," I said.

"That was insane…We got shitfaced at ten in the morning. I remember my armoire was too heavy to carry down the stairs, so we just sort of rolled it," he said, laughing. "I don't think I got any of my security deposit back on that one."

I smiled, thinking back on the memory.

"Man, I miss those days," he said, rolling the luggage cart into my room. "We never thought about the consequences of doing things."

"And somehow it always worked out," I replied.

"Considering some of the stuff we did, you'd have to say that life looks out for the young and crazy ones."

I pointed out the rest of the things I needed to take with me, and Gary stacked them onto the cart.

"The dog's coming, right?" he joked.

"Mattie," I called, not seeing her. After calling her name a second time, she appeared in the doorway with an old doll of my mother's in her mouth. I quickly grabbed it from her and started to laugh.

"I bet your mother's having a drink somewhere, celebrating that you're temporarily leaving," Gary said.

"Probably," I replied.

"Okay, let's roll," he said, reaching down and lifting Mattie onto an open space on the cart.

On the ride over to Gary's house, I expressed my gratitude to him. "Thanks, this is a huge help," I said. "I was losing my mind there."

"No problem," he replied. "You've been through a lot. I was just telling Carmen yesterday that you inspire me."

"Really?" I said. "How can a guy on a bridge contemplating ending his life be an inspiration to anyone except the severely depressed?"

"I wasn't including that," he said, with a laugh. "I was talking about everything else."

Neither of us said anything for a few stop lights, which was a rare occurrence when I was with Gary. Finally he asked, "Would you have really jumped?"

"Yeah," I replied, waiting to see how he would respond before saying anything else. When he kept his eyes on the road and didn't show any noticeable reaction, I said, "I can't explain what it's like to wake up after that many years and have to start over. Then to be shot in a mall...and then the press...it put me over the edge."

"I think we need to have that sports night," he offered.

"You know where I live...anytime."

THIRTY-FOUR

When we pulled into Gary's driveway, Todd and Hannah were outside playing. As soon as they spotted the car, with Mattie's head poking out of the back window, they ran over and clamored to meet her. The feeling was mutual—once Mattie made it out of Gary's SUV, her tail was wagging and she was up for anything.

"What's wrong with her leg?" Hannah asked me.

"She hurt it somehow, before I found her," I explained.

"Did her owner give her away because she was broken?" Hannah wanted to know.

"I'm not sure," I replied, "but she's a great dog."

"Can she play fetch?" Todd asked.

"Definitely—here," I said, handing him a tennis ball from a canister I had in one of my bags.

While the kids played with Mattie, Gary brought me to the guesthouse. Fortunately, it was accessible through the side of the property and it wasn't too difficult to navigate.

"Is Leslie home?" I asked him.

"I doubt it," he answered. "She's never around on the weekends, when I'm here."

"Where does she go?"

"Who knows," he replied, becoming agitated. "Listen…just so you know, one of my hesitancies in having you here is for you to see our marriage—if you want to call it that—up close."

"Don't worry, you know me…I can hole up and keep to myself pretty well."

"At least you're far away from the house," he replied, taking my things off of the cart and then handing me a notepad. "Here—jot down whatever you need from the market and Leslie will get it."

"Hey, I really appreciate this," I said, reaching over to wrap my arm around his midsection to hug him.

"You got it buddy," he replied. "I'll let you get situated. When I see Mattie, I'll send her back here."

A few minutes later, after I came out of the bathroom, my dog appeared on the other side of the glass door. Just seeing her peer inside, with her tail wagging, lifted my spirits.

I let her in, gave her a treat, and then orientated myself to my new surroundings. Incredibly, for a guesthouse, it wasn't that much smaller than my mother's condo. And for the moment at least, it was peaceful.

Later on, Gary sent me a text, saying he was going to order a pizza and bring it over for our sports night.

While I waited for him, I spent some time working with Mattie on her manners. She knew all of the basic commands, but she only complied with them when she felt like it, or after I asked repeatedly.

Although it would have made things easier if she were trained, what endeared me to her was the trust she had in me after being neglected and most likely mistreated.

When Gary walked in with the pizza, Mattie got on the couch to get closer to the arriving aroma.

"Hey—get her down from there," he said. "Leslie will flip out if she sees that."

I tossed a training treat onto the floor and Mattie followed it.

Gary went to set the pizzas down on the coffee table before realizing that with Mattie around, the kitchen counter was a better option.

"She needs training," Gary said, stating the obvious.

"I'm supposed to be getting a walker in two weeks, so hopefully that'll make it easier for me to work with her."

"Dude, that's huge!" he said, putting out his open palm for a high five. "That's definitely something to celebrate…let me grab a couple of beers."

Pizza and beer. It was like old times, with Gary and I shooting the breeze and laughing.

Once we finished eating, he turned on an enormous-sized flat screen TV that was more like a mini movie screen. I was amazed when he connected the internet to it.

For the next few hours, using YouTube videos and games he had taped, Gary relived for me some of the Cleveland sports highlights and lowlights that I had missed.

"One of the first things I asked my mom after I came out of the coma was about the Browns," I told him. "I can't believe they still haven't won, or at least gone to, a Super Bowl."

"It's pathetic. Out of the old school teams, it's just them and the Lions now that haven't won one. The closest we got to a championship was the 1997 World Series. The Indians were ahead in the 8th inning of Game 7…but you can guess how that ended."

As we started to watch basketball footage, I almost fell out of my wheelchair when I saw Michael Jordan tormenting the Cavaliers again.

"I thought he retired!" I yelled.

"Yeah, well, he unretired the year after you went into your coma," he said. "We did make it to the finals in 2007, but got swept by the Spurs."

While Gary went to the bathroom, I watched a hockey game on ESPN.

"I can't believe this," I said once he returned, pointing to the coach of the Rangers being interviewed.

"What?" he asked.

"They're interviewing the coach during the game," I replied.

"They do it now in every sport, except football, I think."

"During the game?" I reiterated. "That's crazy."

"A lot of changes, dude," he replied, taking out his phone. "I looked this up for you earlier. Remember Bobby Bonilla? He made 6.3 million in 1994 with the Yankees. Alex Rodriguez, who now plays with the Yankees, makes 29 million!"

By the time we called it a night, I was zonked. I took Mattie to relieve herself on a patch of grass beside the kids' swing set and quickly got ready for bed.

THIRTY-FIVE

The following morning, Gary left on a short business trip. While he was gone, Leslie and the kids came by to check on me, but most of the time it was just Mattie and I hanging out. It gave her and I a chance to bond with one another, and it gave me a realistic sense of what it would take to care for her.

I was amazed by how much joy I felt being around a dog. I loved the way Mattie rested her chin on the mattress and stared at me until I got out of bed in the morning; the way she intently watched me eat a sandwich, hoping that I would share it; the way she dreamed, with her chest heaving and sighing, while her paws jiggled; and the way she would look over at me when we took walks, as if to say, *Isn't this great?*

But more than anything, Mattie's natural inclination to ignore her physical shortcoming gave me inspiration not to let mine define me. After a week with Mattie, it was hard for me to believe that I never had a dog before.

Like a proud parent, I emailed pictures to Kerrie and Aunt Shirley of Mattie doing cute things. I told them about all of her adorable whims and her quirky habits. And how she loved my *scrumptious scrubs*, which was when I would simultaneously rub Mattie's back and stomach, while she lie on her side with a tennis ball in her mouth. I'm sure they and everyone else around me figured my infatuation with my newfound, furry friend would dissipate. But unlike a human love affair that ebbs and flows before most often waning, my feelings for Mattie only deepened with time.

That Saturday afternoon, after Mattie and I explored Big G's backyard, I returned to the guesthouse to find a surprise visitor. Gary's secretary, Carmen, was sitting on the couch.

"Oh…hey," she said, surprised to see me. "Where's Gary?"

"Uh, I don't know," I replied. "I haven't seen him since he left for his business trip."

"Oh," she responded. "Do you mind if I wait for him?"

"No…go ahead."

I don't know if Carmen realized at first that I was living there, but looking around she probably figured it out quickly. I offered her some lemonade, which she accepted. When I brought it to her, Mattie was already at her side, trying to engage her. Carmen gave Mattie a quick pat on the head, and then folded her legs and leaned back on the couch.

The two of us made small talk, which became more labored as the minutes went by. I was tempted to use Mattie as an excuse to go back outside, but I didn't want to risk seeing Leslie, who I thought was home. Gary hadn't said anything to me about Carmen—other than she was his secretary—but I assumed that there was more to her role than the job title inferred.

"Did you text Gary?" I asked.

"Yeah, he should be here by now," she replied.

When Gary came through the door, five minutes later, he acted as if there was nothing unusual or awkward about the scenario. He gave me a pat on the back before walking over and giving Carmen a big hug. Her mood instantly changed from dour to happy and smiling.

"Hey, dude," Gary said, turning back to me, "would you mind giving me a little time alone with Carmen?"

"No…sure," I said hesitantly, looking around for where I had put Mattie's leash.

"Leslie's gone for a little while and the kids are with friends…you can hang out in the house," he said. "I burned another CD for you and left it in the living room. I think you'll dig it."

I entered the house through the sun room and gave Mattie a treat for waiting for me to go inside ahead of her. When I got to the living room, I spotted the CD Gary had mentioned and put it in the side pocket of my wheelchair.

The TV was on and one of Gary's company's video games was on the screen, ready to be played. I picked up the joystick and began fiddling around. It was a different game than the one Todd and I had played, but the amount of blood and guts were the same.

Instantly, the sound of gunfire triggered the terror I experienced inside of the mall. I felt nervous and agitated. I wasn't an expert and didn't know if there was a connection between violent video games and the actions of the gunman I encountered, but the possibility upset me. That my friend produced this stuff deeply saddened me.

The longer I was gone from Hathers, the more I noticed the ways in which the world had changed. Making money, in far more cases than before, had become *the* passion as opposed to the reward for pursuing a passion. Gary had become part of that trend.

I left the living room and went into the kitchen to help myself to a protein bar from the pantry. I was about to go outside to toss Mattie her tennis ball, when Gary texted me, saying to meet him by the pool. I assumed that meant Carmen was gone.

When I reached him, he was alone, reclining on one of the chaise lounges, already talking on his cell phone. Listening to the conversation for a moment, I could tell it was business related. As his tone got more intense, he got up and walked over to the opposite side of the pool.

From where he was standing, I could still hear him. Soon, he was ranting and raving and his mood suddenly turned angry and cold.

A polar opposite of the Big G I had always known now existed, and his old personality and new one were frighteningly interchangeable on a dime.

"Business," he said, returning to me, without elaborating on the issue. Neither of us said a word about Carmen.

THIRTY-SIX

On the way to taking the kids to school, Leslie filled in for my mother, dropping me off at therapy. With the blessing of the staff at Sarswick, I began bringing Mattie along with me. On her third visit, I experienced a monumental moment in my rehabilitation.

Sooner than I had anticipated, I was given the go ahead to begin using a walker. My physical therapist told me I would need to slowly build up the distances I could walk with it, but nothing could put a damper on my accomplishment.

Dorothy's prophetic words—*Great strides are nothing but small steps taken over time*—came back to me as if they were written across the sky on a summer day.

My progress had been anything but a straight line, and it took far longer than I wanted it to, but I had made the journey and taken those steps.

Best of all, I had someone to share it with. After I completed my first lap around the gym with my walker, I got down on my knees, wrapped my arms around Mattie and cried into her coat.

Once I got back to Gary's guesthouse, I called my mother to tell her the news. She seemed genuinely happy for me and suggested we go for dinner to celebrate. I told her I needed to see if someone in

Gary's family could let Mattie out while I was gone.

"You can bring her with us if you want," my mother said.

"What?" I asked, obviously surprised.

"We can leave her in the car—it's not hot out."

"Did you rent a car?" I asked sarcastically.

"No… I've just reconsidered some things," she replied.

Gary's kids were excited to watch after Mattie, and I thought she would be happier with them as opposed to sitting alone in a car.

Once my mother picked me up, I asked where we were going but she wouldn't tell.

"It's a surprise," she said.

The surprise turned out to be the Sushi restaurant she had pointed out to me on our drive home from Hathers.

"I don't like Sushi," I said, as we pulled into the parking lot.

"Have you tried it?" my mother asked.

"Yes. I told you, Lauren used to have it all the time."

"It's really popular now," my mother reminded me.

"I don't think that's going to make it taste any better," I replied.

After I pointed out that we were celebrating *my* accomplishment, we settled on a Chinese place, a few doors down.

Over dinner, I told her what I was working on in therapy, now that I had my walker. Normally, she would subtly or suddenly shift the topic of conversation to something having to do with her, but I could sense that she was trying her best not to.

"I want you to come back home, with Mattie," she said, once I finished talking.

"Really?" I asked. "What changed?"

"Nothing changed. You're my son and I want to be here for you."

"Wow," I replied, figuring Aunt Shirley must have said something to her to change her mind. I refused to believe that my mother had softened on her own.

I knew Gary's guesthouse was only a temporary solution, and that my mother was the most available person to help me until I could help myself.

I agreed to move back, but I wanted to stretch out my vacation a little bit longer.

"I think I'll stay for a few more days," I told her. "Gary's kids love Mattie, and she's really enjoying the open space."

"Can I ask you a question without offending you?" she asked.

"I guess that depends on what the question is," I replied, smiling.

"Since when do you love dogs so much?"

"Since Mattie," I replied.

Thirty-Seven

Staying at Big G's a few extra days was good for Mattie, but in hindsight I wished I had left sooner.

Carmen made another impromptu visit. As soon as I saw her waiting inside the guesthouse—returning from a game of fetch with Mattie—I sent Gary a text to let him know. He wrote back, *Sorry dude, be there soon.*

When he showed up, Carmen approached him like a dog who had just been shown a tasty treat. While Gary wrapped his arms around her, he glanced at me as if to say: *You know the drill.*

On my way to the main house, Mattie and I crossed paths with Hannah and a friend of hers, who were outside playing.

"Can Mattie play hide and seek with us?" Hannah asked me.

"Sure," I said.

I went inside and picked up a guitar that Gary had in a small room off of the living room. To blow off steam, I strummed a few simple chords and made up lyrics about what an asshole I thought my friend had become.

After I put down the guitar to go to the bathroom, I returned to find a text from Gary saying, *WTF—Get Hannah away from here!*

I didn't know what *WTF* meant, but I knew what had happened.

As quickly as I could, I went back outside and called for Hannah. Mattie heard my voice, and like a good girl immediately came to me. I yelled again for the girls, but still couldn't see or hear them.

"Let's go find them," I said to Mattie, and she followed alongside me. After we went about ten yards towards the guesthouse, Hannah and her friend came running our way.

"What's my dad doing inside the guesthouse?" Hannah asked me, out of breath.

"I think he's taking care of some business," I said.

"He closed the shades and wouldn't let us in," her friend pouted.

"Don't worry, he'll be out soon," I said. "In the meantime, Mattie wants you guys to play with her some more."

The girls went over to a patch of grass by the swing set and Mattie followed after them. Watching her, I smiled at how sweet she was with the kids. She had also made peace with Gary's two cats, who were less than hospitable to her. It was hard to believe that someone could have discarded this dog.

I was going to join Mattie and the girls, when the sun broke through the clouds. I rested my hands on my walker, closed my eyes, and leaned my head back. After a morning of unusually cool temperatures and a surprising rainfall, the warmth felt good.

A moment later, I heard someone approaching me and opened my eyes to see Leslie.

"Joel, where's Gary?" she asked, glaring at me.

"I'm not sure…I think he went to the store," I replied, shading the sun with my hand.

"Really?" she asked sharply. "His car is in the garage."

"Oh, then maybe he's back," I said. "I've just been out here with Mattie and the girls."

Leslie turned away and called out to her daughter. Hannah, who was rolling on the grass, giggling with her friend, while Mattie circled them, didn't respond.

"Hannah!" Leslie yelled a second time. "Come here this minute!"

Hannah reluctantly got up and walked over to her mother.

"Where's your father?" Leslie asked her sternly.

"He's in the guesthouse with somebody."

Leslie shot me a dirty look, and then made a b-line for the guesthouse.

I muttered "shit" under my breath, trying quickly to think of what to do. I pulled out my phone and texted Gary, *Leslie's home!*

Several minutes later, Gary and Leslie emerged from the guesthouse. They looked about as happy as two birds drenched in water. Leslie called the girls to follow her inside the house. Gary walked over to me with a sullen look on his face.

"Hey," he grunted.

"Hey," I responded.

"Don't you have the sense to keep my daughter away from the guesthouse while Carmen's here?" he asked, wiping sweat from his forehead.

"I didn't think about it to tell you the truth," I replied.

"Well, *think* next time. *Fuck!*" he said, his voice rising in anger. "She almost saw me naked with someone other than her mother."

"I hope there's not a next time, asshole," I responded, wishing I could have taken back my words as soon as they left my mouth.

It wasn't that I was in the wrong, but in the past Gary and I never got into arguments. No matter what happened between us, we either just let things go or held in whatever bothered us until it passed.

"Man, I let you come and stay here and that's the thanks I get?" he said.

"One thing has nothing to do with the other," I shot back. "You're shtupping your secretary with your wife and kids seventy yards away. It's moronic, not to mention wrong."

"Grow up, dude—married couples cheat," he responded. "It's a fact of fucking life. You seem awfully protective of my wife, though. Why don't you give her a go? She needs someone to fuck that frown off of her face."

"Really? So if you found me with Leslie it wouldn't bother you?"

"Not one bit."

"If that's the case, then get a divorce," I barked back.

"If I didn't have kids it would have happened a long time ago."

"That's a cop out," I said. "Your kids would be better off not being around two people who can't stand one another. Maybe you're just afraid to be alone."

"I appreciate the free psychoanalysis," he replied, "but Todd has a little league game in less than an hour and I got to shower."

"Pussy," I said, as he turned away.

Over the next couple of days, the tension between Gary and I dissipated somewhat. By the time he helped me move out of the guesthouse, both of us had managed to put the incident behind us.

THIRTY-EIGHT

Returning to my mother's, I was surprised to find that she had put a padded blanket for Mattie by the sliding glass door so Mattie could lie down and look outside.

From the get-go she tried harder where my dog was concerned—refilling her water bowl and occasionally taking her outside to do her business, when I was too tired. But there was one habit of Mattie's that continually drove my mother crazy.

After Mattie finished eating her food, she would rejoice by rubbing her chin back and forth on the carpet, and then running the side of her head along the front of the couch.

It was hard to know who got more pleasure—Mattie or I watching her do it. It never failed to put a grin on my face.

The trouble with Mattie's post-meal ritual—as far as my mother was concerned—was that it left a trail of fur in its wake. She tried to get her to stop doing it, and begged me repeatedly to intervene. I made a few lazy attempts to deter her, but felt that joy is too hard to come by to justify stopping it.

There was always comfort in numbers when it came to being around my mother. The more people, the more distraction, and the less friction between her and I. Mattie, of course, wasn't a person (although at times she could have fooled me), but she provided a much needed buffer between my mother and me.

If things got heated between us, I would take Mattie downstairs for a stroll. We would meander along the concrete pathway that wound around the property and stop at the waterfall. There I would sit on the bench and take a break, listening to the sound of the cascading water and the chirping birds. In this instance, and so many others, Mattie had a magical way of slowing down time for me so that I could appreciate ordinary moments.

Mattie however, like every dog and every person, had her issues.

Shortly after I moved back home, she threw up one afternoon and again that night. For the entire next day, she refused her food. When she didn't touch her kibble the following morning, I started to worry about her.

Before calling the Vet, I decided to cut up a chicken breast that my mother had in the refrigerator and mix it in with Mattie's food. In seconds, she went from having no appetite to emptying the bowl.

I continued the same routine for a few meals, and then figured I would go back to giving her just kibble. She stuck her snout into the bowl, sniffed around, discovered that the contents weren't to her satisfaction, and walked away.

Once I acquiesced and gave her chicken again, I tried an experiment of slowly diminishing the amount I gave her with each serving. I thought for sure she would ultimately just go back to eating the kibble without any chicken. No chance.

Not only did she stop eating the kibble again, she began a new routine of eating the chicken first, with just a little bit of kibble, and then walking away. Only when I would put more chicken in the bowl would she eat more kibble. It took a few rounds of me anteing up more chicken before Mattie would finish her food.

As you might have guessed, my leniency and softness with Mattie didn't make me the best dog trainer. Disciplining a dog—from what I had read—required repetition and an alpha dog mentality. I was spotty with the repetition part, depending on the energy level I had on a particular day, but I sucked at being tough with her.

When she did something wrong and I raised my voice to her, she would immediately go and grab one of her toys and stare at me. The pout on her face—with her head ever so slightly tilted to one side, seemingly saying, *What? I didn't do anything*—made me feel guilty for reprimanding her in the first place.

The next time I spoke to Kerrie, I told her about my dog training exploits. After giving me a few tips, she added, "You never had trouble being tough on the people who worked for you."

"What do you mean?" I asked defensively.

"If the records weren't displayed exactly the way you wanted them, you'd give whoever it was a look that made them want to wither away and die."

"No. I wasn't that bad."

"I'm afraid so," she replied. "Thankfully I wasn't on the receiving end of those stoic stares very often."

After I got off of the phone with Kerrie, I took Mattie downstairs for a walk. Once I closed the front door, I turned and saw Don Grainy coming back to his unit.

I hadn't seen him in a while, and he noticed my walker and congratulated me. I told him I decided to keep the dog he had seen on the balcony, and introduced him to Mattie. Don was a little unsteady, but he got down on one knee and stroked the side of her face.

"Ain't nothing like a dog," he said, looking up at me. "Humans…you give 'em an inch, they take a mile. Dogs…you give 'em a morsel of food and show 'em some love, and you got a friend for life."

Don went on to tell me about the dogs he had owned throughout his life. Afterward, I asked him if he knew anything about training them. Hearing that he did, and seeing that Mattie had taken a liking to him, I asked if he wanted to get together and talk dogs sometime.

"Sure," he said. "So long as you're sober and your mother ain't around."

THIRTY-NINE

One morning, just after my mother left to go grocery shopping, there was a knock on our door. It was the first time I ever heard Mattie bark, and it was pretty rapturous.

I grabbed my walker and she excitedly followed me to see who it was. Looking through the peephole, I saw a man wearing a straw hat pulled down to cover his face.

"Who is it?" I asked, leery that it might be someone from the press.

"Flower delivery for a Mrs. Berskin," the male voice said in a heavy English accent.

"You can leave them by the door. Thanks," I said.

"I need a signature," the delivery person anxiously replied. "C'mon mate—you're not the only stop I have."

"I'll take responsibility—just go ahead and leave them," I reiterated, as I backed away from the peephole to pacify Mattie with a pet on the head.

"Man oh man, just open the door," he replied, annoyed. "What are you, a neurotic Jew or something?"

Startled, I put my eye back up to the peephole. As I did, the man slowly pushed the straw hat off of his face.

"Dude, it's me!" he exclaimed, without the accent.

"Brian!"

I quickly opened the door and my old friend rushed inside.

"I had you!" he cried, giving me a hug.

"Not even close—that accent was seriously suspicious."

"Man, it's so good to see you," he said, raising his hand to give me a high five.

I held his grip for a moment and started to get teary-eyed.

"It's okay, brother…let it out," he said, embracing me again. "It's a heavy thing."

"How'd you get this address? Big G?" I asked, as we walked into the living room.

"No, from your mother."

"I should have known."

"How's it going since you came back from Gary's?" he asked.

"Better, but how good can it be for a grown man to live with his mother?"

"I hear you," he replied. "Remember, my offer to come down to Mexico still stands."

"If you're the walking billboard for the place, it looks enticing. Man, you look relaxed, tan, and happy."

"It's the best thing I ever did," Brian said, reaching down to jostle with Mattie over the toy in her mouth.

"I'm surprised it's not lonely living so far away from everything you know."

"It took some adjusting, for sure, but the life I have there is better than the one I had here."

"I still can't believe you just up and left your career," I said, thinking back to Brian the accountant I knew from all those years ago. "Do you ever miss having a more traditional life—the wife and kids thing?"

"Occasionally, but by the time I left here I realized that it just wasn't in the cards for me," he replied. "Now all I have to do is talk to Big G and hear him screaming at his wife and kids to be reminded that the grass isn't so green on the other side."

"Did he tell you about the guesthouse incident?" I asked.

"Yeah. He was pretty steamed, but I think he knows he was wrong."

"When he told me he married Leslie, I knew it wasn't going to be a pretty picture," I said.

Brian nodded his head in agreement. "Unfortunately they decided to do what most miserable couples do—have kids."

"They're sweet kids," I replied. "But I agree, it's like adding kerosene soaked logs to a burning fire."

I grabbed a couple of bottles of home brewed beer that Don Grainy had given me, and Brian and I headed out to the balcony.

We talked about the changes in the world since we last saw one another, specifically technology.

"If you came out of your coma just after the dot-com boom, it wouldn't have seemed so dramatic," he told me. "Smart phones and social media really changed everything."

"Speaking of the devil," I said, hearing my phone alert me of a new text message.

"Who is it?" Brian asked.

"Big G," I said, before reading aloud what he wrote to me. "*Has your surprise visitor arrived yet? Get your asses over here!*"

"We might as well go now, if you're up for it," Brian said. "You know Big G—he'll pester us until we give in."

We talked for a little while longer, finished our beers, and then headed over to Gary's in Brian's rental car. I left Mattie in my room, with the door closed, thinking she would be all right for a few hours.

Gary was outside, throwing the baseball with his son, when we drove up. As soon as Brian got out of the car, Gary and Todd grabbed him and tackled him in the grass.

While the three of them grappled on the ground, Leslie came up behind me. She gave me a hug and didn't show any indication that there were hard feelings from the uncomfortable situation we experienced.

"Fellas!" Gary bellowed, once he and Brian stopped wrestling. "Let's head back to the guesthouse and hang."

He and Brian walked ahead, while Todd tagged alongside me, asking about Mattie.

Once we reached the guesthouse, Gary told Todd that the men needed some time alone.

"But I'm a man too," he protested, wanting to be included in the group.

"Yes, but you're a small boy, and this is for big boys," Gary responded.

"It's a good thing," Brian interjected, consoling Todd, who walked off with a long face. "Hang on to it as long as you can."

Being together in the same room with Gary and Brian, after so long, was incredibly surreal. The last time was a lifetime ago. O.J. Simpson had just been arrested for murder and nobody knew the name Monica Lewinsky.

"Sorry about our dust up," Gary said to me, referring to the incident with Carmen and Leslie, while grabbing three beers from the refrigerator.

"Apology accepted," I replied.

"The truth though is you should thank me," he said.

"Are you serious?" I asked, trying to read his facial expression. "Why's that?"

"By staying here and seeing my life, it made you realize that you and Lauren had a good marriage."

"That's pushing it," Brian cracked.

We started talking about relationships from our past, and wondered how they would have panned out, if they lasted.

"It's funny to look back," Brian said. "We were always searching and thinking we had found *the one*."

"There isn't one…that's the problem," Big G replied. "There's many, and they all drive you crazy."

"Spoken by a happily married man," Brian said sarcastically.

"C'mon, Brian, who have you dated that disputes that?" Big G asked.

"Actually, the women in Mexico are different than the ones here."

"Yeah, the hookers are less per hour," Gary cracked.

"Man, you're jaded something wicked," Brian responded.

"Just keeping it real, brother," Gary said. "Relationships don't work. They're built on a selfish premise—a woman's objective is to get in a man's wallet and a man's objective is to get into a woman's pants. Once one or both of them gets what they want, there isn't much left."

"Friendship's left," Brian replied. "And that's what it's about."

"Who's the last woman you dated that you'd consider as good a friend as one of your buddies?" Gary asked him.

"Give me another beer to think on that," Brian responded with a laugh.

"My cousin gave me a book of quotes for my last birthday," Gary said. "Einstein summed it up best, 'Marriage is the unsuccessful attempt to make something lasting out of an incident.'"

"Didn't he marry his cousin?" I asked.

"I wish I would have married mine," Gary replied. "She's still hot and wild."

"Yep," Brian confirmed, looking down at his phone. "His second wife was his cousin—Elsa."

"How about you?" Gary asked me. "Are you looking forward to dating again?"

"I've actually already found someone," I replied.

"Who?" Gary asked, disbelieving.

"She's a little hairy, but I love her for it," I said.

"Oh brother," Gary said, rolling his eyes and turning to Brian. "I don't know if you know already, but he's crazy for that dog."

"Yes, I've seen pictures," Brian responded.

"Seriously," Gary said to me. "Are you ready to get out there? Is your anatomy in working order…if you don't mind me asking?"

"I think I'm all right," I replied. "But from watching those commercials on TV, I know there's help if I need it."

"Man, that must be strange, waking up and seeing erectile dysfunction commercials every two minutes," Brian said.

"It was! After a few days I asked the nurse what happened to men."

Leslie knocked on the door and brought us some tasty, barbequed turkey burgers that we happily devoured. We continued talking and laughing for a while afterward, and then my energy started to fade. I told the guys that I should get back home.

Unfortunately, I only saw Brian one more time before he left town, because he had a bunch of family commitments. We had lunch at *Frankie's on Fifth*, which was also a favorite of his.

When I hugged him goodbye, he reiterated his invitation to come to Mexico for as short or long of a stay as I wanted. I told him for now I was committed to continuing my therapy and getting stronger, but I appreciated his offer.

"Who knows though," I said, after he got into his rental car. "The only things in life that I'm sure of—after what I've been through—are the ones that have already happened."

FORTY

Unlike me, my mother religiously followed the press coverage of the mall shooting. Embarrassingly, there were times when she seemed to gloat to strangers that I had been involved in it.

"Is there anything new?" I asked, after I walked into the living room and found her glued to a one-hour special on the event.

"They're talking about the killer's background right now," she said.

I decided to sit down on the couch and join her.

Since the shooting and my awful encounter with the press, I'd done everything I could to put the incident out of my mind. But there was a part of me—although I hated to admit it—that was curious about what type of person could kill with such ease and joy.

Watching the program, I knew there were people who would have sympathy for the gunman based on the hardship of his upbringing. At one point in my life, I might have been among them. But after witnessing the horror, the suffering, and the carnage on that day, I could only see evil as evil, without any concessions or caveats.

The longer I sat there, the more I stewed. Knowing that the killer would ultimately become notorious and the victims would eventually be forgotten incensed me.

"I have an idea," I said to my mother, during a commercial. "If this guy's going to sit in jail year after year, watching TV and lifting weights, filing one appeal after another, why not use him for animal testing? That way we spare the innocent animals and society gets something from this vermin and others like him."

"I know you're crazy for Mattie now, but don't you think that's a bit much, Joel?" my mother asked.

"No, I think it's brilliant," I replied.

At breakfast the following morning, my mother looked over at Mattie—who was lying lazily on the living room floor—and surprised me by saying, "I think your dog needs to be more social…play with other dogs."

"I think you're right," I said. "Why not drive us over to the dog park?"

"I don't want all that fur in my car, Joel," she replied. "Can you take a cab?"

I turned to Mattie, and in a sweet, childlike voice asked, "Mattie, do you want to go for a ride in mommy's car?"

She lifted her head a few inches off of the ground and looked at me earnestly. *Are you serious? Go? Now?*

"I wanted grandchildren," my mother said, getting up to take our dishes to the sink. "Instead I got a stray dog that my son talks to like it's human."

I searched on my phone and found a dog park less than five minutes away.

"This place is so close, Mattie won't even have a chance to shed," I told her.

"Honestly, I'd rather you take a cab."

"C'mon," I said, seeing an opportunity to bring her closer to Mattie. "It wouldn't hurt you to be social once in a while."

My mother ignored my sarcasm and walked into her room. When

she returned, minutes later, she was holding a large mound of stuff in her hands.

"What's all that?" I asked.

"I want to put something down so she doesn't ruin the interior of my car."

"Mom, she's a forty-five pound dog, not a bear."

"It's just an outdoor furniture cover, a blanket, and a bath towel."

When I started to laugh, she said, "Joel, please...let me do what I have to do to be comfortable with this. You said you wanted me to go with you."

I got up from the kitchen table and went to grab Mattie's leash.

My mother told me that she needed some time to prepare the car, and said to meet her in front of the building in ten minutes.

By the time Mattie and I made it downstairs, she was waiting. I walked a few feet toward the car and then stopped and lifted Mattie's paw up slightly to wave at her. She grimaced at first, but then managed to force a smile.

I opened the rear door on the passenger side and Mattie hopped onto the heavily padded backseat. As we drove off, I asked my mother to crack the back window for her.

"Is she going to slobber all over?" she asked.

"No, she's just going to breathe," I replied.

Looking in the side rear view mirror, I smiled at the sight of Mattie sticking her snout into the opening. But moments later, she backed away from the window and moved into the space between the front seats, putting her front paws on the center console. My mother didn't notice immediately, but once she did, she freaked.

"Joel! The dog is climbing into the front seat!"

I tried to calm my mother down, while pushing Mattie back with my left arm. In the position I was sitting, I didn't have good leverage and I couldn't get her to retreat. The more worked up my mother became about Mattie being on the console, the funnier I found it.

For the first time since I came out of my coma, I had a laughing attack. The kind where nothing is really that funny, but you can't stop laughing.

Every time I looked over at my mother and saw the contorted expression on her face, I fell to pieces. The harder I laughed, the more animated Mattie became—whining and pacing back and forth in the backseat, before returning to her perch on the console.

After we pulled into the parking lot for the dog park, and I finally got ahold of myself, my mother said tersely, "I'm going to run a few errands…I'll be back in a while to pick you up."

"No," I replied. "I need you to come with me."

"Why?" my mother asked. "You can handle it on your own."

"If I have to pull Mattie away from another dog or something like that, I can't move fast enough. You've come this far…please."

Without responding, my mother turned the engine off and opened her door. Once she handed me my walker, I let Mattie out.

At the entrance of the park there were two gates: one marked for large dogs and the other for small dogs.

"Okay, sweet girl, here we go," I said, opening the large dog gate for her.

Sooner than Mattie could make her first good canine friend, my mother spotted someone that she knew.

"Look, there's Bud Fairy," she said, waving to a tall guy in a L.A. Dodgers hat, ten yards away. "He just got me an incredible rate on my auto insurance."

While my mother walked over to greet Bud, I spotted a row of benches along the fence and headed there. It was nice to sit and watch Mattie play with her own kind, and see how much joy it gave her.

Soon my mother spotted me and came over with a red-headed woman about her age, who had been talking with her and Bud.

"Joel, this is Janice Shapiro," she said, introducing us.

I reached out my hand and said hello.

"Your mother is one special lady," Janice gushed. "You're very lucky."

"Yes…she's a one of a kind," I said, trying to strike a balance between diplomacy and honesty.

"It's just amazing how many people your mother knows," Janice said. "I always tell her she should run for mayor."

"He'd be my toughest vote," my mother quickly interjected.

Although I had been through these types of conversations countless times before, I always dreaded them. But on this occasion, a four-legged savior came to my rescue. Actually, two of them—Mattie and Janice's cocker spaniel, Rudy.

Instantly, Janice and I started talking about dogs, and I realized once again that in Mattie I had found the perfect ally in making coexisting with my mother more tolerable.

The dogs played for a while, and then Janice announced that she had to leave to take Rudy to a vet appointment. My mother and I decided to walk out with her.

Once we were back in the car, I asked my mother if she enjoyed herself.

"Not really," she said. "The smell of that place is atrocious, and some of those dog owners are crazy. I overheard this one lady talking about a gourmet meal she made. It sounded delicious, and then I realized it was for her dog!"

As soon as we got back home, my mother put down her protective dog seat coverings and headed towards the door.

"Now where are you going?" I asked her.

"To the car wash," she replied. "Do you think I'm going to drive around with that odor in my car?"

FORTY-ONE

Over the next couple of months, my mother managed to co-exist with Mattie. Although she never came out and said it, I got the feeling that she had warmed up to having a dog around.

However, one day, while I was having lunch with Aunt Shirley at her favorite health food restaurant, Silby's, I learned otherwise.

After I told her how my mother had been showing me articles about dogs lately, and might become a dog person after all, she said, "Joel, I hate to tell you, but your mother's still hoping that you'll find someone to take Mattie. I don't know if it's the dog hair or what. She seemed better when you first came back, but—"

"I'll find another place to live before that happens," I replied defiantly, while showing my hurt at what I had heard.

"Please don't mention it to her, Joel. I don't want to stir up trouble…I just thought you should know."

"Don't worry. I won't."

"It's none of my business," Aunt Shirley went on, "but now that you're using a walker and hopefully able to drive soon, why don't you find a nice little apartment for yourself?"

"With what?" I asked.

"Isn't there money left from the sale of your store?"

"My mother told me they didn't get much for it."

"What about the lawsuit?"

"Lawsuit?" I asked.

Aunt Shirley got quiet and had a look on her face of a child who just said something they shouldn't have.

"What lawsuit?" I asked again.

"Your parents sued the doctors who cared for you after you got sick."

"Huh?" I responded, stunned.

"Yeah," she said, without elaborating.

"And…"

"And they were awarded three million dollars in a malpractice suit," Aunt Shirley informed me. "It turned out that the doctors were giving you the wrong dosage of medication."

I stared over her shoulder, out the window behind her, and didn't say anything.

"Joel," my aunt said, redirecting my attention. "I honestly don't think your mother hid this from you. I just don't think the right time had come up yet."

"Well, it's come up now," I replied sharply.

I was quiet for the rest of our meal and didn't say much during the ride back home. The wheels in my head were spinning, trying to decide the best way to broach the subject with my mother.

It ended up coming out of me like water from a hose that had just been untangled.

"Why didn't you tell me about the lawsuit?" I asked in an aggressive, accusatory tone the minute after I greeted Mattie.

"What lawsuit?" she asked, looking up from a grapefruit she was cutting.

"You are serious?" I replied angrily. "The lawsuit that you won against my doctors. That lawsuit."

She hesitated and her face tightened.

"I didn't want to overwhelm you when you first woke up," she explained slowly. "I wanted you to focus on your therapy…on getting stronger."

"And after that?" I asked.

"It happened a long time ago, Joel…it's not something that's on my mind."

"You forgot about the lawsuit—did the proceeds also slip your mind?"

"It wasn't that much," she replied.

"Aunt Shirley told me it was three million dollars."

"She's wrong."

"Why would she lie?" I asked.

"Joel, you know she tends to exaggerate things."

"No, I don't know that," I replied combatively.

"I don't want to talk about it right now," she said. "I'm late for an appointment with my hair dresser."

"I don't give a shit what you're late for!" I yelled. "I want to know how much the lawsuit was for and what's left of it!"

"I'll have to talk with my accountant."

"Is it still Paul Frigman?" I asked.

"Yes," my mother confirmed meekly.

"I'll call him myself," I snapped, walking away.

"Joel…please…don't get like this," she begged. "You know whatever is mine is yours."

"It sure doesn't sound like it," I replied.

"It's complicated."

"Everything with you is," I shot back.

My mother didn't respond. She picked up her purse off of the kitchen counter and walked out the door. I immediately grabbed my phone and searched for Paul Frigman's office number. Once I found it, I thought about waiting to calm down before calling him, but I couldn't.

Paul had been my accountant when I opened my music store, but eventually I switched to a buddy of Brian's, who had a smaller clientele and suited my needs better. We had bumped into one another, however, throughout the years, and he was always friendly to me.

When Paul's secretary put me through, he was taken back to hear my voice. We made small talk—mostly about my recovery—before I launched into my questions regarding the lawsuit. Paul was forthcoming and informed me that my store had sold for $235,000, and that my parents were awarded $2.5 million in their malpractice lawsuit against my team of doctors.

"Why didn't my mother just tell me this?" I asked him.

"I think she's embarrassed," he said, making me wait a few moments while he took a drink of something before telling me why. "She lost a tremendous amount of it."

"How?" I immediately asked before he had a chance to explain.

"In the stock market."

"No..." I replied in disbelief. "My father was extremely conservative."

"Are you on the internet yet?" he asked.

"Of course."

"Google *stock market crash 2008 to 2009*," he said.

"I will, but tell me how much of it she lost," I pressed.

"A lot," he replied before pausing. "Everyone lost, Joel. It wasn't her fault."

"Was it yours?" I asked, getting irritated.

"Research it and you'll see that it wasn't," he replied calmly.

"Paul, cut to the chase—how much is left?" I asked.

"I'm not trying to be evasive, Joel," he replied. "But your mother's my client and I'm not at liberty to discuss her finances with you."

I groaned in frustration and then stewed in silence.

"Listen," he said. "I'll talk to her…we'll make this right."

After I got off of the phone with Paul, I took Mattie downstairs for a walk around the building. When I reached the waterfall, I sat for a long time, stroking her coat, and thinking about the situation. My father's voice—as it had so many times since I came out of my coma—spoke to me. "She's still your mother, Joel," I could hear him say.

The truth was the last thing I wanted was to get in to a drawn-out squabble with her. I just wanted to be independent, and to move on with my life. While I felt entitled to the money from the sale of my business, the lawsuit was a different matter. It came about as a result of my unfortunate circumstances, but I didn't earn it. So was I actually entitled to it? There was also the issue of the cost of keeping me alive in the nursing home for all those years. I guess none of this mattered, until I found out what was actually left.

FORTY-TWO

When my mother came home with her new hairdo, neither of us picked up the conversation where we had left it.

"I got a toy for Mattie while I was out," she announced, after putting her things down.

Mattie accepted the gift—a colorful rope toy—without hesitation, but I couldn't help thinking it was an obvious attempt by my mother to smooth things over with me.

Two days went by without hearing back from Paul, and I began to get restless. I decided I couldn't wait any longer, and gave him a call.

After I hit him with another barrage of questions—attempting again to comprehend how my mother lost a large sum of money—Paul told me he was still working out things with her.

"This isn't cut and dry, Joel," he explained. "Your mother obviously didn't know you were going to come out of your coma after so long. She needs to make sure she has enough to live out her life."

I told Paul that I didn't want the issue to linger. I just wanted what was rightfully mine and wanted to be able to move out and subsist on my own.

Over the course of several phone calls, Paul and I agreed that my mother would pay for me to rent an apartment and give me a percentage of her monthly income from her savings and investments to live on. She would also pay for me to lease a car, so I would have one when I was ready to drive. Paul said that my mother preferred that the money come from him, so it wouldn't involve her and I, and I agreed.

Before we hung up, he said, "Joel, the main thing your mother conveyed to me is that she doesn't want to lose you as a son over this."

"Of course not—who would be left to torture?" I replied, unable to resist the jab.

Knowing my mother, I'm sure that shortly after I spoke to Paul she knew that the issue had been resolved. But for whatever reason, she never brought the matter up again, and neither did I.

Having a walker, and not having to worry about getting a wheelchair through tiny doorways, made most apartments suitable for me. But I still wasn't driving yet, so I wanted to find a place that was within easy walking distance to a market and other amenities.

I called Aunt Shirley and asked if she would help me find the right place. She told me about Craigslist, and I set about searching among a sea of possibilities. After I printed out a couple of options, Shirley picked me up to go check them out.

As excited as I was to leave my mother's, there was a trepidation of being on my own. Ever since waking up at Tender Heart, Aunt Shirley, Big G, and Kerrie had been my support system. They were all still there for me, but to different degrees. Getting an apartment needed to signal the start of a new life for me, but the prospect of it seemed daunting.

Out of all of the places Aunt Shirley and I looked at, the best one was a small, two-story apartment in West Los Angeles. It was on the old side, but it wasn't far from my mother's place and it had a strip mall, with a market and a few restaurants, less than a block away. It also had a nice-sized inlet of grass across the street, where I could take Mattie out. I wasn't crazy about living on the first floor and having someone above me, but the building didn't have an elevator so that was my only choice.

After I decided to take it and filled out an application for the manager, who lived in the building, Aunt Shirley and I sat in the courtyard. "The reality of my life is sinking in," I said, looking around at the sparse patio furniture and the entryways to a few of the units.

"What do mean?" she asked.

"That I was married and had a nice house, and now I'll be living alone in an apartment when I turn fifty."

"Plenty of people do it."

"I suppose," I said, watching a couple argue as they came down the stairs and hoping they didn't live above my soon-to-be home.

"Well, you can always stay at your mother's," she replied, smiling.

"If she and I got along better, I probably would."

"Really? Or are you setting me up for a joke?"

"I don't know… I'm just feeling overwhelmed by the idea of moving someplace new and starting over again."

"You won't be alone," she said.

"Who's going to be with me?" I asked.

"Mattie."

"That's true," I replied, comforted by the thought.

"Joel, you're rebuilding your life. It's not easy, but you're getting there," my aunt said, reaching over to give me a hug. "We all love you and we're only a phone call away."

After we left the apartment, we stopped at a few furniture stores. I didn't need much, but I didn't have anything. I called my mother to ask if there was stuff in storage from the house I owned with Lauren, and she told me all that remained was a coffee table and an armoire. When she mentioned the pieces, it immediately brought back memories of Lauren and I buying them on a trip to Santa Barbara, and I wondered if I even wanted them.

Sensing my agitation, Aunt Shirley told me what she thought I needed and I let her make the decisions. My mind was occupied with all sorts of logistical issues that I was about to face, living on my own. Furniture was the least of my concerns.

As my moving date got closer, my mother started to acknowledge the fact that I would soon be leaving.

"Well, aren't you going to show me your new apartment?" she said to me one morning.

"Of course. I haven't moved in yet."

"Shirley's already seen it," she replied like a jealous, bratty child.

"That's because she helped me find it," I said.

"You could have asked me to help, you know."

"You didn't seem like you wanted to be involved, so I didn't bother."

Verbally jostling with my mother was like wrestling someone that you could never pin down. Just when you thought that you had her, she would wiggle away.

"That's not true at all," she replied. "I didn't want to put my nose into your business. But it would have been nice if you had involved me."

"Next time," I said.

"With this condition the doctor told me I have, there won't be a next time."

"Is this the nebulous one you won't tell me about or a new one?"

I asked, trying to be serious.

"There's nothing nebulous, Joel about a fatal disease."

"I see," I replied unemotionally.

FORTY-THREE

Interestingly, the last few weeks at my mother's turned out to be the most pleasant. Maybe it's because we both knew it was only temporary.

Every other day it seemed like she brought home a treat or a toy for Mattie. She and I even had a nice discussion about my father, in which she didn't criticize him a single time, and even seemed to miss him a little.

When moving day arrived, my mother and Aunt Shirley worked together so that I didn't have to lift a finger. My only responsibility was to look after Mattie, which wasn't a responsibility but a joy. She quickly made friends with the movers we hired to transport a few pieces from my mother's place, delighting in the bits of food one of them gave her.

Arriving at my new apartment was chaotic, as the furniture delivery came at the same time as the movers. My mother asked me where I wanted things, and I told her that she and Aunt Shirley could decide. I honestly didn't care—I just wanted to get settled as quickly as possible.

In the afternoon, Big G surprised me and stopped by to see how everything was going. He was carrying with him a large, slender object draped with a brown sheet.

"What do you have there?" I asked him.

"A little housewarming gift," he replied.

With my mother holding one end of it, Gary pulled off the sheet and revealed a classic photograph of me, him, and Brian taken at the sports bar, which he had blown up and framed.

"What do you think…is that around '92?" Gary asked me, taking a hammer from the kitchen counter to hang the picture.

"I think so," I replied, wishing I could climb into the photograph and go back in time. "Man, I used to love those football Sundays, decked out in orange and brown."

"Look at those hairlines," my mother observed.

"I used to complain about how much hair I had then, but it sure looks good now," Gary said. "Going bald is definitely a lesson in appreciation."

Gary hung around until he got a call that led him outside. After not seeing him for a while, he popped his head inside the door—still on the phone—and waved goodbye.

As night fell and we were all getting tired, my mother suggested that I sleep at her place and come back in the morning. It made sense and I agreed.

As we got ready to leave, Mattie started to get nervous.

"Maybe it's easier to just leave her here for the night," my mother said.

"Alone?" I replied.

"No, you can't do that," my aunt immediately objected. "She would feel abandoned and be scared."

"Okay, forget I said anything," my mother replied, throwing her hands up in the air. "I forgot I'm with two dog nuts."

"Dog *lovers*," my aunt corrected her.

I gave Aunt Shirley a smile and reached down to clip Mattie's leash to her collar.

The following morning, my mother and I headed back to the apartment to finish setting everything up. Unfortunately, my aunt had a doctor's appointment and couldn't join us.

The day started out pleasant, but by lunch my mother and I were getting on each other's nerves. As we squabbled about something trivial, someone knocked on the door. Mattie, who was asleep on her bed in the corner of the living room, popped up and went berserk.

"Joel, take her into the bedroom and close the door," my mother instructed me.

"Just answer the door," I replied. "I'll put her on the leash."

When she opened the door, Mattie lunged forward to greet a guy about my age, who was holding a pizza box in his hand.

"You have the wrong apartment," my mother told him, assuming he was a delivery person.

"No," he replied, chuckling. "I'm your neighbor. I just went through moving a few months ago, and knowing how stressful it is I thought you might be hungry."

"Hey, thanks," I said, standing beside my mother.

"It looks like someone's definitely ready for a slice," the neighbor said looking down at Mattie, who was heavily panting.

"Where do you live?" my mother asked him.

"Just across the way—I'm Matt."

After my mother and I introduced ourselves, she asked, "Do you like it here? Is this a nice place?"

"So far, yeah…for apartment living it seems okay," he replied.

"Well, my son found it, so let's hope—"

I quickly turned towards my mother and shot her a look that cut her off. Then I thanked the neighbor again for the pizza and told him I'd see him around.

Once he walked off, and my mother closed the door, I had to restrain myself from saying something about her intended belittling comment.

"I'm tired," I said, instead. "Let's finish up."

I unleashed Mattie and went to refill her water bowl. My mother put down the box of pizza on the kitchen counter, and poured herself a diet Coke.

"I wonder what kind it is?" she asked, walking back over to the pizza.

Seconds later, as I leaned over to put Mattie's water bowl down, I heard her let out a gasp.

"There's a piece missing!" she cried.

"What do you want, it's free," I said, looking over at the mushroom and pepperoni pie.

"Who would bring someone a pizza with one piece missing?" she asked, perplexed.

"I guess my new neighbor," I replied.

"I'm not sure about this place, Joel," my mother said, closing the pizza box and pushing it away.

"Should I move out?" I asked sarcastically. "Maybe there's something in the lease about an incomplete pizza delivery that's grounds for termination."

"Joke all you want, but that's *very* odd."

"I know," I replied. "You can leave now, if you want. I think I'm set."

Once my mother was gone, I sat down on my new couch and Mattie joined me. "I need to create some new memories," I said to her, staring at the old photographs that decorated my walls. "Do you want to be my partner?" She looked at me inquisitively and then lifted her paw for a shake.

FORTY-FOUR

I used to tell Lauren that apartments are a collection of strangers living in too close a quarters. That was when we first met, and I was living in one. The residents there had so many squabbles that I once suggested to the manager that he should regroup everyone according to personality type. Introverts would be on one end, extroverts on the other, and those who were a mix of both in the middle.

In look and feel, my new place was not entirely different than the one I had lived in, in the early 90's. In those days I was hardly at home. I spent seven days a week at the store, working long hours, and occasionally sleeping on a cot in the back.

Now, I would be home most of the time. Thankfully, except for the person above me, who played loud rap music every afternoon for an hour or so, things were pretty quiet.

I pondered how long I should wait to make my first complaint to the manager. I decided irritability was the best barometer, and gave Sally a call. She was receptive to my issue, and told me that she would talk to the resident. The following day, the music was appreciatively quieter.

Mattie adjusted quickly to her new surroundings, making friends with a Golden Retriever named Lucy. Once they met in the

216

courtyard, and Mattie discovered where Lucy lived, she would sit with her chin on the window sill and stare across at Lucy's unit.

As often as I could, I coordinated with Lucy's owner, Patty to take the dogs across the street to the patch of grass to play. While the dogs entertained one another, Patty, who had spent several years training dogs, shared some of her knowledge with me.

Once I got situated in my new place, I began thinking seriously about what to do with my life. Although the most logical thing in starting over would be to get a job, I didn't have experience working in the corporate world or working for anyone, for that matter.

Aunt Shirley talked to her son, my cousin Josh, to see if he could help. Although Josh now lived in Seattle, working as a marketing executive for a software company, he still had a lot of connections in Los Angeles.

Weeks after we spoke on the phone about my situation, Josh sent me a text saying he could get me an interview for a marketing manager position with Front and Center Productions. The company put on music events around L.A., including a popular summer Shakespeare theatre that took place on the Santa Monica pier.

I made sure Josh had told his contact at the company about my background and lack of formal job experience, and he assured me he had.

"Just be yourself—you'll do great," Josh said enthusiastically, when we spoke again on the phone. "And don't worry about dressing formally, it's a casual environment."

I sent an email to the contact Josh had given me—John Curtis—who was the head of marketing at Front and Center, and we set up an interview for three days later.

Afterward, I emailed Kerrie to tell her about the job opportunity and to get her advice. She wrote back, *The good news is you owned a successful business, the bad news is they might not care.* Elaborating on her point, she said, *They may prefer hiring someone who has marketing manager experience versus someone with business acumen—regardless of your potential, talent, etc.*

In preparing for the interview over the next few days, I compiled a list of things I accomplished in my years of owning Good Sounds, and wrote down ten attributes I felt I could bring to the company's marketing team.

My mother called while I was working on how to answer questions I thought I'd face. I didn't mention the job interview to her to save myself from an inquisition or a lecture on my clothes being out of style. Thankfully, she didn't say anything about it, which meant that Aunt Shirley hadn't told her.

The night before the big day, I hardly slept and dragged through the morning. Once I got dressed and ready to go, Mattie got up from her bed and gave me a good sniff over.

"Keep your paws crossed for me, girl," I said to her, while I called for a cab.

Keeping with the Berskin family tradition, I arrived at the company's office, which was above the Third Street Promenade, twenty-five minutes before my interview. I thought about walking into a few of the stores below to kill some time, but I wanted to be physically and mentally rested.

When I entered the company's office, I was immediately taken by the open, airy atmosphere and the walls, which were papered with signage from past events Front and Center had promoted.

Hearing me enter, the receptionist looked up and enthusiastically greeted me. She then got up from behind a sleek glass desk and came over to me. Once I gave her my name and who I was there to see, she glanced down at her tablet and told me it would be a fifteen to twenty minute wait.

I sat down in a cushy chair, sipped a cup of hot apple cider the receptionist brought me, and read over my interview notes one last time.

Sooner than I expected, a thirty-something year old guy, wearing red-framed glasses, appeared in the doorway that led to the rest of the office.

"Joel!" he said in an excitable voice.

"Hello!" I said, trying to match his enthusiasm. "You must be John."

"No, actually I'm John's assistant," he said.

I grabbed my walker, and once I reached him, extended my hand.

"Corrie Breslow," he said, introducing himself with a big smile. "We're ready for you in the conference room."

He walked a few paces ahead of me, as I slowly made my way down the hallway.

I had been anxious about the interview, but not nervous. Now, with each step, I could feel my heartrate accelerate and feel butterflies in my stomach. I was confident in my abilities, but the last interview I had was at a rental furniture company, before I opened my record store, over two decades ago.

"In here," Corrie said, pointing to the conference room and waiting for me at the entrance.

As I tried to pick up the pace to get to him quicker, I felt a bead of sweat falling down my forehead. When I went to quickly wipe it with the back of my hand, I dropped my interview notes and they scattered on the floor.

"Don't worry, I'll grab those," Corrie told me.

I took a few more steps and turned into the conference room. When I looked up, every chair around the large oval-shaped table was occupied. Quickly eyeballing the group, almost all of them appeared to be half my age. In front of each employee there was a yellow legal pad, and most had a large Starbucks coffee and their phones beside it.

My contact person for the interview, John Curtis, was at the head of the table. He stood up and said, "Welcome, Joel…we're excited to have you."

Nervously, I said, "I—I didn't know there would be this many people."

"Oh, I'm sorry," John replied. "I must not have mentioned in my email that we would be interviewing you as a group."

"Uh, that's okay," I said, sitting down in a chair Corrie provided for me.

After a few minutes of small talk, each member of the team introduced themselves and shared what they did at the company. The unexpected number of people had unnerved me, and I didn't take in very much of what anyone said.

Once everyone finished, John asked me to tell the group about myself. I started strong, but rambled on for too long about my experience of owning a record store.

Afterwards, each employee asked me a hypothetical question about a situation I might face on the job and how I would handle it. They all required me to have had past experience as a marketing manager, of which I didn't have any. I tried to counter by highlighting the creative marketing ideas I had implemented to make my business successful, but from the looks on the faces around the table, it wasn't resonating.

Needless to say, the interview wasn't going well and I was extremely uncomfortable.

The last thing I wanted from anyone after I woke up from my coma was sympathy. But as the interview was about to end, I was desperate. I clutched my walker and leaned against it, with an anguished look on my face. If pity from being handicapped could be had, I wanted some.

Once the torture was over, I shook hands with the employees on each side of me. Then John Curtis walked over and thanked me for coming in.

"We're going to make a decision fairly quickly," he informed me. "We'll let you know either way."

In the reception area, on my way out, I passed by an eager-looking blond woman, who probably hadn't celebrated her twenty-fifth birthday yet, clutching an iPad. I assumed she was the next candidate to be interviewed.

"I set the bar very low for you," I said to her, with a sly grin.

"Oh, thank you!" she replied excitedly, although I'm not sure she knew what I meant.

On the cab ride home I got a text from Josh, asking me how it went.

I wrote back, *FUBAR*.

Huh? he responded.

Look it up, I texted back.

FORTY-FIVE

When I got home, Mattie was at the door to greet me with one of her many toys in her mouth.

"I bombed, Mattie girl…absolutely bombed," I said, on my way to the kitchen to give her a treat.

Once I changed out of my interview attire, I took her for a short walk and then sat in the courtyard. I tried my best to decompress and console myself, but it wasn't working.

After ruminating myself into a miserable mood, I went back inside and called Aunt Shirley. As usual, she tried to cheer me up.

"Joel, it's just one interview," she said.

"And Gettysburg was just one battle," I replied, wallowing in self-pity.

"It would be crazy to think that you'd get a job on your first interview," she reasoned.

"Now you tell me… If I had known, I would have skipped this one."

"Joel, it'll happen. Give it time…I'm certain of it."

"At my age, what kind of job I'm I going to find without any formal work experience?" I asked.

She didn't exactly know, but she had faith that something would shake loose.

John Curtis sent me an email three days later, letting me know that I wouldn't be Front and Center's next marketing manager. To his credit, he apologized again for not telling me ahead of time about the group interview.

Over the next couple of months, I endured a few more interviews which came through online job sites. Two were for marketing positions, and one was for a sales job that I probably wouldn't have taken if I was offered it. Although the interviews weren't as painful as my first one, I didn't come away with a job.

I started to feel as if I was trying to re-enter a stream that I didn't fit or belong in.

One day, feeling depleted and depressed after scouring the online job sites for hours, I pulled the mini blinds up all the way so I could see the sky from my couch. I grabbed a couple of beers, put on some music, and sat down.

While I drank, I vented my frustrations to Mattie. She was lying on her bed, listening to me as attentively as any shrink ever had. Of course, she didn't have any words to console me, but just her presence made me feel a little less awful and alone in my struggles.

After making a trip to the bathroom to relieve my beer intake, I noticed for the first time that Mattie's bed had sunken down significantly, especially in the middle. She looked as if she were lying in an inner-tube, with the sides of the bed almost level with her head.

"Man, oh man," I thought to myself. *"What's with these beds?"*

This was the second bed I had gotten for Mattie. The initial one—which I bought after I found her—looked and felt great at first, but quickly lost its shape. I got the one she was laying on when I went furniture shopping with Aunt Shirley, and the gal at the store told me it was the most popular one they sold. Now, not that long afterwards, it had suffered the same fate.

Buzzed and bored, I leaned over to the coffee table for my iPad and did a search for dog beds. Scouring a bunch of links and blogs, I discovered several other dog owners who shared my frustration.

I wonder why they don't make dog beds like human beds? I asked myself.

The wheels in my head started turning.

Mattress manufactures were set up to make human beds, so it wouldn't be that difficult for them to make smaller mattresses for dogs. You could put the mattress on a slightly raised platform, instead of using a boxspring, and sell cute, canine-themed sheets for it. The sheets would be easier to wash than washing the bed. I even thought of a product tagline: *Premium dog beds that never slump, sag or lose their shape.*

"It's perfect," I said to Mattie. "Dogs prefer human beds anyway."

When you're initially high on an idea, everything seems doable and easy. Of course, it's not. That's where the quote *1% inspiration, 99% perspiration* comes from. Opening a music store, I had lived that old axiom.

Still buzzing with excitement hours later, my mother called to tell me she would be a little late picking me up for therapy in the morning. Against my better judgment, I shared my brainstorm with her, including what I thought a *Mattie Mattress*—as I thought I'd call them—would cost.

"Nobody's going to pay that much for a dog bed, Joel," she said. "It's a ridiculous idea."

"I don't know about that—people love their dogs," I replied, in defense of my idea.

"Yeah, but only the crazy ones would spend that much for a bed…and there's not enough of them to make a business."

For the fortunate ones, parental support is automatic; for the rest of us, it occurs as often as a home run with two outs and the bases loaded in the bottom of the ninth inning.

After I came home from therapy the next day, I sent Big G a text, asking him to give me a call when he had some free time. Gary didn't have a dog, but based on the success of his business I thought he would be a good person to run my idea by.

When we spoke that evening, he responded to my brainstorm better than I thought he would.

"Do the research," he said when I finished my pitch. "If you can show me there's a need, I'll fund it."

FORTY-SIX

My newfound love of dogs and my desire for an alternative to finding a traditional job fueled me. In my mind there were two big benefits to starting a business: it was something I had done before, and unlike a regular job, I wouldn't have to leave Mattie home alone.

I immediately began contacting mattress manufacturers about my idea and talking to dog owners about what they liked and disliked about dog beds.

Two months later—after spending all of my available waking hours, outside of going to therapy and being with Mattie—I emailed Gary a business plan.

I felt confident in what I presented him—that we could convince enough dog owners to spend more on a bed that would last the length of their dog's life, versus one that would be flattened and unsupportive in a short time. If we were successful, my numbers showed that there would be a healthy profit margin.

Gary responded to my plan a few days later with a long list of follow-up questions. At the bottom of his note, he wrote, *Keep going...this seems promising!*

I quickly set out to find answers to Gary's issues. As soon as they were satisfied, others surfaced. Having gone through this process to get my record store off of the ground, I was familiar with the routine and relished the challenge.

I took a break from work to go watch another one of Gary's son's little league games. It was a boring, scoreless game until the last inning, when Todd hit a double to drive in the winning run. Todd's teammates mobbed him at home plate, and it was the happiest I had seen him.

Afterward, Gary was in a great mood, and he took the team and the parents out for pizza.

I ended up sitting beside Leslie at the end of a long table, and we talked about how my business idea was coming along. Gary was at the opposite end, reliving the highlights of the game with some of the kids. At one point, we exchanged glances and he quickly pointed to Leslie and me—when she wasn't looking—as if to infer I should hook up with his wife. I looked at him as if he were crazy, and then waved for him to come over.

After he made a nice toast to the team, he joined Leslie and me. I could tell that he had already consumed a few beers.

"My new business partner," he said, slapping my back.

"I hope so," I replied, reaching back for his hand.

"Hey, Leslie," he said, pulling her away from another conversation. "Do you have any nice women you can set my buddy here up with?"

"I swear I thought about that earlier when Joel and I were talking in the stands," Leslie replied.

"Don't bother," I said. "I'm already taken."

"Dude, seriously," Gary responded. "You can't make that dog your whole life."

Leslie stood up, resting her hand on my shoulder, and whispered something in Gary's ear.

The next morning, when I opened my email, I found out what the secret was. Leslie must have told Gary to get me a subscription to an online dating service, because I was now a member of a website called *Intertwine.*

I emailed Big G and wrote, "Thanks. I guess."

When I brought it up the next time we spoke, he assured me that the stigma of using a dating service was non-existent now.

I dragged my feet, but eventually logged onto the website and looked through several pages of profiles. Los Angeles always had unbelievably pretty women, but I was surprised by how many were available and on there.

Digging a little deeper, however, I discovered something interesting. Several of the women looked great in their main profile picture, but the other photographs of them made the first one look like another person or an extremely flattering shot that a friend took.

After a few visits to the website, I came across a red-haired woman named Chloe. She had a coy but inviting smile and piercing blue eyes. Her profile said she was a huge music lover with similar taste to mine and that we both had several other things in common. Spontaneously, I introduced myself with a quick note. The next day, I got an email from *Intertwine*, saying that Chloe had sent me a message.

We sent a couple of messages back and forth, until she suggested that we use the chat feature to communicate. At the end of our first chat, Chloe confessed to be being fifty-two years old, as opposed to forty-nine, which was the age listed on her profile. She explained that she wanted to be included in searches for women fifty and under. Having enjoyed our chat, I chalked up her dishonesty as a strategic move in the online dating world.

We "talked" again the following night and before we signed off, I asked for her number. Talking on the phone was a familiar and easier way for me to get to know someone. She wrote that she didn't feel comfortable giving out her number to a stranger. "I need to feel safe first," she conveyed to me.

I spent the next three evenings trying to be interesting, funny, and charming in my chats with chloe_876. Feeling I had earned her trust, I asked, "What do you think…are we ready for our first telephone conversation?"

"Not yet," she replied.

"Any idea when you might be ready?" I asked.

I didn't hear from Chloe until the following night, when she wrote me a note saying, "Why do you have to be condescending?…you seemed like such a nice guy."

I thought of a few sarcastic responses to severe our tie, but settled for, "Good luck finding what you're looking for—I'm not it."

When I told Brian about my experience, he said, "Chloe could be a two hundred and seventy pound guy named Carl in Cleveland, jerking your chain while he's jerking his." I definitely could have done without the visual, but it effectively made the point that the online world was the perfect place to be someone or something that you weren't.

Although I made contact with a few other women—and even met one for coffee—I found online dating to be like looking at photographs of airplanes and talking about flying, but hardly ever leaving the ground.

Big G encouraged me to keep trying, but I told him, "The real world's hard enough, I don't need to struggle in the virtual one."

The truth about dating—online or off—is that I was self-conscious about using a walker and not having a livelihood. I decided for the time being to focus all of my energy on my business idea and continuing my therapy.

FORTY-SEVEN

My efforts paid off on the work front. After months of fleshing out the details and feasibility of launching a dog bed company, Big G committed money to the venture. When I asked him what made up his mind, he told me that he was blown away by the size of the pet market and the passion of pet owners.

We entered into a 50/50 partnership, with him providing the capital, and me running the business. We had researched the idea of setting up our own operation to produce the product, but decided the optimal way to get started was to find a large mattress manufacturer to make a line of beds for us. To start, we would sell three different size beds and three variations of fitted sheets for each.

When I emailed Kerrie about the news, she was ecstatic. "This is so great, Joel!" she wrote. "Mattie saved you and now she's leading you in a direction you would have never gone." Kerrie suggested that I use Hallie Serenoff, who designed her line of baby clothes, for our fitted sheets and gave me her contact information.

I had kept Aunt Shirley updated on the progress of the business all along, and she was also thrilled for me. I thought about sharing the development with my mother, but figured I would ride the high I was on for a little longer. The road to bringing a product to market would be filled with enough naysayers: why voluntarily add one at the start?

Ironically, Mattie, the impetus for the business, was the least excited about it. She missed the time we used to spend together, and she let me know about it. Whenever she felt I worked too long without a break, Mattie would sit beside my desk and intensely stare at me. If I didn't immediately give her some attention, she would start whining.

To appease Mattie and make up for my heavy workload, I made an arrangement with my mother's friend, Janice Shapiro, to take her dog, Rudy, and Mattie, to the dog park on Saturday afternoons.

Once we arrived, Janice and I would go our separate ways and reconnect a half hour later to leave. Most times, I'd take to the bench along the fence and watch Mattie play, while looking over some business notes.

On one of our outings, Mattie took a particular liking to a frisky Dachshund. The two of them, along with a teenage girl—who I presumed the dog belonged to—were running around in front of where I was sitting.

"What's your dog's name?" I asked the girl, when she sat down beside me to tie her shoe. "He sure likes Mattie."

"PJ," she replied, out of breath. "It's short for Pure Joy. My mom named him."

"Is that who you're here with?" I asked, making small talk and finding out that the girl's name was Tess.

"Yeah, she's over there," she replied, pointing to a red-headed woman in pigtails, wearing a sun hat, ten yards away. "Isn't she pretty?"

"I can't see from here, but I'm sure she is," I said politely.

"She's super cool," Tess said. "Come meet her."

"Uh, that's okay," I said, surprised by her offer.

"Oh come on," she implored, grabbing my hand and standing up.

"Why do you want me to meet your mother so bad?" I asked, leery.

"Cause you seem like a nice guy and all she dates are losers."

I laughed and said, "Actually, I'm about to leave…but maybe next time."

"Why not *this* time?" she persisted.

I looked over at Tess's mother again and she was now facing our direction. From what I could make out, she looked attractive.

"It's a little awkward, don't you think?" I asked Tess.

"No, I don't think," she replied with a laugh. "Just come on…"

"Okay…" I said, giving in to her spunk, but wondering what I was getting myself into.

I put Mattie on her leash and we ventured to the center of the field, where Tess's mother was talking to a guy with long blond hair pulled back into a ponytail. My level of dread grew with each step I took.

As soon as she noticed Tess, the woman turned to greet her daughter. Up close, she was prettier than I imagined she would be. She had captivating brown eyes and a cute dimple in her chin.

"Mom, this is Joel," Tess said, "and that cutie pie is Mattie."

"Nice to meet you, I'm Holly," she said, before turning to introduce me to the guy beside her.

I don't remember hearing what his name was or anything that he said. Like a photograph sharp in on one spot and blurry everywhere else, Holly was all I could focus on.

A minute later, or that's what it seemed like, the guy said something to Holly and then walked away. I didn't see Tess wander off, but in an instant I realized it was just her mother and I standing there.

Holly smiled at me and I noticed for the first time that the right side of her mouth didn't move, and that she had some sort of paralysis.

Always one to clam up in the presence of a woman I was fond of, I thought to myself: *Don't try too hard or try to be funny—just make small talk.* What came out of my mouth was anything but.

"I can't believe you don't have one," I blurted out.

"One what?" she asked.

"A tattoo," I replied. "It seems like everyone has one somewhere."

"Well, you can't see all of me, so how do you know?" she said seductively, or least it came out that way.

"I'd like to...maybe one day," I said, completely out of character for how I interacted with a woman I just met.

The moment became awkward and I felt I had blown it. I remembered what James the bartender at the sports bar used to say about these situations: *If it's meant to be, nothing you say matters; if it isn't, it won't matter anyway.*

I smiled, hoping to get beyond my blunder.

"How about you...do you have one?" she asked, breaking the silence.

"No, they got popular after my generation."

"Mine too," she replied.

If you don't connect with someone in these instances, every second can be drudgery; if you *do* connect, the conversation glides like skates on ice.

As I continued talking to Holly—a stranger minutes ago—I could have stood in the middle of the dog park for a long time and hardly realized it.

I wanted to extend our chance meeting, but I couldn't find the words to ask her out. I kept telling her how great it was to meet her and how I hoped to see her again, and then—before I knew it—Tess had rejoined us and Holly was waving goodbye.

I slowly followed behind them, with Mattie by my side, hoping Holly would turn around and look my way before she got to the exit, but it didn't happen.

FORTY-EIGHT

Holly lingered in my mind after we met. During the week, I contemplated taking a cab to the dog park to see if fate would strike twice, but I was too busy working.

When my regular dog park visit with Janice rolled around, I immersed myself in reading material, like always, while Mattie played.

I tried not to think about Holly and only glanced up occasionally. It was quiet around me and I didn't realize how much time had passed, until I looked at my watch and saw that it was time to meet up with Janice.

As I headed toward the exit, I looked to find Mattie. She had wandered to the far end of the field, where there was a large congregation of dogs. I called out to her, but she either didn't hear me or didn't respond. I made my way to where she was, and after some resistance was able to clip her to her leash.

Once Mattie and I reached Janice, by the exit, she was talking with a friend. Needing to sit down to rest my legs after traversing the entire field, I led Mattie to a nearby picnic bench. I pulled a magazine from my backpack and began reading, until my eyes shut.

When I felt Mattie's snout sniffing my fingers, I twitched. I looked back over at Janice to see if she was ready to leave. She was still engaged in conversation, but and lo and behold, Holly, Tess and PJ were coming through the entrance gate.

I grabbed my walker to stand up, but then thought better of it. I wanted to make our meeting seem spontaneous, rather than me approaching her.

"Look, Mattie," I said, trying to get her to notice PJ. "Look who's here?"

Mattie responded to my voice, not my hand, and looked at me puzzled.

"Mattie, go—over there!" I said enthusiastically, gesturing again with my hand.

She stared at me confused, and then began to whimper.

Janice wasn't far from Holly. I quickly took out my phone and texted her: *Can you call Mattie? I'm over by the picnic table. I'll explain later.* A minute later, Janice glanced down at her phone and began looking around. When she spotted me, she waved. I pointed to Mattie and looked away.

Janice began calling Mattie's name and I felt her leave my side. I waited a few moments and then turned around and looked back at Janice. My childish plan had worked. Tess and Holly had seen Mattie and were petting her, while PJ sniffed her behind.

I grabbed my walker and casually made my way towards them.

"Hello, Holly," I said, once I got within a few feet of her.

"Hey, Joel," she said, glancing up. "I was wondering where you were when I saw your dog."

I knew Janice would probably be ready to go shortly, so I didn't have any time to waste.

"We're just about to leave, but I'd really like to take you out sometime," I said, reaching down to grab Mattie before she ran off.

"Really?" she asked.

"Yeah," I replied, feeling slightly self-conscious by her response. "Why do you sound surprised?"

"I don't know…it seems most guys my age are only interested in some thirty year old hot thing. I see them at the gym all the time, following these young girls around, drooling. I'm tempted to go over and wipe the saliva from their chins."

"I went that route for a while…it was a shallow existence," I said sarcastically. "Now I'm looking for someone who's a little more sophisticated, kind *and* beautiful…and I'm hoping I found her."

Holly laughed and then gave me her number, which I entered into my phone. Not long afterward, Tess came over, grabbed her mother's arm, and dragged her down the field to see someone. I waved goodbye to Holly, and then walked to the exit with Mattie to meet Janice.

When I got home from the dog park, I called Brian and asked him how I should play the situation with Holly. Specifically, how long I should wait before calling her. He chided me that I was no longer in my thirties.

"I thought something like that was relevant at any age," I responded.

"Maybe for some guys," he said. "To me, it's silly…if you want to see her, call her."

If I had taken Brian's advice literally, I would have called Holly that night. I waited until the following evening, and reached her voicemail.

Leaving a voicemail for a woman I was pursuing had always been a dating faux pas for me. My reasoning was if she didn't return your call, you seemed desperate if you called her another time. Better to keep trying, until you connect. But after listening to Holly and Tess giggle through her entire outgoing message, I decided to leave word that I called.

Holly called me back a few hours later and after we chatted for a while, we made a plan to get together. Initially, I thought of going to Will Rogers State Park and having a picnic. But I decided that meeting for coffee, the first time around, was a better idea.

I knew it was a staid, boring plan, but Holly's response took me back.

"Is it that you don't want to risk at least going for lunch, or are you just cheap?" she asked.

"Both," I deadpanned.

There was silence on the other end.

"Holly…are you still there?"

"Yeah…I'm here," she replied, sounding deflated. "I'm just wondering what I'm putting out in the universe that keeps bringing me losers."

"Ouch," I replied, trying not to take her comment too personally. "Your daughter told me that you've dated some real doozies."

"Let's see…in the last year I've met a self-absorbed yoga instructor, a cheapo who's idea of taking a woman out on a first date is to invite her over for a frozen pizza, and a guy who was so sweet he made Liberace seem masculine."

"Well, I hope I can break the mold," I said. "How about dinner at Dontoni's on Saturday night?"

"That sounds great," she replied, brightening. "It's one of my favorite Italian restaurants."

When I asked her for her address to pick her up, she said, "It's okay, I'll just meet you there."

I didn't respond.

"Joel?" she asked.

"Yeah, I'm here," I replied. "I just don't understand why I'm always attracted to women who aren't trusting."

She laughed and then gave me her address.

It wasn't until I got off the phone that it dawned on me that I would be picking Holly up in a cab. Not the impression I hoped to make for our first date.

FORTY-NINE

On the morning of my date with Holly, I thought of ways I could make my means of transportation a little more special. I called Aunt Shirley with the best idea I could think of, and she agreed to help me pull it off.

As the big night drew near, I sat with Mattie on the couch, trying to relax. "I haven't done something like this in a long time," I said to her. "I might want to bury my expectations deep in the ground like a bone." After I sent my friend Patty in the building a text, reminding her to let Mattie out in a few hours, I showered and got dressed.

When I called for a cab, I asked for their most jovial driver.

"What do you mean *jovial?*" the guy who answered replied gruffly. "They all do the job the same way."

The driver who had persuaded me to keep Mattie popped into my head. "Is the girl with short blonde hair still there?" I asked.

"We only have one female—Rory."

"Is she available?"

"Now—yeah. But I don't know where she'll be at the time you want."

"Now is good," I said.

When Rory pulled up in front of my apartment building, she instantly remembered me.

"What ever happened with that dog?" she asked, while taking my walker. "Did you end up keeping her?"

"Yep," I replied with a smile. "Mattie."

"Did it turn out to be a good thing?"

"Better than I ever could have imagined…so thank you."

"That's so cool."

"Listen, I need your help again," I said.

"Okay," she replied, starting the meter. "What's up?"

"I'm going to pick up a woman for our first date and I'm a little embarrassed about picking her up in a cab…no offense."

"Is it a blind date?" she asked.

"No. Actually, I met her at the dog park."

"Awesome…what do you need me to do?"

"I want to make the experience a little more special, if I can," I said, rummaging through my prop bag beside me. "So…I was hoping you wouldn't mind wearing these."

I grabbed the limo driver's hat, the black bow-tie, and the white gloves that Aunt Shirley had rounded up for me, and draped them over the front seat. Rory glanced over at them and started to laugh.

"No problem," she said. "If I can help two dog lovers fall in love, I'm all for it."

"I've got some time to kill before I told her I'd be there. Of course, I'll pay you for that and I'll tip you like a limo driver."

Rory pulled into a strip-mall parking lot close to where Holly lived and we talked about dogs. She showed me pictures of her chocolate Lab, Sammy and her black pug, Ricki, on her phone. I told her about my dog bed company, inspired by Mattie, and she gave me some good feedback.

I looked at my watch and it was time for us to leave. Rory quickly transformed herself into a limo driver, donning a pair of cool sunglasses for added effect.

Holly lived in an older townhouse, and her unit was in the back of the building on the first floor. As I approached her door, I tried to decide whether I should mention the cab before she saw it. Once she opened the door, I was so taken by how pretty she looked, I temporarily forgot all about it.

"The times I saw you at the dog park you looked great, but tonight you look exquisite," I said, handing her a bouquet of wildflowers.

"Flattery will get you everywhere," she said with a smile, taking the flowers and giving me a hug.

Since I had left Hathers, many of the women I had seen my age were obsessed with looking young. Holly had a unique, offbeat style that made her look attractive without having to dress like someone half her age.

While I was admiring what Holly was wearing, PJ came up from behind her. I reached down and gave the dog a couple of pets. As I did, I noticed Tess over Holly's shoulder, watching TV. I called out to say hello to her and she waved back.

"Well, are you ready to go?" I asked Holly. She nodded yes, gave PJ a scruff on the head, and grabbed her purse.

"Was it hard to find parking?" she asked, closing the door behind her. "This neighborhood is the worst."

"No, I'm right in front," I replied. "Listen, Holly, because of my physical condition I can't drive yet, so we're taking a cab."

"No biggie," she replied, as we walked through the wrought iron gate at the front of the complex. "I wish you would have told me—I would have driven."

"Next time," I said, nodding to acknowledge Rory, who was standing beside the open back door of the cab, smiling.

Either it took Holly a few moments to recognize my limo driver in the darkness, or my idea wasn't that good.

"Oh, how funny," she finally said, as we reached Rory.

Once Holly and I got into the cab, Rory continued playing her role.

"Where to sir?" she asked, looking at me through the rear view mirror.

"Dontoni's, please," I formally replied.

The Italian restaurant was in Pacific Palisades, a few blocks from the ocean. It was an intimate, outdoor setting with candles on white tablecloths, beneath a large gazebo.

Over dinner, Holly and I shared bits about our past. I told her about my coma, and what my life was like before it happened. She shared with me the experience of being born and living for a few years in a hippy commune in Hawaii. She also talked about the pain of her divorce from Tess's father, which happened two years ago.

Holly kept raving about the food, but I was so engrossed in our conversation that I hardly paid attention to it. It had been a long time since I was out with a woman, and with everything I'd been through, my adrenaline was pumping like it used to on first dates back in high school.

Throughout the night, she kept coming back to my coma and asking me questions about it. I was curious about the partial paralysis on the left side of her face, but she didn't offer any information, and I didn't inquire.

"This might be a weird question, but do you feel your age or the age you were when it happened?" she asked, while we shared a piece of tiramisu chocolate mousse.

"That's hard to say," I told her. "Sometimes this whole experience feels like a long, bizarre dream."

"In what way?"

"Just seeing how different the world is and seeing how time has changed my friends."

"Probably not as dramatic as you, but I've seen lots of changes in my long-time friends," she said. "We're not in our thirties anymore…that's for sure. You either figure out how to adjust to life or it starts to weigh you down."

"How have you faired?" I asked.

"Well…it took me a long time to get over my divorce. Just accepting that the dream I had as a little girl of having a family being shattered was hard. But I've moved on…finally. And I think I've come through it as a better mother to my daughter."

I glanced down and noticed that our dessert was rapidly disappearing.

"I see that look in your eyes," she said, quickly changing the subject. "You're plotting an advance to my side."

"What are you talking about?" I asked.

"Don't play me for a fool," she said, tapping her spoon on the dessert dish.

Looking down again, I realized that I was a bite away from finishing my half of the tiramisu, and she still had quite a bit left.

"I wouldn't think of it," I replied smiling.

"I had a date a few months ago with a guy who quickly devoured his half of the dessert, and then tore through mine with reckless abandon," she said. "Don't you think there's an unwritten rule that you shouldn't indulge in the other person's portion without asking?"

"I hadn't really thought about it…but I see your point."

She smiled and welcomed me to help her finish. We ate the remaining tiramisu chocolate mousse in a playful spoon for spoon exchange.

After we left the restaurant, I asked Holly if she wanted to walk a short distance down to a spot which overlooked the ocean.

"Are you sure you can make it down that slope okay?" she asked.

"If you hold onto me, I'll be fine," I replied. She intertwined her arm in mine and we began walking in the cool nighttime air.

The ocean soon came into view, shimmering from the reflection of an almost full moon. Once we made it to the lookout platform, we held hands and listened to the waves crashing on the shoreline below.

If you're lucky, you get a couple of opportune moments on a date in which to kiss a woman. My first one was beckoning, and I wasn't going to wait for another.

I turned away from the ocean towards Holly, and gently kissed her lips. She reciprocated and within seconds our tongues were intertwined. I closed my eyes and let a warm feeling of joy wash over me.

"That was nice," she said, as we pulled away from one another.

"Our first kiss," I said.

"Yes," she replied with a smile.

"Don't you think it's a relief to get the first kiss over with?"

"Not really. Why?"

"Well, what if there's no chemistry, or one person feels it and the other doesn't?"

"Then you just don't go back for seconds," she said, slowly leaning in for another kiss.

We had shared a bottle of wine during dinner and I was getting tired. I could have tried to push myself further, but I wanted to be honest with Holly about my physical limitations.

We talked about it on the cab ride back to her place and she was understanding and said she was tired as well.

For the first time all evening, we both got quiet. I reached over, held her hand and squeezed it.

"You know how at the beginning of relationships people try to put on their best face as opposed to their real face?" I asked, breaking our silence.

"Speak for yourself," she replied, before a smile formed on her lips.

"Let's not do that," I proposed.

"You mean just be completely honest with one another about who we are?" she said, with a chuckle. "That's scary!"

"No…scary is falling for someone who isn't what you think they are and finding out six months or a year later."

"I'll try," she said. "But some of the skeletons in my closet might take a while to come out."

"That's okay. I wouldn't want you to let all of them out at the same time and cause a traffic jam at the door," I joked.

"Thank you."

When the cab pulled up to Holly's place, I went to escort her to her door.

"Joel, you don't have to. Rest," she said sweetly.

I put my arm around her, bringing her close to me and kissed her goodnight.

As sad as I was to leave Holly was as happy as Mattie was to welcome me home. She danced, panted, and circled around me, as if she had thought I was never coming back.

After I took her out to relieve herself, she came up on the couch and sat beside me. While I slowly stroked her coat, she looked over at me and said with her eyes, *Don't leave like that again. I'm all you need.*

I turned on the TV and tried to watch the news, but I kept thinking about Holly. I knew it was way too early to know what we had, but it was hard not to be excited. For me, really great dates in which there was a strong, mutual attraction were like lunar eclipses—they didn't occur very often.

FIFTY

The next morning I woke up to good news. Big G had sent me an email saying a business contact of his had gotten us a meeting with Brillman Mattress Company. Brillman was the third largest mattress manufacturer in the country and they were very interested in hearing more about our idea. The meeting would be in five days, Gary wrote, and he wanted us to meet to go over our pitch and proposal as soon as possible.

A couple of nights later he stopped by after work with dinner for both of us, and a chewbone to keep Mattie occupied. Before we delved into business, he asked me about my date with Holly. I tried to be low key about it, but it was obvious that I really liked her.

"Just take it slow," he advised me.

"Wait, weren't you the one who was after me to get out there?" I asked.

"Yeah...I'm just saying don't suffocate her, like you did with Lauren."

"You think I suffocated Lauren?" I asked defensively.

"Are you kidding me? Remember the time she complained that her car was dirty and you snuck it off to the car wash, had it cleaned, and put it back in the garage with a teddy bear in the driver's seat?"

"That's suffocating someone? I thought that was kindness."

"When you do stuff like that all the time, it is," he said. "Listen, do whatever you want—I'm just saying give her her space. Chicks don't like it when guys are too clingy."

I took a few bites of the Chinese food he had brought, and listened as he went on.

"Managing a woman is like conducting an orchestra," he said. "You need to have crescendos, but you also need times when you're so quiet that they don't even know you're there. That gives them a chance to appreciate you, and start to wonder what happened to all of the love and affection. Then—when the time is right—swell the music again. It's a game, but isn't everything in life?"

"I hope not," I replied. "Interesting analogy, though."

I wanted to ask how his technique applied to his marriage to Leslie, but I didn't want to be contentious and get into a riff with him. I figured it was best to just take what he said and get down to business.

We spent the next three hours strategizing on how to present our concept to Brillman Mattress Company. By the time Gary left, we both felt confident in our direction.

Leading up to the big meeting, I continued refining our presentation. All the while, thoughts of Holly kept drifting through my mind like warm, gentle breezes on a spring day. I didn't want to contact her too soon after our date, but I was finding it hard to resist.

I briefly considered what Gary said to me, but acted on my instincts. I thought sending Holly a text was best, and wrote: *Thinking of you and looking forward to next time.* She replied shortly afterward with a smiley face.

FIFTY-ONE

When the day of our meeting with Brillman arrived, Big G pulled up to the front of my apartment to the sight of Mattie wearing a bow-tie, sitting dutifully by my side. He shook his head in disgust and rolled down the passenger side window.

"Dude, there's no way," he said emphatically, looking over at Mattie. "She can't come."

"It's a dog related business and she's the inspiration for it," I asserted, opening the car door. "Trust me on this."

"I don't want to, but I guess I will," he replied reluctantly. "Promise me you're not going to get goofy and start talking to your dog during the meeting."

"Don't worry," I assured him.

I hadn't intended on bringing Mattie with me to the meeting. But I had left her for a few hours earlier in the day and when I got ready to leave again, she hung her head and gave me a guilt-inducing glare. *Not again*, her sad eyes said.

As it turned out, she proved to be an invaluable asset. Everyone from the receptionist to the CEO of Brillman were smitten with her personality and touched by the condition I had found her in. Several of the employees suggested that Mattie would make the perfect company spokesdog to grab the attention and hearts of dog owners.

After Mattie effectively broke the ice, and soaked up all the adulation and pets that she could, we moved from the reception area to the conference room. Gary and I alternated laying out the details of our product and our proposed rollout plan to the Head of Product Development and the Senior Vice-President of Marketing.

Our goal—if Brillman agreed to work with us—was to have prototypes of our three bed sizes in time for the *Paws & Claws* trade show in Los Angeles, at which we had already reserved a booth. Their representatives seemed confident that they would be able to, and assured us they would also be able to fulfill orders we received at the show quickly.

Our fitted sheets and raised platforms for the beds were being manufactured by separate companies in downtown Los Angeles, and both were awaiting our approval to produce them.

Mattie Mattress had been my placeholder name for the company, until we came up with something better. After brainstorming with the Brillman executives, we decided to officially call our company *Canine Comfort*. While the group continued to talk, I thought of a new tagline—*Forever beds for your furry family members*—and everyone loved it.

The CEO of the company, Norm Crownlee, popped in the room towards the end of meeting and came up with an interesting idea. "What if we alter one of our regular mattresses so that a bottom corner slopes down to make it easier for an older dog to get up on the bed?" he offered. Gary and I exchanged excited glances, realizing it could be a great extension to our product line. Norm suggested calling them *Dog-Eared Beds*.

The meeting went incredibly well, and after a month of more meetings and a few conference calls, Gary's lawyer and Brillman's legal department drafted a contract and put us in business.

Gary and I were pumped up on the ride home, recapping how the meeting went, and thinking about the road ahead. Mattie was pooped from all the activity and lay sprawled out across the backseat. The only part of her body that moved was her nose, which wiggled to take in the passing smells of the city.

Fifty-Two

That evening I spoke to Holly and we made plans to go to Will Rogers State Park the next day, which was a Saturday. She agreed to drive and when she picked me up, PJ was in the backseat of her silver Saab.

"He wouldn't let me leave without him," she said, smiling at me through the open top. "You want to make it a double date?"

I leaned over to give her a kiss, and then went to retrieve a surprised and jubilant Mattie.

After we stopped at the market on my corner to pick up some sandwiches, we headed off to the park.

Winding down Sunset Boulevard, we came to a stop light and both immediately noticed the vehicle in front of us. It was a supped up truck, with massive tires and the thickest exhaust pipe I had ever seen. The driver was revving the engine and you could feel the vibration of his music from his open windows.

"So obnoxious," Holly said, rolling up her window.

"The truck or the music?" I asked.

"Both," she replied.

"Did you see the license plate?"

"ELITIST," she replied, reading it aloud.

"He should have opted for ASSHOLE—it's the same number of letters and probably more accurate."

Holly laughed. "It must be strange for you—there weren't trucks like that back in the 90s," she said.

"Yeah, everything got bigger—cars, homes, even soft drinks."

Once we arrived at the park, we let the dogs mill around for a while. Then we grabbed our food and walked to a nice spot beneath a shady tree to spread out a blanket. I don't know if it was on account of it being our second date, but I was much more relaxed.

I told Holly about the positive meeting Big G and I had with Brillman and showed her samples of the fitted sheet patterns to get her opinion.

"I love them all, but my favorite is the one with illustrations of the different dog breeds," she said. "I'm so excited for you, Joel. It's a great idea and I think it's going to do really well. People treat their dogs like family...at least I do."

As she handed the samples back to me, her cell phone rang.

"Sorry—give me one second, it's my ex," she said, standing up and wandering a few feet away.

I called Mattie and PJ, who had drifted off to check out a dog that was passing by, and gave each of them a treat. I tried not to listen to Holly's conversation, but it was hard to avoid it. She and her ex-husband were having a heated discussion regarding their daughter, Tess. When Holly returned, shaking her head, she apologized.

"Are you okay?" I asked, sensing that she was unnerved.

"Yeah, I'm fine. Can we please forget the last two minutes?"

"Forgotten," I replied, pointing over at PJ and Mattie, who were adorably lying back to back.

"Lucky dogs," she said. "They don't have to deal with the complications and drama of being human."

"Speak for yourself—my life isn't complicated," I said playfully.

"That's because your slate is clean," she replied. "Just wait until you get to know me better."

"I can't wait," I said, leaning forward to kiss her.

We kissed passionately and slowly fell back onto the blanket. Mattie came over to lick my ear, and I shooed her away.

"Jealousy won't do you any good, Mattie," Holly said to her. "He's mine now."

I wrapped my arm around Holly and brought her body flush with mine. After we grappled for a while, a smile came to her face. Then she started to laugh.

"What's so funny?" I asked.

"I didn't know if—you know—it worked after being in a coma for so long," she said, referring to a relevant part of my anatomy. "But I can feel that it does."

"If it didn't, would you still go out with me?" I asked. "Be HONEST."

"Of course I would…as friends," she replied, cracking herself up.

"That's honest enough," I said.

"I'm totally kidding…I'm not that shallow. There's way more to a relationship than that."

"Not in the beginning there isn't," I replied.

"That's probably true," she agreed. "My ex used to say that sex is like rocket fuel. You need it to get a relationship off the ground, but it takes a whole lot more than that to keep it going."

"He's definitely right," I said. "Does your ex have a name or should I just call him *your ex*?"

"I call him a lot of different things these days," she said, with a sly grin. "Originally though, he was Michael."

Nothing can kill an intimate moment like talking about a woman's ex, I reminded myself.

"Let's not talk about rockets and space anymore. I liked it better when there was none between us," I said, reaching around her waist to bring her close to me again.

We kissed and then she said, "You're doing pretty well for someone who hasn't dated in a long time."

"I had years to think about all of my mistakes," I said jokingly.

"Do you remember anything from when you were in your coma?" she asked.

"There's two absolute rules to dating and now we've broken both of them," I replied.

"Really?"

"Yeah…one is not talking about your ex and the other is not sharing your coma experience."

"But I find it fascinating," she said.

"C'mon now," I said, acting irritated. "I just told you the rules."

"But you didn't tell me the punishment if I broke them," she said flirtatiously.

"It's so bad that I can't tell you in a public place," I replied, increasing the sexual tension between us.

"Well, I hope you'll remember the next time we're alone in private," she said.

"Trust me, I will," I replied, running my hand through her hair.

Initially, I was going to opt for another dinner and then a movie for our second date. But at this point, I was happy I hadn't.

Unfortunately, as it turned out, my joy was premature. Holly's cell phone rang again. When she turned around to see who was calling, she let out a moan.

"Now what?" she barked into the phone, without saying hello.

I watched as she walked off to talk to her ex again. Sensing that this conversation might last longer than the first one, I decided to get up and throw a tennis ball for the dogs.

Mattie loved to chase after them, but would never bring them back. PJ zipped back and forth, anxiously waiting—with his tongue out and flapping—for me to throw the ball again.

After a while, I looked over at Holly and she held up her index finger to signal she wouldn't be long.

But she continued to pace and argue with her ex. By the time she made it back to me and the dogs, she was sullen.

"I have to go get Tess," she announced unhappily. "She's butting heads with her father."

Is there anything I can do? Do you want me to come with you? crossed my mind and almost came out of my mouth. Instead, I stayed quiet and rubbed her shoulders. It's probably best to give her her space, I thought, remembering what Big G had said to me.

With a scowl on her face, Holly gathered our stuff off of the ground, while I leashed the dogs. The drive back to my place was as cheery as a commute to a burial service. I couldn't think of anything to say, so I just held her hand.

"You're a good guy, Joel," she finally said, breaking the silence. "I don't know if you want to get involved with me. Tess's father and I are divorced, but there's no such thing when you have a child with someone."

"Everybody has something," I offered, trying to be consoling. "I understand."

When we arrived at my apartment, I grabbed Mattie's leash, gave PJ a scruff on the head and kissed Holly on the cheek.

"That's it?" she said. "Just a kiss on the cheek?"

"Go," I said. "Take care of your daughter."

Once I got back inside, I felt deflated. Holly and I had gone from passion to packing up and leaving, in a matter of minutes. I understood her priority, but I had never dated anyone with a child before and didn't know if I could be content with the pecking order.

If there was anything I learned from my marriage, it was that relationships come down to one thing: *acceptance*. How able you are to live with the other person's imperfections, without holding grudges. I would have to see in time if I could accept Holly as she was and vice-versa.

When Lauren and I met, my business was already established. It allowed me the luxury of spending more time with her than I should have. Big G was probably right—my life got out of balance. Now, with a new business and lots of work to do, hopefully I would have something that would anchor me and prevent me from losing myself in a relationship.

I sat down at my desk and worked for a long stretch. I got so engrossed that I didn't realize it was time for Mattie's dinner, until she came over and poked my arm with her snout.

FIFTY-THREE

The 4th of July was quickly approaching. I had hoped to spend it with Holly, but she'd already made plans to go with Tess to be with her mother in Northern California. Big G invited me over for a barbeque, but it was going to be with five families and their kids, and I didn't feel like I would fit in.

So, when the holiday arrived, I ended up celebrating America's independence with Mattie. I would also be celebrating the retirement of my walker, which transpired at my last therapy session. At last, I would be able to make use of the cane Kerrie had given me while I was at Hathers.

For most of the day I relaxed and took a break from working, which Mattie appreciated. In the afternoon, I took her to the grass patch across the way and she played for a good stretch of time with two dogs that walked by with their owner. Later, Aunt Shirley stopped by for dinner, but unfortunately she didn't stay long because she wasn't feeling well.

A while after she left, I walked with Mattie to a small park my neighbor had recommended as a good spot for viewing the fireworks. Along the way, we crossed paths with a rambunctious black Lab puppy, and while I chatted with the owner, the dogs visited.

After they went on their way, I sat down on the curb to take a drink of water and rest for a minute. Mattie was pulling to sniff a nearby bush, so I unclipped her leash.

"I bet we can see the fireworks from right here," I said to her, reaching into my backpack to take out a blanket. There was an ample patch of grass beside the sidewalk in which to spread it out.

A moment later, I heard the whistle of a firecracker and a splash of light exploded above us.

"Did you see that?" I asked, turning back to Mattie and seeing her standing frozen, anxiously looking around.

Stupidly, I didn't make the connection that she was reacting to the sound of the firecracker.

"Up there," I said, trying to direct her attention toward the sky.

When another firecracker went off, she scurried a few feet away. I now understood what was happening.

"It's okay," I said, getting up to put her leash back on. But before I was able to reach her, a flurry of fireworks exploded and she darted into the street.

"Mattie!" I yelled, anxiously looking to see if any cars were coming. "Come here right now!"

She stood cowering, her ears pinned back, paralyzed with fear. As nonchalantly as possible, I walked toward her. I was a few steps from grabbing her, but another loud boom sent her running away and down an adjoining street.

Once I got to the spot where she had disappeared, I looked in every direction but didn't see her anywhere.

I took off down the street as quickly as I could, looking in every driveway and frantically calling out her name. I passed a large group of people, who were watching the fireworks on a balcony, and yelled up to ask if they had seen a stray dog, but no one had.

Shortly after I continued down the street, a car drove up beside me. One of the guys who had been on the balcony was behind the wheel.

"Hop in," he said through the rolled down passenger window. "Let me help you look."

I put my walker in the backseat and got into the car.

"Steve Meckler," the stranger said, extending his hand. "Where to?"

"I have no idea," I said. "I was going to try looking in the alley."

We searched the alley behind the homes on both sides of the street, and the next block down, but there was no sign of Mattie. I was about to thank Steve for his help, when he said, "Let's try one block over."

We didn't have any luck looking on that street either. But when we turned down another alley, we saw someone stumbling from side to side in the distance. Once we got closer, I could see a dog beside the person.

Pulling up to him, I realized that the man was homeless. His face was darkened with soot; he had a wild, scruffy beard; and he was wearing several layers of clothing on a hot, summer night. He had a rope tied around Mattie's neck and she was whimpering, either from the sound of the fireworks or the tension of the rope, or both.

Steve quickly got out of the car and handed me my walker. "Thanks…that's my dog," I said, approaching the man.

"No—this is my dog," he replied, slurring his speech and nearly falling over.

"She got freaked out by the fireworks and ran off," I explained, trying to remain calm. "Where did you find her?"

"I've had this dog since I got back from the war," he said, stammering toward me.

"Which war?" I asked.

"I can't remember…one of those really bad ones," he said, buckling to his knees.

"Well, thanks for serving and thanks for finding my dog," I said, reaching down and releasing his hand from the rope holding Mattie.

Once I got her into Steve's backseat, I pulled out a twenty dollar bill and stuffed it into the homeless man's jacket pocket.

"Take care of yourself," I said.

After we drove away, Steve asked me, "Where do you live?"

When I told him how close my place was, he agreed to take me back home.

Once I got inside of my apartment, I unclipped Mattie's leash and quickly flipped on the stereo to drown out the sound of the seemingly endless fireworks. When I turned around, Mattie was gone! I looked to make sure that I had closed the door and I had. After searching in the kitchen and in the bedroom, I found my poor terrified dog in the bath tub. I tried to coax her out, but she wouldn't budge.

"I'm sorry," I told her, leaning over to rub behind her ears. "I wish those firecrackers made some other sound or no sound at all."

Soon another round of firecrackers broke through the sound of Miles Davis' horn, and Mattie began anxiously pacing in the tub. It killed me to see her so distraught.

I left to go grab her leash, and returned to the bathroom. It wasn't easy, but after I clipped the leash to her collar, I was able to get her out of the tub.

She reluctantly followed me into the living room, where I grabbed my iPad off of the coffee table and searched for ways to calm a dog's nerves. I found a lot of suggestions, but the only one I had on hand was Benadryl. I smothered a 25 mg. capsule in some peanut butter and gave it to her.

My mind flashed on the homeless guy I had left behind and I felt bad. I thought to take a cab to pick him up and bring him to a homeless shelter, but I wasn't sure of the street name the alley was behind. Also, Mattie was finally a little calmer and had momentarily stopped pacing.

Completely exhausted, I lay down on the couch and eventually Mattie settled on the ground below me. Incredibly, there were fireworks still intermittently going off. It was beginning to feel more like a war zone than a 4th of July celebration.

Hours later, I opened my eyes and it was morning. When I looked down for Mattie, she wasn't there. I got up, still fully clothed, and found her sleeping in the bathtub.

I took a picture of her and sent it to Holly, with a note that said: *Rough night. I hope PJ fared better with the fireworks.* She replied back seconds later, saying that PJ didn't mind fireworks and that she missed me.

Brushing my teeth and waving at Mattie in the mirror, I wondered what would have happened if I had gone to Big G's and left her home alone. Reading stories online later that night about dogs jumping through plate glass windows, or fleeing in fear and getting hit by cars, was terrifying and tragic.

FIFTY-FOUR

With Mattie zonked out from the night before, I sat on my couch and brainstormed ideas for Canine Comfort's upcoming trade show.

Although we only had one product, there were a dizzying amount of details and work in setting up a small booth. Everything from signage to order forms to fixtures, not to mention implementing a giveaway to draw people to our booth.

Learning that a number of trade show attendees brought their dogs with them, I came up with the idea of putting a trail of peanut butter scented paw prints on the trade show floor leading to our booth. Of course, once the dogs tried one of our beds, we would reward them with a Peanut Butter treat. It took a few hours' worth of phone calls, but I finally found a vendor who could produce them.

After Holly got back in town, we had a nice, long chat on the phone. She said getting out of L.A. and being somewhere quiet and green was rejuvenating. Tess was still having issues with her father, but Holly seemed less stressed out about it.

A movie seemed like a good plan for our next date, so I mentioned a romantic comedy that Kerrie had told me about. Holly watched the trailer online while we spoke and said she was excited to see it.

I've never liked to cook for myself, but I've always thought making a good meal for a woman was impressive and romantic. So, I invited Holly to come over for dinner before we went to the movie. Anxious to see one another, we made plans for the following evening.

As soon as we got off of the phone, I searched online for recipes. I was going to run a few of them by her, but figured the element of surprise was better. I knew from our dinner at Dontoni's that she wasn't a vegetarian, so I decided I'd barbeque a few chicken breasts and sauté them with a mojito marinade. The recipe for the marinade had a ton of great reviews with almost no negative comments.

A few hours before Holly was set to come over, I went down to the corner market and bought everything I needed. It was only after I printed out the instructions and reread them that I realized I needed a blender.

I knocked on the manager's door to borrow one, but she wasn't home. Next, I tried Matt, the neighbor who had brought over the pizza the day I moved in. He was super-friendly again, and invited me inside. After rummaging through a couple of cabinets above his stove, he handed me a blender that was dusty, but looked fairly new.

"Here you go—this should do the trick," he said. "Keep it as long as you want."

I went back to my place and spent the next hour prepping everything, so that I would be ready to make the mojito marinade easily once Holly arrived. Mattie keenly followed my every move, hoping that her self-anointed role as support chef would earn her sampling privileges. Thinking the ingredients for my recipe might not be good for a dog, I reached into the refrigerator and grabbed a couple of baby carrots for her.

Once I finished the prep work, I sat down on the couch and Mattie retreated to one of the Canine Comfort prototypes I now had in the living room. As I reached over to grab my phone from the coffee table to take a picture of her, the doorbell rang.

I had been training Mattie not to go berserk when someone came to the door, and she seemed to be getting better. I pointed my finger for her to stay and got up to let Holly in. After I gave her a hug hello, I turned to praise my star pupil, only to find she was already at my feet.

Holly squatted down and she and Mattie greeted one another enthusiastically. I smiled watching the two of them interact, while admiring the sexy summer dress Holly had on. After she stood up and brushed herself off, she followed me into the kitchen and put a bottle of red wine she had brought on the counter.

"Look how organized you are," she said, taking note of my prep work.

"Yes. A master chef at work," I said in jest.

"What are you making for us?" she asked.

"We're going to have barbequed chicken with my secret mojito marinade. I hope you like it. And a chopped salad to start with."

"Don't worry, I eat everything," she responded. "I hope you can't tell."

"C'mon," I said, grabbing two wine glasses from the cupboard. "There's not an inch of fat on you."

"Thanks, but I need to lose at least five pounds."

"By your standards most of us would be considered obese," I replied.

I led her back into the living room and we sat on the couch, sipping wine. She showed me pictures from her 4th of July trip on her phone, and I told her more about my ordeal with Mattie.

"I wish I had known what fireworks can do to a dog," I said.

"Next year, you should go up to the forest," she suggested. "My neighbor does it every year with his Chihuahua, Henry. They don't allow fireworks up there."

We talked for a while longer, then I asked if she was hungry. She said she didn't have lunch and was starving, so I went out to the patio to turn on the barbeque. When it was time to cook the chicken, I asked if she wanted to join me outside.

"It's okay," she said. "I'll stay in here with Mattie and let you do your thing."

"Step one completed," I announced, when I came back into the kitchen and put the plate of cooked chicken breasts on the counter.

"Just let me know if you need any help?" Holly asked, looking over my shoulder.

"Actually, in a second here, I will," I said, heating olive oil in a saucepan. "Would you rather pour or receive?"

"Pour, I guess... Are you sure this recipe doesn't call for a hazmat suit?" she asked, realizing that the contents in the mixing bowl—garlic, onions, orange juice, and lime juice—were going to be poured into the saucepan with hot oil.

"Wait—I'll be right back," I said, leaving the kitchen and returning with a sweatshirt. "Put this on."

"Okay," she said willingly, but reticent.

"Let me just grab these other potholder mitts and we're ready."

I cued Holly with a nod, and she began slowly pouring the contents from the mixing bowl into the saucepan I was holding. The oil began to crackle and splatter.

"Are you okay?" she asked, when I turned my face away from the intense heat.

"Yeah," I said, feeling drops of oil stinging my skin. "Keep pouring."

Once she finished, my forehead was dripping with sweat.

"Did you get any on you?" I asked, turning back toward her.

"A little, but I'm fine," she said, grabbing a napkin from the counter to wipe her face.

I stirred the ingredients in the saucepan for a few minutes with a wooden spoon, and then added the spices.

"Okay…last step," I said, looking up from the instructions. "Can you hand me that blender behind you?"

She grabbed it, removed the lid, and plugged it into the wall. I slowly emptied the saucepan into the blender.

"Now we just need to mix everything together and we're finally ready to eat," I said.

I looked down at the buttons on the blender and pulsed everything for a quick second.

"This is going to be good," I said, before pressing down the button again to blend the ingredients.

The blender rumbled loudly, which I assumed was normal. But in a split second, I heard a crack and saw mojito marinade spraying everywhere.

"Oh shit!" I yelled, quickly hitting the off button and stepping back from the blender. The marinade that splattered on my arms and face was hot, but thankfully not to the degree that it was when we poured the ingredients into the saucepan.

I grabbed a dish towel that was hanging on the oven handle and handed it to Holly.

Feeling like a complete idiot, I began profusely apologizing to her, as I quickly headed to the bathroom to get a large bath towel.

"Don't worry about it," she said, when I returned to the kitchen.

"Oh man!" I said, seeing splotches of brown marinade all over her white dress. "You got it much worse than me."

"It's okay, I'll just have it dry-cleaned."

"Do you want to put on a pair of my jeans and a t-shirt?" I offered, while trying to get Mattie to stop tongue-cleaning the floor.

"What about dinner?" she asked.

"Do you still want it?"

"We have to try it after all that," she replied.

I walked back over to the counter and inspected the blender. "I just hope there's no pieces of plastic in there," I said.

"Do you have a strainer?" she asked.

"I'm not sure—my aunt got most of this stuff," I replied, opening a couple of drawers and eventually finding one.

Holly strained the remaining marinade and then poured it over the room-temperature chicken, and dinner was served. After she took a bite, she surprised me by saying, "Joel, this is delicious!"

"*Really?*" I replied, curious to try it. Once I did, I agreed with Holly—it was incredibly tasty. But a hotter chicken and a more cautious execution would have made it infinitely better.

For the remainder of our fragmented meal, we talked about our families. I told her all about my father and how much I missed him. She told me she hadn't seen her father since she was seven years old, and she didn't know where he lived.

"He's the dark side of the 60's and free love," she said. "He wanted to be free to do whatever he wanted…unfortunately that didn't include being a father."

I was about to launch into the exasperating explanation that is my mother, when an idea struck me. Why not describe Aunt Shirley as my mother, and have her fill in if Holly ever had the occasion to meet my mother?

"She sounds like an incredible woman," Holly said, after hearing about my aunt. "I'd love to meet her one day."

"Oh, she is," I said, wondering what I had gotten myself into.

Once we finished eating and brought the dishes to the sink, Holly thanked me for making dinner.

"Anytime," I told her, with a chuckle. "I'm sure it's one you won't forget anytime soon."

"It turned out okay," she said with a smile.

Noticing that her wine glass was low, I grabbed the bottle and refilled it. Then I lifted my glass and made my second toast of the evening.

"To the beautiful woman in the mojito marinade stained dress who's still smiling."

After we clinked glasses I noticed a small red mark on her cheek, most likely from the cooking accident. I leaned over and kissed it.

"That's sweet," she said. "What did I do to deserve it?"

"You have a red mark—probably from the marinade. I just wanted to kiss it to make it better," I said, reaching for her hand.

As we walked into the living room, she said, "I think I should take you up on your offer to change clothes before we go to the movie."

"Good idea," I replied. "Come...we have an open dressing room for you in the back."

Holly followed me to my bedroom and Mattie tagged along. After I handed her something to change into, she headed into the bathroom. Mattie tried to join her.

"No, Mattie," I said, briefly holding her collar. "She'll be right back."

While I waited for Holly, I changed my shoes, which were sticky from the marinade.

"How do I look?" she asked, reappearing with my clothes on.

"Absolutely adorable," I said, noticing that her hair was no longer in a ponytail.

I got up from the bed and walked over to where she was standing.

"I like your hair down," I said, running my hands through it. She smiled and I leaned in to kiss her.

Once our lips parted, I sat back down on the bed to finish tying my shoes. Holly sat down beside me.

"Okay, I'm ready to go," I said, turning toward her. She didn't say anything and we stared into each other's eyes. We kissed again, and slowly fell back onto the bed.

Passionately groping one another, we began to take off each other's clothes. Things were moving fast and I was glad that I had bought a box of condoms, if the occasion arose.

While Holly was pleasuring me, I reached over and grabbed one from the nightstand drawer. After I finished going down on her, I asked if it was okay to use it and she nodded that it was. I tore open the condom and put it on. We tenderly kissed as she got on top of me.

The last time I had sex was at least a month before the illness that led to my coma. Unfortunately, Lauren and I were like many married couples who had been together for a while—sex was more of a duty than a natural desire.

I cradled Holly's face in my hands as I entered her. She rode me slowly to start, but then quickly picked up the pace. I felt like I was going to have an orgasm, so I brought her body flush with mine and held her tight, stopping her motion. "It's been a while," I whispered in her ear. "Can we take it slow?"

"I'm sorry," she said. "It just felt so good."

We lay still until I felt the urge to come had passed. Then I clasped my hands in Holly's and we began gently thrusting back and forth. As the rhythm picked up, she pushed herself up to ride me again. I closed my eyes and felt the sensations throughout my body.

As she started to moan with pleasure, I felt something cold and moist brush against my right arm. I looked over and Mattie was staring at me. I tried to shoo her away, but it only worked her up. Once Holly realized what was happening, she slid off of me.

"It's okay, sweetie," she told Mattie, reaching over to pet her.

It's not okay if you have a hard on that you want to keep that way, I thought to myself, as I felt my penis beginning to soften.

"Maybe if we ignore her, she'll lay back down," I suggested.

Holly got back on top of me, but within seconds Mattie became more animated and began to whimper.

"I'll have to bring PJ next time," she said.

"Good idea," I replied, getting up to go to the bathroom.

Once I closed the door, I quickly opened the cabinet beneath the sink and riffled through my toiletry bag in search of one of the little blue pills Big G had given me.

"Even if you don't need it, it'll help you last longer," he had told me.

I found the pills and popped one in my mouth, swallowing it with a handful of water.

Returning to the bedroom, I had a jealous dog, a willing woman, and a half hour to kill before the medicine kicked in.

I called Mattie to follow me into the living room, where I went to change the music. We had been listening to Steely Dan's *Aja*, but I remember how Mattie had mellowed out to Joe Sample's *Carmel* on the 4th of July, so I put that on instead. When she tried to follow me back into the bedroom, I closed the door.

After several minutes of foreplay, Holly and I picked up where we had left off. This time there were no interruptions, just warm feelings and joyful climaxes.

Drenched in sweat, we blissfully lay next to one another on our backs, holding hands.

"I guess we're not going to the movie," she said with a laugh.

"This was way better than any movie could have possibly been."

"I agree," she replied, turning to rest her head in the crook of my arm.

Before long, we both drifted off to asleep. We awoke to the sound of Mattie sniffing under the door at 6:15 in the morning.

Once we got up and got dressed, the three of us walked down to the corner store. For the next hour, Holly and I sat enjoying coffee and bagels, while watching the traffic begin to swell on Wilshire Boulevard.

Shortly after we returned to my apartment, Holly gathered her things and left.

FIFTY-FIVE

With the *Paws & Claws* trade show a little over a month away, my goal for the new day was to replicate how our booth would look in my living room.

Mattie would have much preferred doing something else and displayed her displeasure by pacing around where I was working, constantly getting on and off of the couch, and sitting and staring at me as if I had lost my mind.

By four o'clock that afternoon, I had finally erected the booth as it would be experienced by buyers at the show. I leaned against the door of my apartment to take everything in.

"What do you think, Mattie?" I asked her, while she stood beside me, hoping we were about to go out.

"Oh, come on," I said in response to her dour expression. "Can you at least give me a wag of approval?"

She gave me a lazy wave of her tail and I dug into my pocket and gave her a training treat, and then grabbed her leash.

We walked across the street and met up with a St. Bernard named Sully, who lived a few doors down. He and Mattie happily romped around, until Sully's owner had to leave.

As I came back to my apartment, I was surprised to see my mother walking across the courtyard towards me.

"Hello stranger," she said. "I was in the neighborhood…I thought I'd drop by."

I waved and then looked down at Mattie and asked her in a playful voice, "Who's that?"

"Is she talking yet?" my mother asked jokingly, after I gave her a hug hello.

"Yes, but only to dog lovers."

"Oh well," she replied.

I was about to open the door to my unit, when I turned to my mother and said, "I just finished constructing the booth for our upcoming trade show in the living room. Let me know what you think."

Once we walked inside, my mother put down her purse in the kitchen. After I handed her a glass of water, she went back into the living room and looked around, without saying a word. I curiously watched her to see what a potential buyer would gravitate toward and to gage her gut reaction.

"It looks nice, but I can't believe you actually went through with this." she said, picking up one of our brochures.

"Couldn't you have said, 'It looks nice, *and*', instead of 'It looks nice, *but*?'"

"What do you mean?" she asked.

"It looks nice *and* I'm proud of you."

"Well, I am proud of you," she said. "I just can't believe you started a business making human beds for dogs."

"What does it matter?" I bristled. "If I won the lottery, you'd ask why I didn't win it in a state with a larger jackpot."

After waking up from my coma, I had done everything in my power not to let my mother get to me. But this time, she had gotten under my skin. I told her I needed to get back to work, and after several hints and a little prodding, she left.

I was yearning to see Holly again after our intimate night together, and sent her a text to see what she was up to. When she replied that she'd love to see me but had Tess with her, I suggested that the three of us go to a movie. I added, "I can even pick you guys up. Surprise! I'm able to drive now!"

She called a second later to congratulate me on my milestone and to make sure I didn't mind hanging out with Tess. I told her that Tess was our matchmaker and her daughter, and I wanted to get to know her better.

When I picked the two of them up a few hours later, Tess was chatty and excited. I could tell she felt comfortable with me, which Holly seemed to appreciate.

We hadn't decided on a movie yet, and after Holly read the list of possible films from her phone, Tess said from the backseat, "We have to see *A Day in Dogtown*."

"I don't think Joel wants to see an animated movie, Tess," Holly replied.

"It's okay," I interjected, wanting to be agreeable. "What's it about?"

"It's about a neglected dog that runs away from his owner to Dogtown," Tess explained. "Dogtown's a place where only dogs live. The preview showed a bunch of dogs sitting in a movie theatre and you see their heads and ears from behind. It's the cutest thing!"

Holly looked over at me and smiled.

"It sounds like my kind of movie," I said. "I'm excited…I haven't seen a movie in a really long time."

I had been by the Southland Stadium Cinemas, where we were going, once when Kerrie took me to my father's gravesite, but didn't know what *stadium* exactly implied.

After we bought our tickets and I got over the fact that it was twice as much to see a movie as in 1994, I found out.

"Wow," I said when we entered the theatre and I noticed how spacious the seating was, and realized that the person in front of you couldn't block your view.

"Can we sit up there?" Tess asked, pointing really close to the front.

"Wherever you guys want," I said.

Once we settled on a spot, I sat on the aisle, with Holly beside me, and Tess next to her.

The film was silly with a predictable storyline, but the concept was sweet. The animation, however, blew me away. It was light years beyond what it used to be.

During the movie, I felt I had tempered my displays of affection towards Holly, but she told me later that Tess referred to me as "Mr. Frisky."

Once the credits rolled and the light came up, I offered to buy yogurt for Tess and Holly at a place that just opened by my apartment. Tess got all excited, but Holly quickly nixed the idea, saying that they had to get home and do a lot of things before school the next day.

After I gave Tess a hug goodbye in front of their place, Holly signaled to me that she would come back out once she took her daughter inside.

"Thanks for seeing that," she said, when she returned.

"I loved it," I said with a straight face.

"No you didn't. It was pretty awful."

I smiled in agreement. "The worst part was not being able to kiss you all night," I said.

"Nothing's stopping you now," she replied with a seductive smile.

I wrapped my arms around her waist, and brought her lips to mine.

"Much better," I said, after we kissed.

"Unfortunately, now I have to go," she said. "I hate Mondays and tomorrow's a long one."

Holly squeezed me tight and then turned to leave. I got into my car, rolled down the passenger window, and watched her walk away. Before she lifted the handle of the entrance gate, she turned around, waved, and blew me a kiss.

FIFTY-SIX

The next morning, an hour after feeding her breakfast, I took Mattie across the street with a tennis ball to tire her out. Big G and I—along with the execs at Brillman—had decided to make Mattie an integral part of our marketing efforts and I had an appointment with a photographer to get some shots of her.

Before going to Doug Korsmann's studio in Venice, I stopped by the groomer's first to have Mattie brushed out and prettied up.

Doug had shot the Brillman Mattress Catalog for years, as well as many other well-known furniture companies, and he came highly recommended.

Mattie was excited and curious to enter the photography studio, which had the open feel of an airplane hangar. Roni, the tall blonde receptionist, welcomed us and then helped me unload the prototype beds and marketing materials from my car. She said that Doug would be just a few minutes.

Once Mattie sniffed the room out to her satisfaction, she settled beside the cushy couch I had plopped down on. Leaning back and staring across the way, I checked out Doug's work, which covered the walls. All of the images were of furniture, and I wondered how he would handle a shedding, drooling, excitable dog.

After what seemed like a long wait, Doug appeared and introduced himself. He was about my age, with salt and pepper hair pulled back in a short ponytail. He had the look of a creative professional, wearing jeans, a black t-shirt, and white Converse tennis shoes.

"Sorry for the delay," he said, shaking my hand. "This catalog I'm working on for a new chair manufacturer just won't end. Maybe that old saying—perfect is the enemy of good—has some merit."

Mattie immediately vied for Doug's attention, and he got down on his haunches to greet her. You could instantly tell that he was a dog lover.

"This must be our star," he said, scratching behind Mattie's ears and talking to her. "Other than my own dog, you'll be my first canine model."

I asked Doug what kind of dog he had and he pulled out his phone to show me some photos he had recently taken of Ernie, his ten year old black Poodle.

"I wish I could make a living working with animals or something else, but I fell into a niche photographing stationery objects," he told me. "It's boring as hell, but at least desks and beds can't complain or tell me to hurry up."

Roni, who turned out to also be Doug's assistant, brought a bowl of water for Mattie and we all walked down a short hallway into the studio.

When I saw the photo shoot setup—two strobe lights, reflectors, and a wide roll of white paper—I wondered how Mattie would respond to quick flashes of light, especially after her reaction to fireworks. But it turned out that they didn't bother her in the least. She posed and hammed for the camera, as if she had done this sort of thing before.

It took Doug about an hour to get what he needed. Afterward, I gave Mattie a proud hug and rewarded her with the remaining dried Salmon treats I had brought for her.

Once I gathered up my stuff to take back home, Doug called me into an adjoining room to look at the images he had shot. Even after seeing so many pictures on smartphones, I momentarily forgot that cameras were now digital.

Doug scrolled through the photographs on a large monitor and we commented on the ones we liked. While he burned a disc of the images for me to take and show Gary, I looked at a few framed prints he had hanging on the wall above his workspace. When I spotted one of Holly, against the same white backdrop that Mattie was just on, I did a double take.

"You know Holly?" I blurted out.

It took Doug a few seconds to look up and realize who I was talking about. "Yeah…" he replied, "she's my girlfriend. How do you know Holly?"

"Oh…I met her recently at the dog park," I answered, after a pregnant pause.

"Then you've met PJ," he replied. "I love that dog."

"Yep," I said, wondering to myself if I should dig for more information about his relationship with Holly.

"Alright…here you go," he said, handing me the completed disc. Then he reached into his drawer and handed Mattie a large heart-shaped treat. "One for the road, right?" he said, giving her a rub on the head.

I thanked him and Roni for their time and work, and then Doug helped me out to the car. Before I drove off, we talked for a minute about the recent, strong Santa Ana winds we had been having.

On my way back home, I passed by a small park and pulled over. I let Mattie off of the leash to explore, and sat down at a picnic table to digest what I had just learned. In the past, when things like this happened with women, jealousy would get the best of me and I'd handle myself poorly. I wanted to call Holly and ask her about Doug, but I resisted.

Holly and I had only been on a few dates and weren't exclusive to one another: she had every right to see whoever she wanted. But I wasn't the type that could be okay falling for someone who was sleeping with other guys. By nature I was a one woman man, and I preferred to be with a one man woman.

Later that night, I went over to Gary's to show him the photographs from Mattie's shoot. We needed to decide which ones we were going to use and get the files to the printer in order to produce our signage and marketing materials in time for the trade show. We quickly agreed on the best ones, and moved on to discuss other issues pertaining to our booth.

As Gary walked me to my car to leave, I told him about the ironic connection between Holly and our photographer. After telling me what I already knew—that Holly hadn't done anything wrong—he said, "You can still have fun with her."

I knew if I saw Holly, the issue of Doug would come up. I wanted to step back and give myself time, so that I wouldn't come at her from a place of envy.

The upcoming trade show gave me a legitimate excuse to focus on my work. The truth is, even if I hadn't found out that Holly was dating somebody else, it was best for me to put all of my energy and focus into making sure our product had a successful launch. For the next few days, Holly and I texted one another, but I didn't initiate any plans. When she eventually asked why we hadn't gotten together again, I explained that I was buried in work.

The printer turned our job around amazingly quick and I was excited to pick up the materials. Before I left their office, the sales rep pulled out a few of the pieces. A large poster of Mattie—looking regal on one of our beds—which was going to be erected in the front of our booth looked great, and hopefully would draw buyers in.

When I added the items I got from the printer into the makeshift trade show booth in my living room, I was psyched by how they fit in. I felt a tremendous sense of accomplishment, having taken an idea and bringing it to fruition. It wasn't easy, but I had done it. Despite my personal dust up with Gary, his guidance and business acumen had been incredibly helpful and had been the perfect counterbalance to my creative nature.

Mattie, as if preparing for her upcoming role, sat in the middle of the booth, panting in a way that made her look as if she were smiling. I opened a beer, sat down on the couch and tried to relax. But my mind—always running—was already thinking ahead to what was to come.

FIFTY-SEVEN

The days leading up to the trade show were a blur and passed quickly. While the preparation was mostly done, I still needed to insure that all of the components came together without a hitch.

When the big day finally arrived, Mattie and I got to the convention hall at 6:30 A.M. to supervise the booth setup. She had no idea what we had come to do, and wanted to inspect everyone and everything within nose reach.

A friendly woman across the way—who sold dog bandanas—brought her bulldog, Rusty over to say hello. She had erected a fenced in area beside her booth, where the dogs could visit and stay out of the way of the workers. It was amazing to see the time and toil it took hundreds of exhibitors to prepare for an event like this.

An hour before the show attendees began filing in the convention center, our three sales reps arrived, looking dapper in their brown and orange Canine Comfort t-shirts. I had hired the three women and met with the group several times to educate them about our product. In addition to the sales team, an employee from Brillman was going to be on hand to answer technical questions about our dog mattresses.

Big G arrived fifteen minutes before the show opened, clutching a big cup of coffee and fired up with enthusiasm.

"This is it, buddy," he said, patting me on the shoulder. "It's game time—you ready?"

"I have a few jitters, but I'm ready—we're ready."

"What are you nervous about?" he asked, petting Mattie, who had come over to greet him.

"Every dog lover I've shown the idea to loves it, but this is the only audience that matters."

"Don't worry," he replied, with a self-confident grin. "I've got a great feeling about it."

Gary wasn't planning on being at the show for the entire time—but he intended to come for a couple of hours each day. We agreed that he would be best using his schmoozing prowess to talk up our product to buyers wandering the showroom, and handing out raffle tickets for our giveaway.

The two of us were sitting in a couple of chairs at the back of the booth, when I looked up and saw Brianna, one of our sales reps, talking to a lady with a buyer's badge on. Canine Comfort's time to shine had arrived. Gary and I high-fived and got up to go to work.

We had placed a full-page ad in the trade show directory, and judging by the early flow of traffic to our booth—in comparison to those around us—it had paid off. The crowd helped to draw even more attention to us.

In my experience from trying various promotions at the record store, I always felt I could tell how something would go over from a small sampling of people. Before lunch—I'd say around 11:00am—I felt confident from the initial reactions we had received that our product was a winner.

Affable and an attention whore in the sweetest way possible, Mattie did a great job of attracting buyers to our booth. Ideally, having her lay on one of the beds, showing off our product was best, but she couldn't stay still with the steady stream of visitors.

When the show closed for the day, it was clear to everyone on our team that it had been a huge success. I was happy and relieved, but completely wiped out. Once I got home, I devoured a frozen dinner and went to sleep shortly afterward.

Opening my eyes the next morning, I immediately felt that I had physically overdone myself. Figuring I'd be on my feet a tremendous amount during the show, I had gotten a motorized cart from the convention hall but didn't bother using it.

I spent the first few hours of the second day hanging out in the back of the booth, only engaging buyers if the sales team needed my help. Sometime after lunch, while I was eating a nutrition bar, I heard someone call my name in a familiar voice. It was Holly.

"Hey!" I said surprised, getting up to give her a hug. "What are you doing here?"

"I wanted to surprise you and see how everything was going," she replied, looking adorable in jeans, a t-shirt, and a baseball cap.

"How'd you get in?" I asked.

"A friend of mine who makes really cool fish tanks got me a pass."

"Have you looked around our booth yet?"

"No, not yet."

Holly had seen one of the prototype beds at my place, but she hadn't seen the final design of our booth or any of the marketing materials. When we came to the large poster of Mattie, she said, "You used Doug Korsmann. I can always recognize his style instantly. Isn't he a great guy?"

"Do you know him?" I asked innocently.

"My ex got me a photo shoot for my birthday a few years ago."

"Oh…I thought he only shot furniture," I said.

"Mostly…occasionally he does portraits of people."

I wanted to ask her a few more questions, but it wasn't the place or the time.

"How's it going so far?" she asked, as we continued walking through the booth.

"Really well. Beyond my expectations, that's for sure."

"That's fantastic!" she said, leaning over to give me a quick kiss. "We'll have to celebrate once the show's over."

"That sounds good," I replied.

"Well, I don't want to get in your way," she told me, once we were back where we started. "I just wanted to say hello and cheer you on."

Before Holly left, I took her back to meet Big G. He was on a phone call, but I quickly introduced the two of them. After Holly left our booth, I looked over at Gary and he gave me a thumb's up.

By the end of Day Two even Mattie seemed worn out.

"One more day, sweet girl," I told her once we got home. "And tomorrow thank God is a short day."

I was going to eat something and go straight to bed again, but the adrenaline of another successful day had me wired. Instead, I sat on the couch for a couple of hours going over our sales. Although many of the orders we received were small—typical of buyers wanting to try out a new product—several of them were from large, national pet store chains that had multiple locations.

As I brushed my teeth the next morning in a heavy fog, I remembered a dream I had about my father during the night. I was at the trade show, standing in the front of our booth, when I saw him slowly coming down the aisle towards me, with the aid of a walker. When he got to within a few yards, he stopped, smiled, and held out his hands as if to say with pride, *Will you look at this?*

The final day of the show started off incredibly busy, but by lunchtime the traffic had slowed significantly. During the last couple of hours, there was only a trickle of buyers left roaming the hall. It gave Big G and me a chance to sit in the back of the booth and talk.

"I told you there was nothing to worry about," he said, while texting someone. "If we don't win best new product at this show, the voting is rigged."

"We passed our first test with flying colors," I replied. "If dog lovers take to the product, like I think they will, we have a business."

"You did a great job, buddy," he said, reaching over to pat me on the back. "Lighten up and spend some time with that pretty woman you introduced me to yesterday."

As the booth was being broken down and I was gathering my things to leave, my mother called. She asked how everything went and I gleefully told her that the product was a huge success, and that within a few weeks our dog beds would be in pet stores and boutiques across the country.

"That's great," she replied, managing a slight elevation in enthusiasm. "I hope they sell."

Aware of my mother's ability to strangle joy and needing to speak briefly with one of the sales reps before I could go home, I quickly ended the call.

FIFTY-EIGHT

For the next few days I continued to be super busy, working with our fulfillment contact at Brillman to make sure that the orders we received at the show were shipped quickly.

Holly and I continued to talk and text, but I still hadn't asked her out on another date.

Is something wrong? she texted me one morning. When I wrote back that I was still consumed with work, she replied, *We don't have to do anything special, I just want to see you.* In the late afternoon, when I had finished most of what I needed to do for the day, I picked up the phone and told her that I would come by later that evening.

When I arrived at her place, after we greeted each another, I said, "Mattie's in the car—grab PJ and let's take a drive."

"That sounds great," she replied. "Can we end up watching the sunset somewhere?"

"Absolutely, but it'll cost you one kiss now and many more later."

"Deal," she replied, leaning over to fulfill the first part of the agreement.

We walked out to my car hand in hand, and once Mattie spotted PJ she got animated in anticipation of seeing him. Once the two of them settled down in the backseat, we headed for the ocean.

I don't know if it was the high I was on from the success of the trade show or how casually Holly had mentioned Doug Korsmann's name, but I didn't feel like asking her about his claim that they were dating. I couldn't tell if I was taking the high road or the naïve road, but that's the choice I made in the moment.

After I turned onto Pacific Coast Highway from Sunset Boulevard, I navigated over to the far left lane and rolled down all of the windows. It was one of those golden evenings in Southern California that convinces countless people from all over the world to move here.

I turned on the stereo and forwarded one of the CDs Kerrie had made me to the first track. "Today's weather calls for blue skies," the voice announced before ELO's "Blue Sky" pumped out of my speakers.

As I picked up speed, I looked in the rear view mirror and saw Mattie and PJ happily sniffing the ocean air. I reached over, held Holly's hand and smiled. Then—scaring her to death and probably startling the dogs—I yelled at the top of my lungs.

"Whoo-hoo! Whoo-hoo!" I cried out, over and over again, until I felt satisfied.

"What was that about?" Holly asked with a bemused expression on her face.

"*That* was for Dorothy," I said, with tears streaming down my face.

Holly had heard several stories about my cherished physical therapist at Hathers. She squeezed my hand and then lifted it up in the air. When I took my eyes off of the road for a split second and looked over at her, I could see that she was teary-eyed.

"Great strides are nothing but small steps taken over time," I said above the roar of the wind. "Never forget it."

About a mile up the road, I made a left turn and pulled into a parking lot. "Who wants to GO down to the water and play?" I asked, looking in the rear view mirror at the dogs.

Holly opened her door and PJ quickly scrambled into the front seat and out of the car. To my surprise and delight, Mattie waited until I opened the backdoor. "Good girl," I said, praising her and digging into my front pocket for a treat.

As soon as we got past a volleyball tournament that was going on, the beach wasn't too densely populated. Once we reached the water, we unclipped the dogs. Holly and I sat down on the sand nearby and watched them chase one another and splash around in the aftermath of the crashing waves.

When I turned to face Holly, she looked beautiful in the soft sunset light. I pushed a few strands of hair away from her face and kissed her. We slowly fell back onto the warm sand, and huddled together like two giddy kids.

"I love you, Joel," she whispered.

I was shocked to hear her say it and almost responded with something sarcastic. Instead, "I love you too, Holly," came out of my mouth, with sincerity.

Although I chose not to address it, Doug Korsmann telling me that Holly was his girlfriend obviously impacted my feelings for her. I also felt that love was much further down the road from lust, and we had a ways to go. Nonetheless, we had now both made that intense declaration.

We continued to cuddle, kiss and laugh, until the dogs came over and reminded us that we weren't alone. Once we sat back up, the orangish-red sun was beginning to dip below the horizon.

"Would you say the sun is half way above the water or half way below it?" Holly asked, when it reached the mid-point of its descent.

"Hmmm… Is that a trick question?" I replied, without answering.

"To me its half way above the water. How do you see it?"

"Well, it's about to set—not rise—so I'll say it's half way below the water."

Holly continued staring out at the ocean, without saying anything.

"Does that make me a cynic?" I asked.

"Not necessarily," she replied. "You have a good point."

Holly changed the subject, and told me that her mother was coming to town in a few weeks. She wanted me to meet her. I, of course, said I would look forward to it. It made me think about how I had misrepresented my mother to her, by describing Aunt Shirley. I decided it was a good moment to come clean.

After I did, Holly said, "For some reason, I'm not surprised."

"Why not?" I asked, sounding purposely outraged.

"Just what I know of you, it didn't sound like what your mother would be like."

"You mean it would make more sense for her to be neurotic and kind of crazy?"

"No...that's not what I said."

"But that's what you were thinking, right?" I asked, getting defensive.

"Wrong," she replied, leaning over to kiss me on the cheek.

Shortly after the sun went down, we slowly trekked back to the car. The dogs slept on the drive home, and Holly leaned her head back and stared out at the passing scenery.

Once we got back to her place, she invited me inside. After putting our things down, we showered together and then crawled into her bed, still warm and moist.

FIFTY-NINE

Over the next week, I visited several local pet stores who had already received their shipment of Canine Comfort mattresses. I wanted to introduce myself and support the product in any way I could.

The first place I went to was a trendy boutique two blocks from my apartment called The Thingery. As I approached the store, I was elated to spot one of our beds in the display window. They had a German shepherd stuffed animal lying on it, tucked beneath a blanket. For an added touch, they put a treat packaged to look like a hotel pillow mint beside the dog.

Inside I met Janine, the owner of the store. Actually, I met her dog Ruffus first, who wouldn't stop poking at my pockets until I coughed up the remaining treat I had. Janine and I hadn't met at the trade show, but one of our sales reps had informed her that we were a local company.

"We love spotlighting local companies," she told me enthusiastically. "We've already sold two beds and I have a few friends coming by later, so hopefully I'll sell more!"

We chatted for a few more minutes and she recruited our company to be one of the sponsors for an annual Spay & Neuter awareness event she held at the store. Before I left, I took a photograph of her and Ruffus, and one of the display window for our Facebook page.

By the end of the week, I had gone to ten other stores. The excitement for our beds, as well as strong early sales, greeted me at each one. Between store visits, I made calls to West Coast accounts to make sure their orders had arrived and that they were happy with our product.

With fulfillment running smoothly, I began focusing my attention on bolstering our social media content and presence. Big G emailed me a few ideas he had, and Mattie and I began working on the first one—a short promotional video to upload onto YouTube. After I finished it, I launched a giveaway on our Facebook page for thirty free bed sets, which significantly increased our number of likes.

The launch of Canine Comfort had gone better than I could have scripted it. Once our product had reached every part of the country, and had been in stores for a while, I began getting emails from suppliers, saying how much their customers loved our beds.

In an informal focus group I conducted a month later—by talking to twenty stores—I learned that over 85% of customers who bought one of our mattresses, also purchased a fitted sheet to go with it. Not all of the stores carried our mattress platforms, but the ones that did were selling them half the time they sold a mattress.

Big G and I had analyzed the pricing for our product countless times, and our belief that dog lovers would pay more for a high quality bed that would last the lifetime of their dog had proved to be right.

I was thoroughly enjoying the process of running and building a new business and being able to do it with Mattie by my side. For the first time since I had come out of my coma, I was feeling truly alive and fulfilled.

Kerrie was back in town for a few days before leaving again—this time to tour the Midwest. People our age and older, who made up most of her audience, were hungry for music they could relate to. And Kerrie was having a great time playing it for them.

It was great to see her again, even if she brought her boyfriend, Jay along for our lunch.

"I can't tell you how much better you look and sound," she told me, after we sat down.

"Man, it's like you're a different person," Jay added.

"Well, time helps…and working again has given me a purpose. And my co-pilot here has a lot to do with it," I said, reaching down to pat Mattie's head.

"It's so cool that they allow dogs on the patio," Kerrie said, slipping Mattie a carrot from her salad.

I opened up to the two of them about Holly and the likelihood that she was seeing someone else. They both thought I shouldn't stop seeing her over it. We talked about music for the rest of the time, and I surprised Kerrie by presenting her and Jay with a CD that I had burned for them.

"The shocking part," I told them, "is that every song except for one was released in the last five years."

Life was good, but on a Saturday night, after I came home from a date with Holly, I turned on the TV and learned that another tragedy had struck.

At the Flix 24 Cineplex in Granada Hills, in the San Fernando Valley, there had been a shooting. The first news reports were confused and conflicting, but you could sense that the magnitude of the situation was massive and that the outcome would be horribly grim.

When the details emerged, it turned out that three teenagers, who worked as ushers at the theatre, had chained the exit doors and blocked the entrances to three separate theatres, and began shooting. Two of them were ultimately restrained by moviegoers, and one was shot in a standoff with the police. The projected death toll continued to climb as I watched, and by the following morning it was confirmed that 127 people had been killed. Among the victims were the daughter of a high-ranking National Rifle Association executive, and the son of a prominent Democratic senator from California.

I sat at my desk, but I was numb and unable to work. The aftermath of the shooting was a replay of the mall shooting with the media providing incessant coverage, filling the public's insatiable desire to know all of the gory details. Sadly, this time I was among them. All I could manage to do all day was watch in disbelief and horror.

To see the young, seemingly innocent faces of the three theatre ushers being flashed on the screen was stunning. Learning later that they had purposely executed their demented and cold-blooded plan during the showing of movies geared toward their own age group made it that much more chilling. Hearing the countless stories of young victims—including a teenage couple who were on their first date—tore your heart out.

Within a day, the media had dubbed the teenagers *The Cinema Psychos*. Like with the mall shooting, cries for stronger gun control laws and less violence in the culture immediately ensued.

It wasn't difficult to foresee the outcome of the tragedy. The trials of the two teenagers would drag on. And in spite of their criminal outcomes, they would be infamous forever, most likely inspiring others, while the families and loved ones of the victims would spend the rest of their lives in torturous, unending sorrow.

SIXTY

Two days after the shooting, my mother emailed me a story from *The New York Times*. It was about violence in the culture, and at the bottom of the article it listed violent video game manufacturers and gun manufacturers, along with profiles of their top executives. The video game companies were listed in order of which were considered to have the most sadistic content. Sharp End Interactive, owned by Gary Wycoff, topped the list. With games like *Thrill to Kill*, *Die Begging* and *Trigger Happy*, it wasn't hard to see why. The article unfortunately also made mention that Gary owned Canine Comfort.

I immediately called Gary, but got his voicemail. I left a message and also wrote him an email to let him know that I was available if he needed to talk.

Meanwhile, *The New York Times* article spread like wildfire throughout traditional and social media, and a boycott of Gary's company and others began to take hold. The pressure forced major online and offline retailers to stop selling their product.

Every pundit and person the media spoke to agreed that things in America were terribly wrong, but pointing fingers was far easier than making changes. Day after day, experts and advocates of opposing views argued their case on the news, on talk shows, and in specials about the killings, which aired seemingly overnight.

It looked like a familiar scenario in which the story would soon recede into memory and life would go on. But something about the nature and the scale of the shooting wouldn't leave the public's consciousness. The desire to make someone accountable for what happened heated up, and the boycotts branched out to include movie studios that made violent films.

After a miserably unproductive work day, I flipped on the local news to see if there was anything new on the shooting. I was stunned to see a reporter finishing up her report from outside of Gary's house. I immediately tried again to reach him, but he didn't pick up his phone or respond to my email or text.

After I ate dinner, I decided to drive over to his house. When I got within a half block of his address, I could see hordes of media camped outside. I drove past them until I reached the house Gary told me Carmen used to clandestinely access his guesthouse.

I easily found the path off to the side of the large property and traversed down a short trail, until I reached Gary's backyard. Shading my eyes from the glare of the sun, I looked inside the guesthouse and saw Gary sitting in the dark with his feet on the coffee table, cradling a bottle of whiskey. His Sharp End Interactive baseball cap was pulled down, covering his eyes.

"Hey," I said, stepping inside and announcing my presence.

He looked up without saying anything, and I could see that he was completely wasted.

"How you holding up?" I asked.

He grunted, but didn't respond. I walked over to the kitchen, poured myself a glass of lemonade, and sat on the couch across from him in silence.

"Fuckers," he finally let out, pushing the bill of his cap back. "They make me out to be the devil. I didn't create the culture we live in…I just saw an opportunity and capitalized on it."

"I think the implication is a company like yours negatively influences the culture," I replied gingerly.

"If I didn't start this company somebody else would have," he slurred.

"Isn't that sort of a cop out?" I asked.

"I don't give a shit—it's the truth."

"That's like Hitler saying if he didn't start the Holocaust somebody else would have," I said.

He didn't respond at first, he just glared at me with hate and rage in his bloodshot eyes.

"Fuck you for saying that!" he then yelled, jabbing his finger in the air at me. "Get the fuck off of my property and never come back!"

I knew as soon as the comment came out of my mouth that it was harsh. But I was only trying to make him see something he had successfully separated himself from—his conscience for what he had put out in the world. As I stood up and headed for the door, for a split-second I thought to apologize, but instead turned the handle and left.

The mood in the country remained the same. There was a mix of sadness and anger everywhere I went. People I talked to said that it was similar to the days after 9-11.

I had become totally distracted by the tragedy, and I needed to get back to the business of Canine Comfort. There was a lot that had to be done, and I hoped that being engaged in work would take me out of my funk.

After uploading another video to our YouTube channel, I went to post it on our Facebook page. I was stunned to be greeted by a flurry of angry posts.

This company is guilty of murder by association. Boycott them and tell every dog person you know.

I just bought one of these beds for my dog. He loves it, but now I'll either burn it or return it.

If you buy this product, you're aiding and abetting killers.

As I read through the messages—my heart sinking lower and lower with each one—it dawned on me that the people boycotting Sharp End Interactive must have picked up our company name from *The New York Times* article.

I started responding to each post, arguing that Sharp End Interactive had nothing to do with our dog beds, until I had to take Mattie out to do her business. When I sat down again at my computer, I counted the number of angry messages we had received. I stopped at seventy.

I called Kerrie, who was in Stillwater, Minnesota doing a show, to tell her what had happened. She told me to immediately change my Facebook settings so that only I could make posts on our page, and to make one passionate statement defending our company.

"After that all you can do is wait and hope this blows over," she said. "I don't know though…the public's outrage seems to be challenging the status quo like I've never seen before, and anything that gets in its way is going to get hurt."

"Including our company," I replied mournfully.

"I'm afraid so," she said.

SIXTY-ONE

In the weeks to come, Kerrie turned out to be right. There was a powerful groundswell forming and elements of the culture deemed by many to be sinister and salacious were being questioned, vilified and scorned. Reality TV, music that glorified violence and disrespected women, violent video games, violent movies, and the seductive way young girls dressed were all under fire. A citizen started campaign called *Let Kids Be Kids* went viral and became a national rally cry.

As a result of immense pressure from the public, every traditional and cable news network agreed to no longer show any footage or images from the theatre shooting or any mass killings in the future. The networks would only announce the incident when it occurred, without any supporting coverage. Newspapers, magazines, and websites eventually followed suit. The Homeland Security Office announced plans for a dedicated public TV channel and website which would disseminate pertinent emergency information in the event of a mass shooting.

I wanted to wait for things to simmer down before calling our contact at Brillman, but it didn't look like it was going to happen anytime soon. I decided a Friday afternoon was as good a time as any.

I asked the receptionist if I could speak with Hal Ernstein, who was the Senior Vice-President of Marketing and among the most enthusiastic in our initial meeting with the company.

When he got on the line—before I addressed the elephant in the room—I gave him some impressive sales reports from local stores as well as a list of large chains that had already placed follow-up orders. I then made the obvious point that Sharp End Interactive and Canine Comfort were separate entities with entirely different products. I finished by asking for the company's support, until the storm passed.

He didn't interrupt me once while I spoke, but when I was through he exploded like a dam breaking.

"You must be living under a rock!" he barked. "Sharp End and Gary Wycoff are all over the news! Don't you understand that the public's made the connection between Sharp End and Canine Comfort?"

I calmly countered by reiterating that we were making dog beds, not video games. Sharp End Interactive may not survive, but Canine Comfort had done nothing wrong and deserved the right to.

"Have you read the paper today?" he asked me.

"Not yet," I replied.

"Well, pick up the *Los Angeles Times* or go online and read their headline story on the shooting."

After we hung up, I went to the newspaper's site and read that the police had discovered a slew of Sharp End video games in a hidden underground fort that the three teenage killers had hung out in. The story included several photographs of the dark, creepy place, which had violent mantras from Sharp End Interactive video games scrawled on the walls.

I grabbed Mattie's leash and we went for a walk. The reality of Canine Comfort's future was sadly sinking in. Save for finding another mattress manufacturer that was unaware or didn't care about our connection to Sharp End or raising capital to do our own manufacturing, the business likely wouldn't survive.

A little while after dinner that night, Holly called to check on me. After I told her about my conversation with Brillman, she asked if I wanted to bring Mattie over to play with PJ the following day. When I said I wasn't up for it—that I'd be rotten company—she replied, "Joel, there's nothing else you can do right now. We can sit in the courtyard with the dogs and I'll make lunch for us. I know it's hard, but try to let go for a while."

I told her that I'd sleep on it and let her know first thing in the morning. After I had breakfast, I turned on the TV to see if the coverage of the killings was still continuous. It was still being talked about on every news channel, but it didn't seem like there was anything new to report. When I went online, other stories were starting to get attention. I texted Holly that I would come over around 11:30.

When Mattie and I arrived, I unclipped her leash as soon as I saw PJ standing at the gate. Holly walked up a few seconds later, smiling, and greeted me with a big hug.

"I'm sorry," she said. "I know how hard you worked on this business."

"In the end it's just a business," I said, trying to make myself feel better. "All those people lost their lives. I can't get the images of the kids that were killed out of my head."

"Come," she said, taking my hand. "I'm making a delicious, healthy lunch for us."

"Do you mind if I stay out here with the dogs?" I asked. "I'm tired of being inside and staring at the walls."

"Sure," she replied. "I'll bring the food out in a few minutes."

Holly turned to go back to her place, and I sat down on one of the wicker chairs in the courtyard. A nice breeze was blowing through and the joy of interacting with the dogs made me relax a little. Soon a neighbor of Holly's walked by, carrying a load of stuff to her car.

"I bought one of your beds for my dog!" she said to me excitedly.

"Oh…thanks," I replied. "Did Holly tell you about it?"

"No, I saw it at Petz World," she told me. "Holly was so excited to see that I had one. My dog LOVES it."

After the neighbor walked off, I closed my eyes and tried a meditation technique I read about in an article that Brian had sent me. I lasted about four breaths before I started thinking about ways our company could be salvaged.

PJ brought me back to the moment, when he bounded up beside me with a soggy tennis ball. I tossed it for him a few times and then started to get restless.

I got up to go inside to see how Holly was coming along with lunch and to get a bowl of water to bring outside for the dogs. When I walked into the kitchen and didn't see her, I called out her name.

"I'm in the bathroom," she answered. "I'll be right out."

I looked over at the Greek salad she was preparing and grazed a few pieces of feta cheese. I didn't see PJ's water bowl anywhere on the ground, so I opened the cabinet above the sink to find one.

As I reached up to grab a large soup bowl, Holly's cell phone vibrated on the counter below me. After I filled the bowl with water, I glanced over at it. The message on the screen said: *Doug Korsmann, Voicemail & Missed Call.*

Just then, Holly walked into the kitchen.

"Hey," she said, coming up behind me and rubbing my neck. "Whatcha doing?"

"Just getting the dogs some water."

"Okay," she said, surveying the food on the counter. "We're about ready to eat…I'll start bringing this stuff out."

The time to ask Holly about Doug Korsmann was now. Except I

just didn't have the desire or energy to do it. The whirlwind of the trade show, followed by the theatre shooting and the repercussions to our business, had completely drained me. Obviously Doug telling me that Holly was his girlfriend, and then seeing that he had called her made me pretty certain there was something between them.

As we sat and ate, I was quiet and withdrawn.

"Are you okay?" Holly asked.

I nodded noncommittedly, concentrating on my food.

"Can I do anything?" she asked.

"No," I replied. "I'm just dealing with a lot and it's probably best if I'm alone right now."

"I understand," she said. "Give me a minute…I'll be right back."

I looked up and watched her walk back inside. I tried to feel what my gut was telling me—is she going to respond to Doug's call or am I reading something into this that doesn't exist?

A few minutes later she returned and said, "Tess just called. She needs me to pick her up from her soccer game. Her friend's mother had an emergency and can't get there."

Case closed, I thought to myself, feeling more sadness than anger.

I put down my fork and got up to get Mattie's leash.

"We can finish eating," Holly said. "I told her we were in the middle of lunch."

"No, I think I'm going to take off now," I said, moving away from the table.

"Okay," she said meekly. "Are you sure there's nothing I can do, Joel?"

"No," I replied, clipping Mattie's leash to her collar and giving PJ a rub on the head.

Holly followed me to the front of the complex and before I lifted the latch on the gate, she leaned over and gave me a peck on the cheek. I might have mumbled something—I don't remember. In my mind I was already gone.

On my way home, I pulled beside a car at a stop light that was blaring rap music. I rolled my window down half way and tried to make out what the song was saying. The rapper was talking about having his way with a lady, to put it cleanly.

Inside there were two white suburban-looking kids, who were probably still in high school. When our eyes met, they started saying something to one another and laughing. I got the feeling they were about to make a smart ass comment to me. *I feel you, fellas—I was once your age*, I conveyed with a knowing glance.

When I looked away, they turned down the music and one of them yelled out, "Did you say something to me gramps?" I smiled, but didn't reply. As the light changed and we drove off side by side, I treated them to Jimi Hendrix's version of "All Along the Watchtower" at full volume. *Take that youngsters—sadly your generation was deprived of rock 'n roll.*

SIXTY-TWO

The next morning, feeling depressed, I decided to take Mattie to the beach. After parking in the same lot as the time I came with Holly, I traded my tennis shoes for a pair of sandals. Once I reached the sand, I plopped myself down and leaned back against the cement wall that separated the walkway from the beach.

For a long while, I stared at the ocean, trying to sort out my feelings about everything that had happened. Soon I was so inside my head, trying to process the past and ponder the future, that I was wasting the view.

Be here now, I told myself. *Feel the sun, smell the ocean, pet your dog.*

I took off my shirt, rested my phone on top of it, and put on some mellow instrumental music. I closed my eyes and took in a deep breath. Before I could take a second one, the phone rang. I looked down and saw that it was Brian.

I answered, pretending he had reached *Sal's Surfboard Shop*, and then painted a picture for him of where I was at. We talked for a while and I told him what happened with Holly and updated him on the business.

"Imagine the setting you're in right now," he said to me, "but in a less crowded, more beautiful place, hanging out with your old buddy. C'mon man—it'll do you good to get away. Come down to Mexico."

I was in a better and stronger place physically than when Brian first made me the same offer. I told him that it sounded great, but I didn't know what to do with Mattie and I wasn't sure I wanted to leave her.

Over the last few weeks my sweet dog hadn't seemed herself and occasionally wasn't finishing her food. I had taken her to the vet and although Sima didn't find anything wrong, she reminded me that Mattie was getting up there in age and time was precious. I suppose that was obvious, but hearing it was hard nonetheless.

I ended the call with Brian by telling him that I'd think about it.

After I put the phone down and turned the music back on, I looked over at Mattie, who was lying on her side in the sand, gazing out at the ocean. *What is it about a dog that can fill you with so much joy even when they're doing nothing?* I reached over and slowly started petting her coat. She poked her head up and looked at me.

"I wish dogs lived as long as people," I told her, "but it's not the years in your life, it's the life in your years that matter. Right Mattie?"

She cocked her head and after I rolled over to give her a hug, we went down to the water. Once she was tuckered from chasing her new Frisbee toy, I gathered my things and headed back to my apartment.

I wanted to ignore anything work-related for the rest of the day, but couldn't resist checking my email. Among them was one from Hal Ernstein from Brillman, letting me know that his company would be severing its ties with Canine Comfort as soon as their current inventory ran out. The email included an attachment, which was a letter from their legal department. I glanced at it to get the gist, but didn't read the entire thing.

I closed my email and looked online for possible places to board Mattie. After reading reviews on several of them, I called a homey-looking one that was run by a woman named Jessica, out of her house. She lived within a mile of me.

After asking Jessica a few questions, I made a reservation for Mattie. I knew if I didn't act at the moment, I'd find reasons not to leave her and visit Brian. Immediately afterward, I booked a flight online to Puerto Vallarta. From there, Brian would pick me up and take me to Sayulita, where he was living.

Once I arranged for transportation to the airport, I emailed Brian to tell him I was coming to see him. He was psyched, lauding me for making a good decision and promising that we'd have a great time. He wrote me a quick follow-up message reminding me that I needed a passport.

I thought for a moment, certain I had had one at some point. But when I called my mother, she refreshed my memory. I had planned to take a trip to Europe with a group of my friends, but decided instead to work on opening a record store.

SIXTY-THREE

That afternoon I called the Passport Agency to make an appointment for the following day. When I found out that the soonest I could get a passport was three weeks, I changed my flight and called Jessica to switch Mattie's boarding dates.

The next morning I went back to work, researching mattress manufacturers who could possibly replace Brillman. My hope was that when everything calmed down, if our brand was not irreparably damaged, I would approach them.

After I took Mattie for our ritual post-lunch walk, I drove to the Federal Building on Wilshire Boulevard to apply for my passport. Once I went through the security check, I took a seat and waited to be called. I always figure these places to be a long wait, so I brought a draft of the book you're now reading to look over.

I couldn't concentrate and kept having to re-read each paragraph on account of a young girl sitting beside me, who kept intermittently singing aloud. She had earbuds on and her voice was probably louder than she realized. I was going to tap her on the shoulder to ask her if she could keep it down, but she seemed happily in another world so I didn't bother.

I put down my book on the open chair on the other side of me, and scrolled through my phone to find some music to listen to.

When the girl started to sing another song, I was surprised that I recognized the lyrics. I smiled at the unlikely occurrence of someone her age listening to a song from Joe Walsh's first solo album.

I waved my hand to get her attention and she removed one of her earbuds.

"Sorry to bother you, but can I ask you what you're singing?" I asked, even though I knew.

"Oh…it's called Birdcall Morning…it's by Joe Walsh," she answered, while leaning down to pick up a pack of gum that had spilled out of her purse.

"You're way too young to know that song," I said to her. "Was your mother a fan of his?"

"No…it's a long story," she said.

"Well, it looks like we're in for a long wait if you want to share it. I'm curious."

"I used to work at a place called—" she said before suddenly stopping and looking at me strangely.

When she remained silent for a few more moments, I prompted her to continue. "And?"

The young girl's lips started to quiver and within seconds she was in tears.

"What's wrong?" I asked, puzzled.

She wiped the tears from her eyes, and then leaned over and gave me a hug.

I started to think that maybe she was high on something.

Things got stranger when she pulled away from me and said, "Joel…I can't believe this."

"Wait—do I know you?" I asked.

"Sort of…it's a long story."

"Another one," I said with a laugh.

"No, actually it's the same one I started to tell you."

"Okay," I replied, probably looking at her as if she were crazy. "I'm ready."

The young girl then told me how she had cleaned at Tender Heart Nursing Care during the time I was in a coma. She explained how she discovered the newspaper article in the *Santa Monica Outlook* about me, which included my last music mix. And how she played those songs for me on her iPod every night while she cleaned. That's how she knew Joe Walsh's "Birdcall Morning."

When she finished talking, we were both in tears. I reached over to embrace her.

"What you did…" I got out before breaking down again, "was so thoughtful and kind. It means so much to me."

"It wasn't anything really. I just hoped somehow you could hear the music, cause I knew if you could you'd appreciate it."

We sat silently looking at one another, her hands in mine.

"I wanted to contact you after you woke up," she said.

"Why didn't you?" I asked.

"I wasn't sure how to and I figured you'd be overwhelmed by everything."

"Wait…" I said, laughing. "I don't even know your name."

"It's Maya…and guess what?" she asked, her voice rising with excitement. "I'm a music therapist now!"

"You're kidding!" I replied.

"And I sing some of the songs from your playlist with my patients."

"That's awesome!"

Maya asked me what my life had been like since I woke up, and then told me she was getting a passport to go see her father in Guadalajara.

"I'm nervous," she said, standing up after the woman behind the counter called her number. "I haven't seen him since my mother brought me to America."

"You'll be fine," I told her. "You're an angel, and always remember Maya, angels are rare. Your father's a lucky man to have a daughter with such a beautiful soul."

We quickly exchanged contact information and made a plan to have lunch once we returned home from our trips. After Maya walked away from the counter to leave, we met to hug and say goodbye one more time.

A few minutes later, my number was called. The clerk asked me a few rudimentary questions, but my mind was elsewhere.

I was back in my room at Tender Heart, where I had spent all of those years. I pictured Maya tucking her iPod beneath the sheets and gently placing the earbuds on me. I heard her talking to me in a comforting voice.

"Mr. Berskin?" the clerk said, redirecting my attention.

"Yes," I replied.

"Are you okay?" she asked.

"Yeah...sorry. I drifted off."

"I hope you went to a good place," she said with a smile.

"It used to be dark and lonely, but it just got brighter."

"Oh, that's good," the clerk said. "How'd it change?"

"The kindness of a stranger," I told her.

Once I finished up and left the Federal Building, I immediately called Kerrie to tell her what had just happened. Next, I phoned Aunt Shirley. "That's unbelievable," she said, starting to cry. "Maybe that's what helped bring you out of your coma." I left a message for Gary and told him I wanted to share something miraculous with him, and that I loved him in spite of our last encounter. I was about to call Brian, but decided I would tell him the news in person. My mother was having lunch with a new friend, when I reached her. She was in a hurry because they were about to eat, but she seemed truly touched by the story. "Maybe you could write a book," she suggested. "There's a lot to tell."

"I could," I said with a chuckle.

Instead of getting in my car, I decided to walk over to the grass field just beyond the parking lot. I climbed onto the first picnic table I came to and sat down. I closed my eyes and was again overcome with emotion.

Finding out what Maya had done for me released so much of the sorrow I had been holding onto. The struggle to rehabilitate myself, the angst in dealing with my mother, the heartbreak of losing my father, the anger at the mall gunman, the awfulness of the theater shooting and how it affected our business, and the sadness about my relationship with Holly, poured out of me.

Over the next couple of weeks, I worked on a survival plan for Canine Comfort. The boycott of our product and others was still going strong, but perhaps, in time, there would be collective realization that we were just selling dog beds. I still had hope.

Big G eventually called me back and we had a good conversation. He told me that Sharp End Interactive was inundated with lawsuits from family members of the victims, and his company most likely wouldn't survive. He said he was trying to reevaluate his life and his marriage.

"Do you know anything about pugs?" he asked before we hung up.

"Not much, but I know they're always friendly when Mattie and I come across one. Why?"

"For whatever reason, my kids really want one."

"I bet if you go to the shelter and search online, you can rescue a great one. Any dog would love having your backyard to play in."

"I'm not sure how much longer we'll have this house," he replied somberly.

"Well, wherever you are that dog will be happy to be there," I told him.

"Are we good?" he asked, changing the subject.

"Always," I replied. "I'll never forget you being there for me after I came out of my coma. I cherish your friendship."

Once I got off the phone with Gary, I continued preparing for my trip to Mexico. Mattie anxiously followed me from room to room and didn't like what she suspected.

When my travel day arrived, I took Mattie to Jessica's place early in the morning. She was antsy on the ride over, but quickly warmed up to Jessica.

Before I left, I asked Jessica if she wouldn't mind leaving Mattie and I alone so I could say goodbye. Once she left the room, I got down on my knees, cradled Mattie's head in my hands, and told her that I loved her and would miss her the minute I walked out the door. Then I gave her a special treat I had been saving for the moment.

Back at my apartment, while I waited for the airport shuttle, I watched Mattie on the webcam that Jessica had on her site. She had already made friends with a yellow Lab and was happily playing.

When the shuttle arrived, there was only one other person in the van. Surprisingly, the traffic on the freeway was relatively light and I made it to my gate early.

After I checked in, I pulled out my iPad, hoping to get more glimpses of Mattie on the webcam. I was so caught up in watching her that the guy sitting next to me had to nudge me to let me know I had missed the seating announcement for my row.

I hurried to board the plane and got situated in my window seat towards the rear. Exhausted, I closed my eyes and drifted in and out, while the stewardess went over the safety instructions.

As I felt the plane slowly backing away from the gate, I reached for my phone to turn it off. When I glanced at the screen, there was a text from Kerrie. It said, *Broke up with Jay. Ugh… I'm getting so tired of this. Remind me again why friends don't end up together. We could find a little piece of paradise somewhere away from the city, have a bunch of dogs, and live happily ever after.*

I looked out the window, thought of my father, and smiled. Then I replied to Kerrie's text with a smiley face and a couple of x's and o's.

Note from the Author

Thank you for reading *Birdcall Morning*. If you know of another reader who might enjoy it, please pass the word, or if the mood strikes you post a review on Amazon or Goodreads.

Writing is a solitary endeavor, but having a book come to fruition is anything but. My utmost gratitude to the following people for their time, insights and talent: Christine Olen, Courtney Silviotti, Robyn Kohl Van Dusen, Pamela Tamulevicius, Rodney Wishart, Colin Hunsberger, Stephanie Demello, Keri Knutson, and Jesse Hanwit.

Narrated by a rescue dog that ends up at a home for seniors, *All That Ails You* has now received over 400 five-star reviews!

"Every thoughtful, carefully placed word engaged me, from the first to the last. Beautifully written. It is a book that will make you smile, laugh, cry and hug and kiss your own dog!"
—One of over 400 Five-Star Reviews

Made in the USA
Columbia, SC
06 October 2018